"Nice won't keep you alive."

"And you will?" she asked.

Time for a little reassurance. Not his best skill.

He lifted her chin until she stared up at him. "Yes, Lexi. I will."

And that was a vow.

She smiled then, a bit lopsided and not all that convincing, but at least she tried. "I like your confidence."

"Consider it a promise."

"But you don't know what's going to happen when the army finds the bodies or—"

"You will stay alive." He couldn't let her mind wander to any other place. The could-be and what-if possibilities were pretty awful. "I guarantee it."

By HelenKay Dimon

FALLING HARD
PLAYING DIRTY
RUNNING HOT (novella)

Coming Soon

FACING FIRE

FALLING HARD

BAD BOYS UNDERCOVER

HELENKAY DIMON

AVONBOOKS

An Imprint of HarperCollinsPublishers

AVON BOOKS
An Imprint of HarperCollins*Publishers*
195 Broadway
New York, New York 10007

Copyright © 2015 by HelenKay Dimon
ISBN 978-0-06-233007-9
www.avonromance.com

First Avon Books mass market printing: June 2015

Avon Trademark Reg. U.S. Pat. Off. and in Other Countries, Marca Registrada, Hecho en U.S.A.
HarperCollins® is a registered trademark of HarperCollins Publishers.

Printed in the U.S.A.

10 9 8 7 6 5 4 3 2

To my nieces Jennifer, Barbara and Danielle—
may you be fierce in your determination
and fearless in all your choices.

FALLING HARD

1

AFTER SPENDING most of his adult life in the Marines, Weston Brown recognized a shithole when he stepped right in one. He had no one else to blame for this assignment. Just his piss poor decision-making. Next time his team leader told him about an optional operation, he'd take a pass. Wouldn't kill him to sit one out now and then.

With his gun in his hand and his finger skimming along the side, right off the trigger, he scanned the area, squinting to check his surroundings in the fading light. Skardu, Pakistan. The town served as the launching area for high-altitude climbing expeditions. Dusty and barren, filled with grayish-brown boulders and outlined by a towering mountain range. A few rivers and bursts of green provided by man-made irrigation systems broke through the rough landscape.

This was not his idea of the ideal vacation spot, and that's what he was supposed to be doing—taking mandatory leave—forced rest between assignments with the Alliance, the elite black ops fighting force put together mostly from the United States' CIA and MI6, the British intelligence service.

The work suited him since he wasn't a desk guy, but it wouldn't be a bad thing to go a week or so without choking or shooting someone. When his eyes locked on the target dead ahead, he knew the no-violence thing wasn't going to happen today.

He'd done this a million times. Careful steps, slowed breathing. A mental countdown to impact. Calculating the risks and preparing a second option if this one went sideways. He'd been trained to be ready—always. To kill without thinking.

His boot hit the ground right behind the armed unknown leaning against a tree and aiming his weapon at the building in the distance. The guy must have sensed him because he flinched a second before contact. Started to turn. West locked his arm around the guy's neck before he could call out and bring his friends running.

Flailing and full of panic, he had one last burst of energy. The bottom of the guy's shoes scraped against the loose pebbles on the ground as he beat his fists against West's arm. West pressed harder and the guy fell in a heap in the dirt.

West had been using the choke hold since boot camp. Just shy of thirty-four and he could still take a man down in less than four seconds.

Oorah.

"Nice, now stay low." Josiah King, clean-cut, British, and one of the toughest men in Alliance, issued the order.

"It's not my first day on the job." West wasn't accustomed to following Josiah's lead. He directed Delta team's operations. While the men could be moved around as needed, West generally worked on Bravo.

He'd been home, lifting weights and sitting out an enforced break with the rest of Bravo following a successful operation in Germany when he got the call. Between his knowledge of the region and his preference to keep moving, tagging along seemed like the right choice. Problem was, volunteering put him smack in the middle of the one place he never wanted to see again.

Josiah shook his head. "You're a big target."

"Good thing I run fast." West pointed off to his right. "India's that way, right?"

"Funny." Though Josiah's tone didn't say funny.

But if the Pakistani army unleashed its fury, that was exactly what they'd be doing. Burning for daylight. They weren't exactly in-country on tourist visas or with the government's knowledge. Any government.

That's how Alliance worked. Underground and answering to few. Lethal but expendable, so everyone in power could maintain plausible deniability. For this assignment, they'd hooked up with a team of charity workers and flew in over the Karakoram mountain range and right past K2, the second highest mountain in the world.

The long and breathtaking trip from Islamabad ended here, in Pakistan, eighty miles from the ongoing conflict with India over a strip of wasteland called the Siachen Glacier. People referred to the conflict as the highest battleground on Earth because it took place 20,000 feet in the air. West viewed it as a fucking nightmare he'd vowed never to return to.

It sucked that his nightmares haunted him longer than his promise to stay away.

Josiah gave the hand signal and they headed out, moving fast, doubled over and crouched down, all while continuously scanning the landscape. They took cover behind rocks and an occasional shed as they made their way over the span of open area between them and the one-story beige building in the distance.

Intel pinned this place as a clinic. The one place other than the state-run Combined Military Hospital in Skardu where injured hikers were brought when they were rescued. Most came here off K2, but hikers ended up here from a few of the thirteen other highest mountains that loomed nearby, known as the eight-thousanders. The clinic looked like every other building, as far as West could tell, only spookier since there was no sign of life around the place.

Josiah rushed up to a group of trees and hid behind them. He motioned for West to follow. "I'd prefer if we didn't turn this into an international incident, so try not to draw fire," Josiah said.

"That's a reasonable position." But since military battles waged in the mountains nearby, and armed officers walked the streets, the boss might be asking a bit much.

Only Alliance would send in a two-man team to attempt this kind of motherfucking retrieval madness. West loved that about this group. No weakness allowed.

"Nothing can go wrong," Josiah said.

"You should have thought about that before we decided to kidnap a doctor out of Pakistan." As far as West was concerned, damage, collateral or not, had to be expected.

Josiah's gaze flicked away from the building to West's face. "Rescue, not kidnap."

Yeah, right. "We'll see if the guy's using that word when we interrogate him."

"Talk with." Josiah emphasized each word as if he were addressing a confused child.

If his temporary leader wanted to engage in verbal gymnastics, West would comply. "We both know the truth."

"That you're a pain in the ass?"

"That's not news." Neither was the suicidal nature of this mission. So much for all the rah-rah bullshit about it being a quick in and out. Tell that to his nuts, which were in the process of freezing off.

Despite it being May, he could see the snow piled on the mountain range around him. In this part of the world, seventies during the day and forties at night were normal for this time of year. He expected that. He didn't plan for the unseasonable cold snap that ushered in blustery winds and frigid temperatures well below normal. He blew a warm breath into the palms of his black gloves.

Josiah glanced over then did a double take. "You okay?"

"I hate this place." Spent the worst damn three weeks of his life hunkered down in this area, alternating between pulling bodies out of the ice and hiding from the Pakistani army.

"Skardu?"

But now wasn't sharing time. They were almost on top of the building and anyone could be lurking, so West kept it short and sweet. "Anywhere with mountains and snow."

"Be happy it's not winter. The whole place is impassable then."

Sweet damn this was a lot of talking. Ford Decker, West's team leader on Bravo, knew not to engage him in mindless bullshit. Josiah would learn. "I have the itch to shoot something. Wanna volunteer for my target practice?"

"Keep in mind I'll shoot back." Josiah scanned the horizon and checked the coordinates on his GPS watch. "This is definitely the right location."

As the wind whipped over the scarred land, West wondered what the hell was so right about it. Nondescript and squat. Plain with few windows and no discernable signs of human life.

As a clinic, the building should be buzzing with activity. A steady stream of locals and climbers seeking treatment. The usual check-ins from the military stationed nearby.

But they had no movement. Hard truth was they might be too late to call this part of the mission a success. Their witness could be dead.

Josiah must have reached the same conclusion because, though his frown didn't lessen, his grip on the gun tightened. "We go in and grab Alex Palmer, then get out."

The whole reason for this fucked-up venture. "The doctor with the intel."

"The doctor in trouble."

"We're basically saying the same thing." West didn't separate the doc from the information he'd relayed through back channels and coded chatter. Risky and brave, but the doc had to know the dangers going in for an American working in this part of the world. "Let's grab him."

They skipped the front door and circled around to the side, checking for tracks and finding a mishmash of prints. Their footsteps landed in almost noiseless thuds on the dirt over the others. No extra movements or stray comments. They stayed focused and clear, the sole objective being to get in there and get the doctor out.

Ducking, Josiah moved to the far side of the window. He pulled the fiber-optic camera out of the utility pocket of his pants. New tech and pretty damn impressive. Nothing more than a thin wire. Thinner than West had ever seen. Harmless, unnoticeable to anyone not looking for it.

With an expertise and patience West admired, Josiah

screwed on the tiny lens no bigger than a mint that he kept in a separate pocket and eased the end up until it touched the edge of the glass. Whatever he saw on the monitor on his watch had him nodding. He motioned for West to take the back door.

The tension thumped around them, broken only by the stark silence. West knew they could be walking into a bloodbath. Or worse, a trap. Last place he wanted to die was on this forsaken strip of land. But if it was his fucking time, so be it.

He made his way to the corner, keeping his back tight against the building but careful not to shuffle or create noise. His gaze bounced from the open dirt-covered area around them to the empty few feet in front of him. A quick peek to check behind him, then he rounded the building and stepped up to the open door.

Bad sign. A smart doctor would keep the door locked, if only to protect the meds.

Every little noise echoed to a deafening roar in his ears. A pebble here. The creak of the hinge as the wind knocked the door back and forth there.

He half expected the entire Pakistani army to pour out of the building. Instead, more quiet greeted him. A stillness that reeked of death. He was far too familiar with that stench.

He squinted, looking between the crack and the edge of the door. A man in uniform held a gun to the back of a woman's head. From the position and where she sat in a chair, West could only see her hair, long and brown.

That didn't tell him a damn thing other than they had a hostage situation, which ranked pretty low on his list of favorite things.

He scanned the small room, taking in as much information as possible. Overturned furniture, glass shattered and covering the floor. The worn soles of sandals sticking out from under an overturned chair. From the size, probably male, which suggested they already had one down.

It looked to be an operating room of sorts. Equipment, all with plugs ripped from the walls, placed in a circle like a shield between the hostile and whoever might come storming in. Tables and supplies strewn around.

Someone came looking for someone or something, and since West didn't see an older white male, he guessed the hostile found his target, and now was biding his time.

One faint click came from his watch. Well-timed, just as expected from someone of Josiah's expertise. Between the wind and the crunch as the gunman shifted his weight and crushed whatever lodged under his foot, the sound barely registered. West answered with two clicks. The prearranged signal.

He started the mental countdown. When he got to one, he crossed the threshold and slammed his shoulder against cabinet blocking his path to the hostile. With access open, West dropped. Gunfire pounded over his head in rapid succession. Panic firing.

Then came the swearing. West couldn't make out

the words or nail down the dialect, Urdu or Balti, or maybe a regional dialect, but he knew ticked off, and this guy sounded like that.

The hostile shouted as West slithered across the floor on his stomach. Fast and unconcerned about sound now, his knees thudded against the wood as he scrambled over the lifeless body he saw earlier—definitely male—and headed for the woman. Shots pinged around him and Josiah yelled for the guy to stop firing. Yeah, this one wasn't going without a fight.

Launching his body, West switched from prone to the balls of his feet, hitting the hostile square in the side and driving him into the wall as the man aimed at Josiah. The guy's assault rifle dropped then clattered against the floor. West saw the flash of movement as Josiah jumped over a broken desk on his way to provide backup.

West stayed focused on knocking this guy out. Registering the glint of steel, he pivoted as the hostile's blade sliced through the air in a wild arc. West heard a rip but didn't feel pain. He slammed his body over and against the smaller man, crushing him into the thin wall.

The hostile groaned and shouted, but the frantic knife-waving didn't cease. West caught a nick along his chin. Felt the blood swell. Got really fucking pissed off and the rage went nuclear when the hostile shoved against him and tried to knock his head back.

When the guy's fingers brushed against the extra gun West kept at his side, he stopped trying to take him alive and fired. A single shot rang out. A boom, and the guy's hands dropped. His balance faltered as his head lolled to the side. Unsteady on his feet, he smashed into the wall and stayed pinned there by West's hand.

Blood seeped through the hostile's fingers where he covered the wound, and the color left his face. A second shot, this time from Josiah's gun, nailed the guy in the forehead and took him out for good.

Breathing in, forcing the adrenaline buzzing through him to slow, West eased his grip on his gun. The whole attack probably took less than two minutes, but it dragged in West's head. He lived every second in slow motion. Always did.

Suddenly he was facing down the barrel of a nasty assault weapon. An AK-103 or something similarly problematic in the hands of someone aiming it at his head. To add to the fun, this one had a grenade launcher attached to it. Which was just fucking fabulous.

West's gaze traveled over the shaking arms to the white-knuckle grip on the plastic. Then to her face. A brunette of the shockingly hot variety. Not that he cared about that on a job.

He didn't like shooting women, but he would. He had. An enemy was an enemy, and he waited to see if that's the tack the victim-turned-potential-attacker took.

"Two roads diverged." She spit out the not-so-random sentence, and the dark energy spinning around the room eased.

"Well, damn," West whispered, stunned to hear the code from her.

Josiah lowered his gun as he finished the agreed-upon signal. The one the doctor provided and insisted on, citing faulty short-term memory and a love or Robert Frost. "Sorry I could not travel both."

She blew out a long breath as the stiffness across her shoulders eased. "Thank God you're here."

West tagged her as American but definitely not male, which made little sense under the circumstances. But she wasn't firing at random, so he considered that a bit of good luck.

Still, a potential novice with a weapon was an invitation to get his nuts blown off, and he sure as hell didn't agree to that when he signed Alliance's employment contract. "Ma'am, I need to you put that gun down."

She blinked a few times before her gaze went to her hands. It was as if she forgot she took it off the dead guy when he dropped it. "Why?"

West chalked the confusion up to the chaos of the last few minutes. Still, shock and bullets rarely mixed well. "I don't want to be shot."

Her chin came up as she nodded at him. "That makes two of us, so you lower your weapon first."

Okay, chaos or not, her attempt to order him around was pretty fucking hot. Kind of brave, too. "No."

Not dropping his guard, West took a second to study her. Long hair, half in and half out of a ponytail, huge whiskey brown eyes, and the sexiest pouty mouth he'd ever seen. He couldn't make out her frame under the olive pants and oversized long-sleeve tee but he guessed curvy.

Not just pretty but lose-the-ability-to-spell sexy. Of course that could be the gun. Something about a woman holding a weapon turned him on, sick twist that he was.

"I'm not really giving you a choice," he said, more to stall than anything else.

Josiah moved in, step by small step, as if not to scare or rattle her. Pretty soon two trained men would almost be on top of her, and then it was just a matter of time until one of them wrestled the weapon away from her.

And that's how it would end because there was no way West was heading back home after this and listening to the shit he would get from Bravo if he let a hot brunette get the jump on him and take a shot. He had a badass shoot-anything reputation to uphold.

"At this distance I can blow your balls off," she said, looking ready to do just that.

Then again . . . "Okay, that's a solid argument."

That fast West held up his fist to stop Josiah's attack. Thought he saw Delta leader's lips twitch in a smile, too.

Josiah circled wide around her and dropped next to the men bleeding on the floor. He grabbed paperwork out of their pockets and checked pulses. West decided to keep his eye on the woman with the gun instead of moving around.

After a few minutes she lowered the weapon. Didn't put it down or ease her grip, but it no longer aimed at his groin, and he was pretty damn grateful for that.

"You're American." Josiah made the obvious call, which sounded ridiculous in his British accent.

She frowned at him. Gave him one of those you're-an-idiot expressions women did so well. "And you just killed a man."

West looked down. Saw the blood. "Yeah, but he attacked first. Well, maybe not technically."

"It's his country."

True, so West didn't debate the point. Also held off on the fifty or so questions bouncing around in his head about her and the urge to demand answers, including the identity of the guy he shot as well as the other guy on the floor. Not to mention the part where she looked to be a captive a second ago but seemed just fine now.

He ignored those and zipped right to the heart of the mission. "Dr. Alex Palmer?"

Some of the tension around her eyes disappeared and the barrel of her gun tipped until it aimed at the floor. "Sort of."

Now West knew they were in trouble. "What the hell is a 'sort of' doctor?"

"Ma'am." Josiah stood up again. "You knew the code but are now saying you're not the doctor. You care to explain that?"

She winced. "Sort of not the doctor."

Josiah took his place next to West. Tall with a could-kick-your-ass attitude, Josiah looked every inch in control. "Stop saying that."

"Yeah, wrong answer," West said at the same time.

When she just stood there, he tried again. "In case you're not clear, this conversation is not going well for you."

Her gaze moved back and forth between the men. "Do you two practice that act? The rapid-fire question thing combined with the disapproving looks and the semithreatening comments?"

Josiah exhaled as he hitched his thumb in West's direction. "You have two seconds to say something that doesn't make West, here, twitchy."

Her gaze switched back to West. "He doesn't look like the nervous type."

Never mind that "he" was standing right there.

Josiah snapped his fingers, probably to regain her attention, but the move earned him a glare instead. "You don't look like a sixty-year-old male doctor from Seattle, so talk. Who are you and where is he?"

"He's on his way to Everest. He won't be available until he reaches base camp, which is days away."

The shitty news just kept coming. West was ready for a little luck. "That's just fucking fabulous."

She stood up straight enough for her back to snap. "I'm his daughter. That's how I knew the signal."

Josiah didn't move. "Uh-huh."

"My dad is Alex. I'm Alexis. You can call me Lexi."

West had studied the file. Knew all about Palmer and his kid and where she wasn't supposed to be—here. West didn't think he could hate this assignment more than he had, but right then it took another step into crapville. "You're saying a lot of names but not explaining anything."

"Does it help that I can press one button and bring the Pakistani army running?" She picked up a small black box off the floor. It could have done anything, been anything. "As far as I'm concerned that means I'm in charge right now."

Josiah's hands went to his hips. "Oh, really."

West understood Josiah's reaction. She was dead wrong about her role in the power structure, but West admired spunk. "The dead guys on the floor suggest otherwise."

Her eyebrow lifted. "Don't let the breasts fool you. I know how to use the gun I'm holding."

Well, damn. Now West had no idea where he should look.

"Noted." All of it. The breasts, the gun, the face. Pretty or not, smooth-talking or not, this woman was trouble. A warning sign flashed above her head, and he added a mental *Stay away* to keep from becoming the world's biggest dick.

But the ticking at the back of his neck warned of an impending screwing, and not the good kind. No, this land had fucked him over once before. He had a feeling he was headed straight for round two.

2

LEXI TRIED not to heave. The air jammed in her throat and her heartbeat hammered hard enough to rock her whole body. Not that she would let these two guys know it.

She'd gotten the call out for help and shouldered some of the risk while using her dad's connections. Just as he taught her. Also dropped his name in the right international circles to make sure the right people in power took the warning seriously. Gave the emergency signal and called in favors, all in his name because like it or not a man's name got you further in these parts than a woman's.

Never mind that she ran the clinic right now while her dad acted as the medical representative for expeditions on Everest and Lhotse, two of the world's highest mountain peaks. The clinic was his baby, but left alone, she dealt with the local political operation and waded through all the restrictions about things she had to do to blend in and be a part of a community.

And as soon as she could reach him at base camp she'd fill him in.

Thanks to her chronic insomnia, she'd noticed the late night convoys and watched as the trucks rolled into the base of the mountain. Saw the men unload what looked liked weapons. Town-destroying, war-starting weapons.

In her place, she knew her dad would have made the call to report the odd shipments. He'd probably have tried to shuffle her out of the country first because he still saw her as a confused girl of fifteen instead of a twenty-six-year-old adult. She'd long ago decided to think of the overprotectiveness thing as charming rather than what it was—annoying. But there were days her tolerance ran low.

The two guys in front of her? She hadn't decided what they were yet. They worked for some agency. They weren't aid workers or doctors. They were trained killers with guns, which didn't matter. What they lacked in charm they made up for in firepower. And really, she needed lethal, not likable.

She'd hoped for black ops experts and expected fighting machines. Seemed like her wish had been granted.

As she looked now, she pinned them as the grown-up Boy Scout type and the hot could-lift-a-truck type. One of those sounded like he could be the right guy for this job.

Since knowing their real names might be easier than her assigned nicknames, she tried that. "Who are you two? And by that I mean what do I call you?"

Her gaze traveled between them but kept landing on

the big one. Tall, well over six feet, with broad shoulders big enough for her to climb and sandy brown hair in a military cut. If there was an extra ounce of body fat on him, she couldn't find it, and God knew she kept looking for it. No, those muscles bulged just fine through the thin fabric of his form-fitting athletic jacket.

For women who liked their men brawny and quiet while wearing a fierce glare, he'd be a dream candidate. She generally went for the studious, researcher type who never stepped foot inside a gym. Still, there was something about this guy—his demeanor, the way he answered every verbal shot she threw out with either one of his own or a confused frown . . . the whole big and hot and protective thing—that had her staring.

While the silence dragged on, the one who looked kind of proper and a bit more refined, though that could have been the British accent, studied the documents he'd picked off the dead guys. She ignored him and continued to analyze the man locked with her in a staring contest.

No, there was nothing pretty about him. He possessed a rough-around-the-edges look and seemed unapologetic about it. He held that gun like . . . well, like he slept with the damn thing. Maybe that's what drew her. If a battle came, he'd be a good guy to stand behind.

Then a thought broke through the adrenaline rush of confusion and frustration. They hadn't answered her simple question. She was about to pipe up and ask again when the dark-haired one spoke. Didn't bother to lift his head. "I'm Josiah. He's West."

She'd expected last names. First or not, these sounded fake. "Those are . . . unusual."

The corner of West's mouth twitched. "You should be more interested in what we can do with a hand grenade."

Okay, she'd bite. Didn't look like they were moving until these two said so anyway. "And the answer to that is?"

"Anything." He made the word last for what sounded like fifteen syllables.

Yeah, he'd be a good shield. "That's strangely comforting."

And if her instincts were right, they were going to need one. She'd been waiting for the CIA or SEALS to storm in. Maybe these guys were one of those. She still didn't know but at least someone listened and sent reinforcements. It would suck if she'd gotten this whole convoy thing wrong.

"Happy to help." This time West smiled.

At least she thought he did. It came and went so fast it could have been anything. Gas, boredom . . . an inner need to kill things. Maybe he remembered shooting the guard and that made him chuckle, who the hell knew.

The next two seconds might give her an answer. She blinked, losing the staring contest, but only because her eyes started to water. "Then lower the gun."

Josiah glanced up and watched. She watched. Minutes of silence ticked by, then a few more. She couldn't tell the exact number. Couldn't look away from West's intense green eyes either.

For a big guy he could hold still. Not move or talk. The quiet made her head pound, and his ability to prolong the waiting without flinching made being patient that much harder.

Just when she thought her insides might crawl out from the building tension, West nodded. The gun, at least the one in his hand, disappeared into the holster at his hip. Impressive that he listened but not a miracle. From this angle, about three feet away, she counted three other weapons on him. And those were the ones she could see.

"You obeyed her order?" Josiah asked with more than a little awe in his voice.

West shrugged. "Yes."

Since there was no need to tick these two off, she tried to tone the language down. "It was more of a request."

"Because she told you to?" Josiah's blue eyes bulged. "Since when do you listen to unknowns?"

"I'm an unknown?" That didn't sound very promising.

"For now," West said.

She had no idea what that meant or what question he was answering. "Okay, then."

The odd male interaction suggested she'd won the debate, but she doubted it. The big guy struck her as someone who didn't do anything without having four backup plans ready. He could probably slice off her nose without moving his arms. She wasn't in the mood to test him, so she handed him the gun she swiped off the floor during chaos while bullets had ricocheted around her.

Good thing she wasn't the pass out, throw up, or run away type. She'd grown up hearing about surgeries and seeing blood, then enjoyed a front-row seat to it all while in school. She remembered all those photos of climbers who came off the mountains with frostbitten limbs and devastating injuries. She'd seen split skin and cracked bones that would make most people lose a month full of lunches.

Her father had an odd sense of what constituted appropriate vacation photos. As a young girl she used to heave as she flipped through those albums. Training and lots of heavy inhaling helped. Now she saw things that might take down even this big guy West. Though probably not. He didn't look as if he'd fall all that easily.

The one thing she'd learned while working in and around Skardu—don't show fear. Deference and respect, yes. Defiance and ego, no. The people who lived there were decent and generous, but you did not mess with the military. The presence and power proved stifling.

"I know the hostile who had you captive was part of a patrol. Can tell by the uniform and papers." Josiah pointed to the body that was already on the floor when they stormed the building. "But who is this guy?"

She'd asked the same question a few minutes earlier. "No idea."

West frowned at her. "Seriously?"

"He came in and started shouting, then the guard burst through the back door and shot him." She shook her head as she studied the carnage around her, blocking out the human toll and trying to concentrate on pure facts. "I couldn't pick up the dialect or understand what he was saying."

"We need to move."

With comments like that, West looked smarter and smarter to her. Getting them to follow her might be trickier. "Agreed. Here's the plan—"

"Excuse me?"

She ignored the Brit and the accent and the whole talking-down-to-her thing. She lived here. She knew the people and the danger. Maybe these two shot people for a living or wrestled lions or whatever—fine, she wouldn't judge—but she followed the rules, and that included knowing where and when to go places. All their intel couldn't give them a global look at the reality on the ground.

There was only one way to get out of this without endangering her father's work or risking her ability to stay in-country with him. "We're going to finish ripping this place apart."

West moved his foot and something crunched under his heel. "That shouldn't take much effort."

At least they were still listening. "Make it look like

someone came in here searching for drugs and killed the guard and that guy, whoever he is." She struggled to remember him from anywhere but nothing came to her.

Josiah frowned at her. "We need—"

"Don't use anything that can be traced back to you, or your group, or even the United States, or Great Britain, though I'm unclear on how you fit in here." She waved her hand at Josiah as she said the last part.

"You're not alone," West said in a dry tone.

She kept right on talking, somehow knowing if she stopped they'd jump in and she'd never get the floor back. "You need to wipe out any sign that I was here at the time. That might work since the clinic was supposed to be closed hours ago."

There. Now she'd finished, though the sudden silence following the reveal of her big plan did unnerve her.

Josiah glanced at West. Neither man said anything as the quiet ticked on. When Josiah started talking, he hesitated over the words. "You're a 'sort of' doctor? You sure you're not CIA?"

"Or a drill sergeant?" West asked.

If they thought that was bossy now, they were going to love the next few minutes. She pointed at West. "You're coming with me, getting me out of here in one piece."

That sexy lip twitch of his came back. "How did I get so lucky?"

She didn't see a reason to pretty it up. "You're big."

"So I've heard."

Didn't sound like she'd offended him . . . yet. "I figure if someone shoots at me they're more likely to hit you. That makes you the most valuable man in my life at the moment."

That was the reason for finding him compelling. Some sort of anthropological trigger. Like a survival instinct. It had to be.

She tried to put all the pieces together and make her reaction to him fit. The unwanted smack of interest. The whole couldn't-stop-staring-at-him issue. It all boiled down to his size. Being big and loaded down with weapons, West would protect her. He'd been trained to do so.

Even if the guy wore a bag over his head it wouldn't matter. Getting her out was his job, and she had a feeling he excelled at the whole rescuing thing. No way would someone high up in the U.S. intelligence community send a novice in to get the intel she claimed to have, or they thought her father had. No one knew about her, apparently. Of course, that didn't explain why the Brit tagged along.

Josiah shook his head. "The idea of using West as a shield sounds pretty bloodthirsty for a doctor, sort of or not."

"Smart, though," West said.

She skipped over the doctor part and long-winded explanations about her dad being unavailable as he hiked to the base of Everest for fun. There would be time for twenty questions later . . . she hoped. "Besides that, I think I can probably outrun you."

This time West scoffed. A big hearty tone that sounded as if it rolled from deep in his chest. "You would lose that bet."

There it was. Self-confidence. A good thing to possess in this situation. West was definitely the right answer for her human shield.

They could debate the details of her life and his running skills later. Right after the get-to-know-you talk, which she planned to avoid altogether. "Either way, we only have a few minutes."

"Because?" Josiah asked as he held up the edge of the worn curtain and checked outside.

"These guys patrol in groups of two. The one you both took a shot at is the more agreeable of the two on the night watch." The one not in the room was a complete ass who used intimidation to get whatever he wanted in town. "His partner will kill us without asking questions. Or arrest us, and here that's much worse."

Josiah finished scanning the outside through the window and turned back to face them. "Good news is we neutralized the other guy."

West frowned. "We?"

"Neutralized?" she asked at the same time.

Josiah spared them both a glance before returning to informal guard duty. "As soon as this one doesn't check in or the other one wakes up—"

"Wait, you didn't kill his partner?" Sweet damn. Now there was a mistake. She valued life and worked hard to save everyone that passed through the clinic, but this was not a place where you could silence a military officer and expect to live.

"—we'll have guards up our ass if we don't get moving."

Josiah had a point there. Only a stupid person would argue when they should be running, and she was not stupid. "This time I'll agree."

If West's eyebrow lifted any farther it would hit his hairline. "You don't get a choice. Besides, you have enough problems without causing more."

She stopped in mid-stride on the way to her overturned desk and shot West a glare. Caught him staring at her ass. "Meaning?"

Josiah groaned. "Children—"

"You shouldn't be here. You have unverified identity, questionable intel, and bodies scattered across the floor." West ticked off her alleged sins. "You could be friend or foe, and we won't know until we interrogate you."

He used that word on purpose. To terrorize her. She'd bet on it. "I think I want the gun back."

"In that case I'm thinking I should frisk you for other weapons." West managed to deliver the line without sounding threatening. Didn't move a muscle either.

But the more he morphed into superwarrior, the less compelling she found him . . . or that's what she tried to tell herself. That should have been the case, but something about the tone, the command, worked for her. Damn him.

Still, no way was she getting felt up in the middle of a crime scene. "Touch me and I bite off your hand."

After a second he nodded. "Fair enough."

When she blinked again Josiah stood between her and West. Probably a smart move.

Josiah touched his watch as he talked with West. "You take Dr. Palmer—"

"Ms." No need to let that misconception linger on too long. This happened to be a touchy subject for her.

"So, not just 'sort of a doctor,' you're actually not a doctor at all. Looks like we found something else we need to talk about." West's dry tone didn't exactly hide his frustration. He may as well have said, *She's working on my nerves,* and been done with it.

She wasn't offended because that grumbly sensation deep in her belly hadn't eased since she watched him fly across the room to nail the guard to the wall. "Fine, but I have a few questions for you as well."

Josiah talked right over both of them. "Lexi, take only what you absolutely need because the point is to make it look like a normal night."

Hearing her name with the accent threw her for a second but she quickly got back on track. "Right."

A mental list came together as she conducted a visual search of the room. She needed the usual, like her bag, but the jump drive mattered most. She didn't need to hunt that down because she'd tucked it into her pocket when the bullets started flying.

"I'll stay behind and clean up the scene," Josiah said. "We'll rendezvous in fifteen at the planned spot."

That grabbed her attention as much as the touch of West's hand on her elbow. She blocked the odd sensation spinning through her as her gaze bounced between the two men. "Which is where?"

West shook his head. "You don't need to know right now."

He didn't pull or grab, but he brought her in closer to his side before she could put on the brakes or jerk away. She stared at his hands. Long fingers. Tan. Calluses. Workingman's hands.

"So that you're clear." She glared at his hand, trying to send a message. "I hate that in a guy."

"What?"

"Bossiness."

West flashed her an actual smile. Not a half. Not a smirk. "Then the next few hours are really going to suck for you."

3

GETTING LEXI out of the clinic took another three minutes. Minutes West wasn't convinced they had, but she'd insisted on grabbing a few things. Since one item turned out to be a medical kit and the chance they'd need one of those grew with every passing second, he gave in without too much bitching.

But then the talking started. Sure, she kept the unending stream of chatter to a whisper as they walked, but still. A man needed peace every now and then, and he craved silence more than most.

Ducking behind trees and keeping her shielded half behind him, West guided her through the open area to a line of houses. Darkness had fallen and the cold wind turned frigid. She'd grabbed a jacket but her teeth still clicked together.

The wicking material of his shirt helped, but the thin jacket could only block so much. Still, he'd dealt with freezing temperatures before. The bone-chilling cold this time came as much from memories of his last stay in the region as from reality.

They slipped through a gate and into a rough courtyard. Two rows of guest houses faced each other. He knew from the operation briefing that the mountaineering crowd used these. The rooms looked as if they'd been patterned after inexpensive motel rooms in the U.S., rotating door then window then door again.

Equipment balanced against the outer walls near the doors. Ice axes and trekking poles. Water bottles sat on plastic chairs scattered around the grassy area. Someone had set up a yellow dome tent in the center of the makeshift common yard.

The place was small and practical, and not the set meeting place. He grunted as he nodded in the direction he wanted them to go. Straight through to the opposite end.

"Where are we—"

"Quiet." He slipped his fingers through hers and gave them a gentle squeeze.

Before she could complain or yell at him, he pulled her through the night. Stepped over discarded gear and across the uneven turf that served as the lawn as he picked up speed. Kept going until they reached the end of the row and turned right toward a separate building set back from the rest. The manager's office for the guest houses. The meeting place sat behind the office.

They'd slipped around the side of the office before she began to launch into a new conversation. "If you would listen to—"

He pulled her to a stop and pressed her back against the far corner of the building away from the road into the property and just outside the bright circle of the security light. Even with limited illumination, this close he could stare into her eyes.

Her chest rose and fell on hard breaths as her hands rested against his forearms. Soft breaths blew across his chin.

Well, this position was a big fucking mistake.

"What are you doing? Why are we stopping here?" The words sounded labored, as if she struggled to get them out.

He didn't want to scare her, but shaking some sense into her quickly moved up his To Do list. "I'm thinking you're confused by the definition of the word quiet."

She thumped a fist against his chest. When he didn't move, a certain wariness fell over her. Narrowed eyes and lips in a thin line. "Are you always this difficult?"

"Yes." Better that she knew now. The next few hours would be rough for her. He'd keep her safe but he couldn't promise she'd enjoy how he made that happen.

"At least you're honest."

Jesus, that mouth. Always moving and so fucking hot. A sudden kick of need to taste her hit him out of nowhere. "Uh-huh."

He shook his head to knock the stupid thoughts out. The intelligent eyes. The sharp comebacks. The way she walked, slow and lingering, with her hips rocking a gentle sway from side to side.

Not that he noticed.

"Could you—"

He put a finger over those lips. "Wait."

Even on the verge of losing his mind, he heard it. The rumble of male voices hit him first. Low but there. Then the footsteps, crunching against the stones and not bothering to hide the trail straight to them. As the sounds drew closer, West pressed her tighter against the building, covering her body with his and ignoring the heated friction as they rubbed against each other.

"What are you doing now?"

That fast he clamped his palm over her mouth. Her cheeks heated under his hand as she pushed against his chest. When he put his finger to his lips, she stilled. She morphed from pissed to something else. Her nails dug into his skin through two layers of clothing and her eyes widened as her gaze locked on his face.

He mouthed, *It's okay,* and she nodded. Dropping his hand, he reached for his gun. With his body still pressed into hers and one hand balancing on the wall next to her head, he waited. Listened. Prepared to shoot then grab her and run like hell. He'd carry her if he had to.

Seconds ticked by. The voices grew louder and his finger inched closer to the trigger. Taking down two wouldn't be a hardship. The numbers didn't faze him. But handling hostiles while guarding Lexi from stray bullets was a bigger concern.

He widened his stance, covering as much of her body as possible with his. He'd slide off her and . . . but then the voices faded. He strained to hear the conversation. To pick up snippets. The footsteps retreated and the wind covered every sound except her heavy breathing.

When a tremor ran through her and into him, he glanced down. One of her hands rested on his belt and the other clenched his hand, an inch away from his gun. Both were a problem. One needed to stop right now . . . but for some reason he mentioned the other one. "Don't touch my gun."

"What?"

"A man's weapon is sacred." True, but his mind flicked away from the small armory he carried and back to her. A smart-ass comeback caught in his throat. Something about what he wanted to do to her once they were somewhere safe.

"I'm not touching that comment." Her hands dropped to her sides and her back stayed pressed deeper into the wall. "Just don't shoot everyone who crosses our path."

"I can't promise that."

She froze. "Try."

He shrugged even though the adrenaline pulsing through him called for him to do something else. "If they start it . . ."

She treated him to one of those long and tortured sighs. "I know you're big on death and all, but—"

That shook him out of his poorly timed lust. "No, I'm not."

The sighing turned into a frown. "You're also a bit of a pain in the ass about not letting me finish a sentence."

The woman had a point, but he refused to smile. Not

while they were out in the open. He couldn't afford to let her think the danger had passed. "Go ahead. Say whatever you want to say."

"You kill for a living."

He hit the brakes a second time. "I don't."

"No?"

An innocent sounding question but an insult nonetheless. He fought for a purpose. He had a debt to repay, and somehow he'd bank enough goodwill to extinguish it. "I'm not a fucking mercenary."

He expected her to back down. He barked, women cowered. The cycle rarely broke down on him. His size and tone combined and people made assumptions. He used them to his advantage.

She eyed him up, letting her gaze wander over his body, over, around, and down. "You look like a former soldier."

He hated that description. "I'm a retired Marine."

"Aren't we saying the same thing?"

He bit back a string of profanity. "Not even close."

The whole checking-him-out thing continued for another few seconds before she folded her arms over her stomach and leaned into him. "I'm starting to think you like to argue."

Between the talking and the touching she had him spinning. "Not really."

"Was that supposed to be funny?"

This woman was going to be the death of him. Rather than yell or order or knock her out and throw her over his shoulder—which was pretty damn tempting—he reached for the last bit of patience he could muster. "We need to get you to—"

"I have a place." She smiled at him. "Yeah, see? The interrupting thing is annoying, isn't it?"

No way was he answering that. "We have a set rendezvous site."

"You find it on a map, big guy?"

He planted both hands against the wall and stared down at her. Maybe intimidation would work. God knew nothing else had with her. "Excuse me?"

"Have you ever even been here? To Pakistan, let alone Skardu?" Instead of backing down she poked him in the chest. "Do you know anything about the people, the area? I happen to live here part of the year."

This is the kind of shit that happened when he got dragged into a conversation. But, big news, this was not a topic he planned to have with her now or ever. "Yes."

Her head snapped back and she swore when it smacked against the building. "What question are you answering?"

Much more of this and she'd injure herself. He slid a hand under her head to keep that from happening. Soft hair fell over his fingers and he massaged the spot where she hit. "I've been here before."

"Don't sigh at me." Most of the heat had left her voice but the color in her cheeks brightened. "Wait, do you mean in Pakistan?"

"Yes but also right here."

"Skardu?" She whispered the word.

Yeah, that was enough of that. He slipped his hand out from behind her. "Can you move?"

Anger flashed across her face again. "What kind of question is that?"

She was so damned prickly. Talkative and sensitive and hot . . . Jesus. He exhaled, long and loud enough for her to know he was done with this. "A simple one."

He held out his hand, surprised when she threaded her fingers through his. Not that he intended to walk this way. They weren't on a date. This was combat. But he needed her to follow his direction, and since telling her to do things didn't work, he tried showing her.

"What's happening right now?" Her words stumbled but she didn't shrink away from him.

"Follow me." He guided her hand to his back and hooked her fingers under his jacket on the top of his belt. "Preferably without all the whining."

"You're wearing a vest?"

He assumed she meant the Kevlar. "Of course."

"Should I have one?"

He let the question sit there because she wouldn't like the answer. Rather than batter him with a million more comments, she treated him to a few blissful minutes of quiet.

Shortening his stride, he maneuvered them away from the building and through the overgrown yard separating the office from the shed on the other side of the fenced-in property. She stumbled into his back and he stopped until she regained her balance.

He kept his hands free for his weapons and scanned

the area as they moved. She walked so close to him, so tight against his back, she kicked the heel of his boot several times. Knowing she had to be scared, he ignored it. Pretended he didn't feel it. Even the kick that had him wincing.

The shed door opened without trouble. He'd conducted a quick surveillance. The lack of a lock made an out of the way property the place perfect for a rendezvous spot. He ushered her inside and sat her down on a stack of boxes. After a few seconds of hugging her bag to her chest she dropped it on the floor.

The place reeked of fish, which explained the rod that poked into the side of his head. If there was a light, it was staying off. The only brightness came from the cracks in the wall where the security lights beamed in.

She rubbed her hands together, blowing on them before tucking them under her armpits. "I should have picked Josiah. He's smaller but seems nicer."

"Nice won't keep you alive."

Some of the tension snapping between them decreased. West didn't know if that was good or bad. With his luck, she'd fall asleep on him.

"And you will?" she asked.

Time for a little reassurance. Not his best skill.

He lifted her chin until she stared up at him. "Yes, Lexi. I will."

And that was a fucking vow.

She smiled then, a bit lopsided and not all that convincing, but at least she tried. "I like your confidence."

"Consider it a promise."

"But you don't know what's going to happen when the army finds the bodies or—"

"You will stay alive." He couldn't let her mind wander to any other place. The could-be and what-if possibilities were pretty fucking awful. "I guarantee it."

"Oh."

He skimmed his thumb over her chin, then across her lips, watching her mouth drop open at his touch. His brain telegraphed message after message, telling him to back away, but his body refused the call.

He had no idea how her skin stayed so soft or why her eyes grew so wide. Still, his thumb brushed over her . . . then he heard it. A slight change in the usual sounds of the night. Little more than a whisper.

He'd fine-tuned his ability to pick up on discreet shifts during training and practiced the skill in weekly drills. He used it now, though he'd been a half step too late to get them out of the building before the person or people out there closed in.

She stood up. "What is it?"

"Someone's here." One person and someone with training. Not Josiah because he'd use their signal, but someone who knew how to circle and hide sounds. Just not well enough.

"How can you know that?"

"I should have picked up the cues before now." When he realized his fingers still touched her cheek, he dropped his hand and reached for his gun. "You threw me off."

She made a face that consisted mostly of frowning, squinting, and doing this weird thing with her lips. "I'm not sure if the blame thing is flattering or annoying."

Talk about having the wrong priorities. "Me being off could get us killed."

Some of the color left her face. "Then I'm against you ever being off."

"Ms. Palmer, you need to come out."

West took in the accent and pegged the speaker as a local. That qualified as a pretty big problem. So was the fact that someone had managed to follow them. He had doubled back and covered tracks, so he knew they shouldn't have company.

"Oh no. It can't be." She moved around West but he caught her before she opened the door.

"Who the hell is that?" he asked in a rough whisper.

She looked past him to peek through one of the cracks in the wall then sat back down again. "It is."

As intel, that explanation sucked. "You need to use more words."

"Raheel Najam." She bit down on her bottom lip.

West picked up on her nervous energy but still had no idea what he was dealing with here. Since he had more than one problem at work, he needed specifics to at least handle this one. "Who exactly is Raheel Najam?"

"He works with someone I know." She kept up the biting thing, tapped her foot against the floor . . . ran through an entire repertoire of panicked gestures.

He finally pressed a hand on her knee and got her to stop moving around. "Lexi?"

"A friend of a friend?"

Much more of this and his head would explode. "Are you telling me or asking me?"

"You don't get it." She knocked into his shoulder as she stood up again. "This is bad."

As she turned, he caught her shoulders and forced her to face him. "Why?"

"The friend he's a friend of is in the Pakistani army. So is this guy."

That should have been confusing. It scared the hell out of West that it wasn't. "I can't believe I followed that explanation."

"Do you need assistance?" The male voice called out again, this time only a few feet from the door. "There's a problem at the clinic and I've been looking for you."

That's the part West didn't get. Skardu was about twenty-five miles long. While an American woman might stick out among the two thousand or so people who lived there, they'd been tracked.

"I'm fine." She yelled the answer then put a hand over her mouth.

West nodded to let her know her answer sounded fine. Last thing he needed was her getting plowed under by a new wave of panic.

"I'm here to help," Raheel yelled.

Of course he was. The bastard. The familiarity ticked West off and he refused to think about why.

West watched the guy move around out there instead. "Exactly how well do you know him?"

"I told you."

She had a habit of saying words and not telling him much, which annoyed the piss out of West. "Not really."

"Stay here." She gave his arm a squeeze then buzzed past him.

"Don't—" He started to follow then shrank back so he wouldn't be immediately visible to anyone in the yard. He'd have to storm out there, and when he did he wanted the element of surprise on his side. Easier to fire a killing shot that way. Though if they had been tracked, Raheel had to know he followed two and not one.

The brief wait gave West a minute to control the explosion of rage inside him. The woman had meandered her way to here from the clinic, but now, when she wanted to move, she darted out of his grasp at record speed. It was good to know she could move when needed. Problem was, she stood outside and he was inside.

West went back to looking through one of the cracks. Saw her rush up to the stranger. A man in uniform. An olive green jumpsuit with a belt and a gun strapped to his upper thigh. A visible gun. The patch stood out even from this distance. What looked like a yellow 5 and a picture of a mountain.

West recognized the insignia of the Pakistani Army Air Aviation No. 5 Squadron, otherwise known as the Fearless Five. The elite team of helicopter pilots that specialized in mountain rescues and could fly up to 20,000 feet. Total badasses. Not the guys he wanted to hunt down and eliminate. He would but he'd be pissed about it.

She didn't touch the man but seemed to bow her head as she approached. "Is something wrong?"

This Raheel kept glancing over her shoulder toward the shed. Right past her. "There's an issue."

"What kind?" With him she sounded deferential, not belligerent.

Smart woman.

Raheel gestured toward the front of the property. "I know you have someone with you and you both need to come with me."

She was not taking even one step with this guy. West silently started a countdown in his head.

"Why with you?" She shook her head. "I don't understand."

"Now isn't the time for questions. We can fix this but we have to leave now."

Raheel reached for her and West lunged. He slammed open the door and flew past Lexi. Not giving the guy time to recover from the surprise, he rammed the heel of his hand right at the guy's neck. One shot and the guy's hands went to his throat. A guttural rattle escaped his mouth but no other sound came out.

West landed a second shot with his elbow. Hit the guy right at the back of the neck, and he dropped in a motionless sprawl in the dirt.

Lexi stared down at the prone form then back up at West. "What did you do that for?"

Not exactly the grateful reaction he expected. "The guy touched you."

"And your plan is to kill everyone in Pakistan who touches me?" She sounded appalled by the idea. The way she screwed up her lips in a look of distaste didn't seem good either.

"He's not dead."

Her eyes widened and her head shifted forward. "What?"

West wasn't accustomed to having his judgment challenged. From the snap in her voice he half expected her to flag down the nearest Pakistani army truck and have him arrested. Which made him wonder what this guy meant to her. "Raheel is only unconscious."

"Are you kidding?"

"You lost me." Not a surprise since she'd been doing that to him almost from the second they met.

"You keep injuring people but not finishing them off."

She was angry he *didn't* kill the guy? "For a *sort of* doctor who is not really a doctor you have a fixation with seeing people die. You also have a tracker on you."

"What does that even mean?"

They didn't have time for him to give her the long explanation or pretty up the words. "Where did the men in the clinic touch you?"

"They didn't." She tried to step back from him.

West caught her before she could get very far. "Lexi, think. Walk through every movement. Did either of the men touch your back or—"

"Just my arm."

That's all he needed. As gently as possible he moved his hands over her arms. It only took a second. There by her elbow. A small black square. High-tech and very effective. Someone had been tracking her movements—their movements—and he wanted to know why.

"Ow . . ." She lowered her head, knocking it against the side of his as she rubbed her arm. "What is that?"

"Looks like your clinic visitors saw you as a threat." Maybe they wanted her to get away. The other possibility was that someone knew he and Josiah were on the ground and on the move. West hated that option because it meant a mole or a break in the communication trail somewhere. Both very bad options.

"How am I going to explain this?" She walked around in a circle, muttering about "idiots" and rubbing her forehead.

None of that clued him into whatever was happening in that head of hers. "When, what, and to whom?"

"To borrow your staccato delivery, injured army guys, trackers, you."

He had no idea what the staccato thing was about, but he did need to make one thing very clear. "You won't because you will not be here."

She stopped and glared at him. "No, *you'll* be gone and I'll be here, which is the problem. I'm thinking attacking Raheel is going to make the clinic break-in story harder to sell." She blew out a breath and went back to circling. "Damn it."

"You're not staying." He caught her at the next turn and lowered his head until she gave him eye contact. This was too important to skip over or let her think she had a say. "Lexi, you know that, right? There are two men from our team working outside of Skardu. We'll pass you off to them and they'll get you out of here and back to the United States while Josiah and I investigate your claims."

They went deep with a two-man team on this operation. Even with the climbers coming in and out, foreigners stuck out in Pakistan. They could disguise a lot but not their lethal nature. Four guys with a military look roaming around would raise questions, so he and Josiah had to handle this one alone. Most of Delta team stood ready nearby to pose as climbers preparing for a July expedition on K2, but they wouldn't take the risk unless necessary. Until then they stayed connected and talked via the communication system—the comm— that tied them all together in-country through their watches and tiny receivers.

"Investigate my claims?" She didn't pay attention to anything but West now. "You're saying you don't believe me?"

"You, or your dad . . . someone, made a pretty serious charge about weapons being moved around up here." The details still didn't make sense but West would get them later.

"That was me."

"Fine." Knowing her stubbornness, she probably

had managed to pretend her way through this, which was quite something in light of the intelligence community firepower aimed in her direction at the moment. "You think we're going to get the intel out of you—"

"Out of me?"

"—then leave you behind?" He stopped because her brown eyes had gone almost black. Looked like her rage matched his, and could, even on his worst days.

She lifted her chin. "I'm ignoring that for now except to say my job is here."

She was a smart woman, and the fact they were spending two minutes on this subject with an unconscious guy sprawled between them made West's head pound. "It was. Not anymore."

"I hate everything about what you just said."

"Okay." To keep from drawing even more attention West linked his hands under Raheel's arms and dragged him into the shed. Didn't tie him down. Didn't need to. Unless Lexi drove him insane they'd be long gone by the time the other man woke up.

She pointed a finger at him. "One final time because I feel the need to have the last word: I'm staying here. My work is here."

Conscious or unconscious, the woman was leaving Pakistan as soon as he could get her safe transport out. "No."

"You can't just say no."

"Watch me." He was done with this topic and he was sure as hell finished standing out in the open. The rendezvous spot was compromised. That meant one thing. He slipped the small silver disk in his ear and tapped the button on his watch. "Scatter."

Her eyes narrowed. They did that a lot when he talked. "What was that about?"

"New orders." The comm and the satphone in his pocket were the only options for staying connected to his team. "We need to find somewhere else to hide before the next set meet-up time."

"I thought that was now."

"We missed this window." West conducted a quick search of Raheel's pockets. He came up with a few folded papers and a wallet. He left the latter. "From what this guy was saying, it sounds like someone found one of the bodies I've left lying around and—"

"Nicely done."

He almost smiled at the load of sarcasm in her voice. "You need to work on your gratitude."

"Or you could listen to me and follow me to the hiding place I was going to suggest. This way." She held the door open and motioned for him to come back outside. "Trust me."

The last time someone said that to him, the day ended buried in a pile of ice and snow. "For the record, I'm not big on trust."

She turned and started walking. "Yeah, well. You'll need to work on that."

4

CLUSTERFUCK. THE word summed up the day so far, and it was just after ten in the morning.

Ward Bennett turned away from the wall of monitors lining the Warehouse and watched Tasha Gregory, the love of his life, the woman he lived with and his boss at Alliance, walk into the room. The swing of those hips. The slim-fitting tank top and dark utility pants. He could watch her move all damn day.

Good thing her office sat a building away in Liberty Crossing, the official home of the National Counterterrorism Center in McLean, Virginia, or he'd break their business-personal separation vow. She had a corner office and a big title. And an ass that made him wild. The combination of her fighter instinct and that face had him going under from the first time he met her.

She stopped right in front of him and picked the file out of his hands. Didn't open it, but took it away without so much as blinking. "What do we have?"

"A mess." He could give that answer almost every day and have it be correct. That's what happened when you chased human garbage for a living and didn't have too many rules outlining how you should do it.

He fucking loved this job.

She flipped the file open and started scanning. "You'll need to be more specific."

Since the information in her hand had nothing to do with the men currently on the ground, he put a hand over the page. "West gave the scatter command. He and Josiah separated and are underground. We have radio silence at the moment."

"And the doctor?" Tasha looked up, kept going as if he'd never interrupted her. She was a woman who knew how to stay on task no matter what. "Where is he?"

And there was the newest piece of interesting intel. "She."

Tasha's eyes narrowed. "Excuse me?"

Yeah, he had her attention now. He could tell in every line of her body. In her sharp focus. "Apparently the good doctor's daughter found her dad's alarm code and passed the intel exactly as the doctor had been trained to do."

"Difference is, the doctor regularly passes intel. He's on the payroll, so how did his daughter get his codes and his contacts?" Tasha shook her head. "Palmer knows better than to share. We use codes for a reason. No one talks directly with him and nothing can be traced back to his clinic."

Ward knew she was venting, but still . . . "I've actually read the briefing file."

"The daughter could have messed up and ruined everything." Tasha swore under her breath. "Got herself or our men killed."

But Ward knew what Tasha really hated. Someone without clearance and out of their control figured out the go command that got the intel to the right people and eventually on Alliance's radar. How that happened was a good fucking question, and he didn't even have a bad answer for her. Dr. Palmer would need to explain his sudden over-sharing issue once someone dragged him off Everest.

Ward had another worry and knew Tasha did, too. "You think this is a setup."

She nodded before he finished the sentence. "Could be."

With other teams, lesser men, he'd be worried. Not this group. Not with Josiah at point and West on mission. They could probably unseat a long-standing government without even working up a sweat. Ward just hoped they didn't try that with Pakistan.

He wasn't ready to sound that alarm but he'd keep a close watch and send in resources if needed. "West is going to question this woman."

"West is the one with her?" Tasha's hands went to her hips and her head started shaking. "Do we think that's a great idea?"

She clearly didn't. Ward was at about fifty/fifty on that one. "He'll keep her safe."

With a flip of her wrist she threw the file, sending it through the air to land on the corner of the desk behind him. "I was talking about the part where he might scare her to death."

Ah, yeah. That was totally possible.

"But she'll be alive, won't she?" Ward leaned against the nearest desk, ignoring the movements of the administrative team around the room·and the rumble of conversation as the rest of Bravo team, led by Ford Decker, walked into the weight room.

Tasha rolled her eyes. "I'm sure that will be a great comfort to her when she's curled in a ball in the corner."

Coming from the woman who once drugged him and tied him to a chair, the comment struck Ward as amusing. "Since when do you care about an asset's feelings?"

She smiled. "Never."

"That's my girl." She was. In every way. And so damn competent.

Tasha pushed for the setup of Alliance after she—as an MI6 officer—and Ward—as a CIA operative—clashed on a job in Fiji. She'd decided the U.S. and the UK should share resources and work together, off the books and without all the confining rules of either agency . . . so Alliance was born.

Now, Ward was just about to break their private agreement and tell her how hot she looked in that shirt when Harlan Ross walked up. He was Ward's co-administrator of Alliance and until very recently a lifetime MI6 officer. Together they took care of the day-to-day operation from the Warehouse, a building on the far side of the locked-down intelligence compound that housed Alliance.

The Warehouse sat surrounded by big gates and

armed guards, with all the high-tech security gadgets of the main building. But there was no question that Alliance qualified as the bastard child of the intelligence community. Almost no one knew of its existence, which meant few rules and little accountability, but also no rescue when things went to shit.

Good thing they only hired the best. People who walked into danger knowing, without flinching, they might never walk out again.

Harlan held out a note to Ward. "Pearce is at it again."

Now that Ward knew who the message was from, he could ignore it. He intended to do just that as he balled the paper in his fist. "I say we just shoot him."

Tasha snorted. "You should have done that when you had the chance."

"Now you tell me." If he had to do it again, he would. Put a bullet right in Pearce's forehead and end the motherfucker and all the grief that went along with him.

Jake Pearce, the piece of shit former agent who tried to single-handedly take down the entire U.S. intelligence network with a toxin set loose in Liberty Crossing. After a lifetime of service he turned and justified the betrayal by arguing that he needed to clean out the community. But his motives were much more basic than that. Greed and hate.

Harlan didn't walk away. Glanced at Ward's closed fist instead. "Pearce says he'll only talk to you."

"Yeah, well, Pearce has been spewing a lot of nonsense since he's been in the cell. Apparently being locked in an eight-by-eight steel box with little access to anyone and no sunshine makes him chatty." Not that Ward underestimated the guy. No, Pearce had serious skills.

They shared similar training through the Farm, the CIA's secret training facility near Williamsburg, Virginia. Interrogation techniques, survival drills, sleep deprivation practice. Pearce could shoot, stab, fly a plane, and launch a rocket. And that was just a partial list. He honed his skills with more than twenty years undercover and in the field.

"He might be ready to say something helpful." Tasha shifted her weight back and forth. "Maybe earn an extra dessert."

She was not the type to fidget. The moving around was a message of some sort. Since Pearce's accommodations were just about the last thing on Ward's mind, he'd bet the same was true of her. This was about an actual visit to the nutcase.

"If I go in, I'm taking a gun, then spraying the guy's brains against the wall." Sounded like a good plan to Ward, which was why he said it.

Harlan shook his head. "You can't see him. He's playing a game and it will give him what he wants."

"He has valuable intel." And there it was. Tasha's point.

When Pearce turned, he didn't do it half-assed. He went right to the one man every intelligence asset hunted. From Mossad to MI6 to the CIA—every country—

wanted a man known as Benton. A man with a hand in everything. Tentacles everywhere. He traded in weapons and lives. He set up an auction for the toxin that Pearce had tried to use to kill everyone in Liberty Crossing.

Alliance brought Pearce down and grabbed the toxin before its widespread release. It qualified as a huge win, but they never got close to Benton. No one ever did. He continued to hide. And every single member of Alliance vowed to bring him down.

But Ward couldn't tackle that today. He had men on the ground and an operation to handle. "Yeah, well, I have other things to worry about. Like, four agents running loose in Pakistan."

Satellite images of Skardu and the surrounding areas continued to flash on the screens on the wall. The analysis of the intel didn't stop even though verbal contact was on hold.

"All good points." Tasha watched the monitors. "Go see Pearce."

"Ward's right." Harlan said. "The timing doesn't make sense."

"You're not in charge. I am." She stopped shuffling around and glanced at Ward. "So, go."

He knew better than to challenge that tone. "Yes, ma'am."

With a nod, she walked away. Went right up to the computer techs and loomed over their shoulders. She had them pointing and explaining and typing.

Harlan swore under his breath, all British and proper

but still effective. "Do you ever get tired of her bossing you around?"

Now there was an easy question and Ward didn't hesitate. "Never."

They circled around. Quickened their pace then slowed it down. Doubled back. Even stopped while West covered their tracks. A trip that would have taken fifteen minutes by foot if they walked in a straight line lasted a hour.

Lexi could walk for miles in heat or cold. Being on the road with her father since she was a kid, she'd learned to adapt. She didn't collect things. She didn't demand certain foods or special treatment. She was grateful and tried not to complain. But the circling thing made her dizzy . . . and a little bit worried they were wasting time that could be spent running away.

That would teach her to go for a walk with an undercover agent . . . or whatever West was.

She guided him down the path to the small one-story building tucked into a grouping of trees. The beige of the walls matched the landscape around it. The place blended in. That was the point. West said he needed safe and quiet. This place should meet the criteria.

"This is it." More of a statement than a question. Nothing in West's tone gave away his mood.

He could be happy or pissed off. She was beginning to think those emotions looked and sounded the same on him. Despite being shot at, taking down Raheel in front of her, and engaging in that winding covert walk here, West's affect never changed. He stayed on task and determined. Exactly what you wanted in a make-shift bodyguard—focus.

While he scanned the surroundings and what could be hiding behind rocks and in trees, she studied him. The firm jawline and massive shoulders. There was nothing pretty about him, but he was compelling. The way he handled the weapon helped, completely in com-mand and ready to kill if needed.

That last part should scare the shit out of her. Her last boyfriend was a botany professor. Nice guy but not exactly a laugh riot at parties. He viewed the outdoors as work and defined date nights as dinner in. Not excit-ing but safe.

She blinked a few times, trying to block out the pounding need to have West strip off that shirt. Adrena-line was kicking her ass and making her reckless. He already viewed her as a wild card. Had basically said so. Now he needed to see that she could handle this life, because she had no intention of abandoning the clinic.

Gravel crunched under his boot as he turned to face her. "Now you decide to be quiet?"

She had no idea what that meant. "What?"

"You're staring at me."

Rather than respond to that, she jumped right into the explanation. "Javed told me to come here if I ever got in trouble."

"That response raises more questions than it an-swers."

This guy liked to fight about everything. "How would you like me to construct the sentence?"

He exhaled. Not short and not quiet. More like a get-your-act-together exhale. "Who is Javed?"

She guessed her friend's last name mattered for some reason. "Javed Gul."

"Keep explaining."

That attitude was starting to get problematic. Made her want to kick him, and it probably wasn't a good idea to nail him in the thigh while he held the gun. "Javed works with Raheel, the guy you took down earlier, which now feels like months ago."

"Not even close."

It would help their communication if West didn't take her so literally sometimes. "What was with the covert craziness getting here? I told you no one knows about this place."

His eyebrow lifted. "You're alive, aren't you?"

Talk about dramatic. "Was there a possibility I wouldn't be?"

With a hand on her elbow, he dragged her off the hard-to-see path and closer to the side of the house. "Why the hell did you bring us here?"

"I just told you." She was not a fan of the manhandling. Or the way he talked to her. "And do not swear at me."

"You've got to be kidding." His eyes bugged out. "I've heard you swear."

The list of things he did that annoyed her grew with each passing second. She shrugged out of his hold and faced him. "Not *at* you. And for the record, you're warning when I first picked you as my bodyguard wasn't strong enough. You're more than difficult."

This time he went with an inhale. She could visibly see him bring his body under control. His shoulders rose and then fell. The harsh lines around his mouth eased. He even lowered the gun . . . a little.

"Okay." His voice continued to sound strained. Maybe even more so. "Tell me why you think this is a smart place for us to be."

"Much better." She treated him to a smile, hoping that might calm whatever seemed to be zipping around inside of him. "Thank you for not being an asshole."

"Don't get used to it."

She decided to ignore the snap in his voice. With this guy she had to ignore a lot in order to keep a massive headache at bay. "Javed is part of the Fearless Five." When West didn't say anything, she tried a little more information. "Do you know who they are?"

"Yes."

That seemed pretty clear. "We met when he brought some climbers to the clinic. He and my dad are close and—"

West held up a hand. "You're with him. I get it."

That made one of them. "With?"

"Sleeping with."

This guy could make conclusion jumping into an Olympic sport. "Women and men can be friends without sleeping together."

This time West screwed up his mouth in a way that telegraphed how seriously he took her comment—not very. "Let's not get into that debate."

She was starting to see why she gravitated toward botanist, researcher, studious types. They didn't argue her to death. "Fine."

"So, Raheel and Javed are both Fearless Five."

"Yes. I told Javed what I saw. About the trucks." West returned to the staring thing. The standing there and not talking. It made her twitchy. "You know what I mean, right? The reason you're here."

If possible, his eyes narrowed even further. "Spell it out."

That set off an alarm bell ringing inside her. "Should I be worried you don't know?"

He shook his head as he dragged her around the side of the house and out of sight of anyone who might wander by, which should be no one. This was not the kind of town where people broke into the home of a Pakistani army pilot. Not unless he did something very wrong and not if they wanted to live.

"You saw weapons being moved. Caravans, late at night, headed toward the base of the mountains." West delivered the explanation as he continued his not-so-subtle surveillance. He looked in windows and scanned the horizon.

Night had fallen. Skardu suffered from a severe electricity shortage. Plans were under way for a massive project, but those would not be completed for years, which meant relying on generators and limited spurts of power. In their case, the light from the gray sky and flashlights.

She could only see his face now because he stood inches away and held a light. Not big. Just a round disk, and when he clicked it, it lit up the small area around him. She'd never seen anything like it before.

Figured he had one. She'd bet he had a rocket launcher in those pants pockets somewhere. He struck her as being prepared for anything, except maybe her.

"At first you thought it was Pakistani movement on the Siachen Glacier, but you—being reckless—followed and saw stockpiles of weapons and an encampment. Things that shouldn't be there." He wasn't listing off direct quotes, but close.

Impressive in a freaky kind of way. But she would not let him see that the realization set off a flurry of anxiety deep in her belly. "Do you even need me for this conversation?"

"Probably not."

"I assume all of that was in a file in a building somewhere." Part of her wanted to know what was in that thing now. The other part wanted to be indignant and ticked off that a file even existed. That part answered him. "Good to know you can read."

"You should be more concerned with my ability to shoot."

She rested her back against the side of the house as he kicked at the ground and took out a small black disk. "I'm guessing you're an expert in that area."

"Yes." The disk popped up, opening a few inches until it looked like a jeweler's magnifying glass. He put it up to his eye and shifted in a circle, watching the world through this lens.

She wanted to ask what he was doing. She really did, but she had so many questions that she jumped to one of the most obvious to make sure she covered it. "You're not going to qualify that by saying you only kill bad guys?"

West stilled for a second, then continued. "Nope."

"I'm guessing your entire team shares these skills."

"We're all trained. All have different areas of expertise. One guy likes to blow things up. This is mine."

He always said just enough to get her interested and listening, then he stopped. "You mean shooting?"

"Shooting, tracking, sneaking up on people."

Sneaking? "But you're so big."

"It's not about size, though I do use that to intimidate people." He shrugged. "Bottom line, I'm the one who goes in first whether I'm taking on one or twenty. I don't hesitate because that's my role on the team. First in. Take out hostiles and provide covering fire."

And she sensed he liked it. Maybe it had something to do with the Marine mentality. "The others hesitate?"

"They're good." West dropped his hand and looked at her. "I'm better."

Something thudded inside of her. It was as if her insides were running at high speed and slammed into a rock wall, leaving her breathless and a little dizzy. "I'm not sure what to say to that."

He flattened the monocle and tucked it into one of his pockets. "I need the location."

She didn't pretend not to follow the thread. She knew what he needed and where the encampment sat, but that was her leverage. The only bit she had. "Not yet."

"We're not negotiating, Lexi."

For once they actually agreed on something. "Right."

He aimed the light straight at her. "I'm serious."

She knocked it away again. "Do I not look serious?"

"It's very tempting to leave you here and head out on my own."

With her hands folded behind her, she pressed her palms against the building. The coolness of the wall seeped into her skin. "I have to take you there. You'll never find it without me."

"Your faith in my skills is heartwarming."

"Which direction are you going to try first?"

He shrugged. "I'll make an educated guess."

"I go or you don't get the information you need to quickly figure this out and then leave Pakistan before the government here realizes there's a spy hanging around."

He frowned at her, which he seemed to be doing with increasing frequency. "We don't use the word spy."

"Maybe you don't but they will."

He shifted his weight, moving in until he almost stood on top of her. "You understand that interrogation is one of my skills."

"You mean torture." A shiver raced through her as she said the word. It was a touchy subject in this area of the world. A lot of nasty history took place in and around here. People in town whispered about what happened when men disappeared. She tried to stay neutral and focus on health issues only. For the most part that worked, but she got questioning looks now and then.

"You are going to give me the data. When we rendezvous with Josiah and the rest of my team, you will be taken to Islamabad, then to Germany for rendition, then—"

"Do you think I don't know what rendition means? I'm not a terrorist." She'd just about had it with the mumbling threats. "And none of that is going to happen."

West shrugged. "Start with the location and I'll see what I can do."

He acted as if she was the bad guy here. Never mind that she was the one to call the problem in. Without her reporting, he would not be here. The way she saw it, he owed her. "Stop threatening me."

"Stop fighting me."

"Sorry to disappoint you." She tried to call up fear but didn't feel it. Not toward him, regardless of what he said. His strength could break her in half, but something in her sensed he was there to protect her, not hurt her. "I'm not afraid of you."

The corner of his mouth kicked up. "You should be."

5

THE STEEL clanked as the pressure lock rods released and the vault door leading to the open area in front of Pearce's cell opened. He stood at the side of his bed, looking down. Not moving.

Ward guessed this was some sort of power play. If so, Pearce would be going it alone. Ward had no interest in giving the guy one more ounce of attention than he had to, which was already more than Pearce deserved.

Ignoring the chair, Ward moved closer to the clear . . . was that plastic? Whatever covered the opening, it allowed him to see Pearce yet kept the asshole locked in there. Well, that and the armed guards who watched over the underground cells beneath the nondescript beige building on the Liberty Crossing campus.

Since he wanted to talk then leave, and do it fast, Ward started. "What do you want?"

With deliberate, almost aching slowness, Pearce lifted his head. Then a smile spread across his lips. "Is that any way to greet an old friend?"

One of Pearce's assignment covers set him up as a professor at a university in Germany. Even beneath the scruffy beard and lose gray pants, he maintained the academic look. Bright blue eyes and what Tasha described as an objective smart-guy attractiveness that had fooled so many people over the years, Ward included. He hated Pearce for that reason alone.

"I should kill you." Ward swore if he could do it and walk out of the building without trouble, he would. Didn't matter that the guards took his weapons and made him all but strip down before walking in the vault. He could choke this motherfucker and not have to beat back one second of guilt.

"You won't." Pearce stood straight with his hands linked behind his back. "You couldn't before and your pretty little girlfriend would get angry with you if you tried it now."

"You think that kind of talk will piss me off?" Ward took good-natured shit from the men on a daily basis about loving Tasha. Did not have any impact. He knew who he was and accepted that in many ways she was tougher than he ever was . . . and that was saying something. "You're going to need to try harder."

Pearce's head tilted to the side. His glasses slid on his nose but he didn't make a move to push them up again. "I can't figure you out. All rah-rah and supporting the team. Is it because you can't lift a gun anymore? Such a terrible injury."

This was so amateur the shots bounced right off. "Want to see what I can do to you with this chair?"

He'd been injured in Fiji and left the field. No secret there and no regrets, since he was on the job and watching out for Tasha at the time. But Pearce knew that, so Ward waited. Whatever Pearce really wanted to say would come out soon enough. Ward just had to be patient, and he could call up a mountain of that if it meant beating Pearce at his game.

"The system you defend so fiercely will screw you eventually. You gave up your hand and you'll sacrifice most of your life, probably lose Tasha in the process. And no one in the intelligence community will give a damn or even remember your name." Pearce remained perfectly still as he delivered his little speech. "You're a number to them. A sacrifice they are happy to make. Expendable."

"I read the same contract you did when I went into black ops. The fact you're all whiny about your choices now is your problem." Ward glanced around, took in the gray walls and gray floors. No windows and air pumped in. He half wondered where he could turn that off. Let Pearce suffocate to death. "Good thing you'll be rotting in here for a long time. You'll have many hours to think about how the world has done you wrong."

"Your time will come."

Ward was already tired of the nonsense. Time to fast forward. He clapped his hands and treated Pearce to a little nod. "Thanks for the warning."

He turned then and reached for the button to call

the guard. He didn't even make it the whole way before Pearce sighed.

"West is going to die out there this time," he said in a flat tone.

There it was. The real reason for the request. Some sort of fucked-up scare tactic. Fine, Ward could handle that. He turned back to face Pearce head on but didn't say anything. He'd rather let this fool talk.

Pearce nodded. "Now I have your attention."

Barely. "West is on leave."

"He's in Pakistan with Delta team." Pearce started pacing, as if delivering a lecture to one of his classes. "Last time he was there he was almost buried alive. For anyone else, going back there would probably be impossible. Not West. He's not human. No emotions in that one."

Son of a bitch. Ward forced every muscle to freeze. Wiped all emotion off his face as he dropped his shoulders.

Pearce could not know that information. West left at the last minute and wasn't even with his usual team. Pearce could guess at some things, but the location and team switch . . . that was too much of a coincidence.

"He's fine." Ward said it but now suspected it wasn't true.

"I gotta hand it to you. You found yourself a fine machine when you brought him into Alliance. The targeting ability. The way he can locate a hostile, pick up signals a few beats before anyone else. The lack of fear."

Ward didn't say a word. Just let Pearce spew. Eventually Pearce would use the one word that would give him the ability to pinpoint where he got his intel on West.

"Is it true he took out a terrorist cell in Yemen while they trained?" Pearce asked. "He actually went in, all alone, and killed them in the middle of the day while they were armed and in the act of shooting. Most people would go in at night. Take the advantage. But not West." He laughed. "That's a big pair of balls.

"I'll let West know you like his balls."

Pearce made a tsk-tsking sound as he shook his head. "Losing him will hurt, but then you're going to lose all of Delta team, which will be quite the blow to your merry band of brothers."

Score one for Pearce.

Ward knew he needed to leave. He had to recheck the intel and try to communicate with Josiah. Find West. "Anything else? If so, say what you want to say."

"I just did."

"You are in here without any contact to the outside world." The guy didn't have family or friends. He hadn't been assigned a lawyer because he didn't need one. Thanks to his work, no one knew who he really was or missed him when he disappeared off the street.

Pearce scoffed. "Don't be so fucking stupid."

Anxiety punched Ward in the gut. "Enlighten me."

"I know everything, including the fact West is about to walk into a firestorm." Pearce's smile came back. "But I can help."

"Yeah, you were really helpful that last time you worked with Alliance."

"You need to get over that. It wasn't about you," Pearce said, as if that made it better.

He'd tried to kill all of them once. Ward would not let him get to West.

Ward turned back to the button. This time he hit it. That gave him less than twenty seconds before the guards stormed in. "Enjoy the silence, Pearce."

"You get me to Islamabad and I will get you to the weapons and give you one opportunity—your only one—to save West."

"West knows the risks of the job." That didn't mean Ward would leave him hanging out there. Not in Pakistan and not vulnerable to someone connected to Pearce.

"Ah, but you're not like West. You do have feelings." Pearce shook his head. "You won't just let him die. Bring them all home and all that."

"Right now the only feeling I have is boredom. Were you always this tiresome?" Ward's nerves pulsed as the need to get back to the Warehouse flooded him. Every second counted now.

"It will kill you to sit in your cozy office and spend your nights fucking Tasha, all while knowing West and Delta are being picked off one by one." Pearce lifted both hands then moved them behind his head as he went to his knees. "But you have the power to stop it. Or at least try."

The locks opened again. Three guards came through the door, weapons ready and aimed at the cell, as they were supposed to every time they came inside. If Pearce somehow got loose, they were under orders to kill him without question. Light it up and take him down.

Refusing to let Pearce see one ounce of concern, Ward smiled at him. "Goodbye, Jake."

"You need me."

Ward refused to let that be true. "Never."

The woman was going to kill him.

West stood there staring at Lexi and forced his breathing to slow. Frustration swamped him when he needed control. Between her eyes, all wide and flashing with anger, and that body, his usual solid concentration blinked out on him once or twice. Something that never happened before. Oh, he'd enjoyed many women in his time, but never on the job. Never did one rock him like this one.

He blamed the smart mouth. Add in her refusal to back down even when he shot her a glare that drove armed men to their knees and his blood caught fire. Standing this close, with his hands on the wall, pinning her there, turned out to be a huge a miscalculation. He could smell her hair. What the fuck was that about?

She put a hand on his chest and pushed. "Stop that."

He wasn't a hundred percent sure that she was talking about—the empty threats or the near drooling. "No."

Didn't move either. She might be fierce but he outweighed her, and his strength might be the one thing that could overcome her sizable will.

"I'm going inside to wait for Javed." She ducked under his arm and headed for the front of the house.

West caught her around the elbow before she could round the corner. Forced his fingers not to tighten, which was tough because the frustration pounding him made every muscle clench. "He's coming here?"

She glanced at his hold then back to his face. "It's his place."

West was half surprised she hadn't marched them right into the middle of a Pakistani army training drill. "This is his house?"

She leaned in until her face hovered right before his. "That's what I just said."

Little did she know how close she was to pushing him to the edge. No one tested him like this. Without ever being warned, his team members knew when to back off. It was as if they understood how he could funnel all his rage, all the fury building inside him, to the subject of his missions.

There was a reason the team called on him to do the dirty jobs. To scare the hell out of people.

But not her. He didn't know whether to be pissed or impressed. Right now he went with demanding. "We're leaving."

With as gentle a hold as he could muster, he started dragging her around to the back of the house. No need to announce their presence and walk out on the open road. They'd cut through the trees. Use the darkness to cover their trail and head for the safest place he could find to stash her.

Would have been a great plan if she hadn't dug her heels in. Literally. The pebbles and dirt crunched under her shoes.

Then she started trying to peel his fingers off her arm. "He's not here."

"Anyone ever tell you that you talk in circles." The guy was there, he wasn't. He lived there, he was gone. "Drives me fucking crazy."

She shrugged at him. Actually shrugged. "Get over it."

Taking a final grab for patience, West started a mental countdown from ten. He abandoned it at eight and dropped his hand. Since touching her seemed to be a very risky plan. "Explain."

"Javed has been doing helicopter training runs. He spends a certain amount of time flying in and around K2, stays at base camp then moves higher, but he has to come back down—"

"Because of the oxygen deprivation. Yeah, I know." West knew far too well what happened at high altitudes. How white uniforms turned black. How men lost their minds. How faulty footing by one person could knock out all those hooked to him.

How the mountain could come down and bury everyone and everything in its path. Expertise and strength didn't matter. Panicked digging kicked in and life turned into a race between speed and suffocation.

"From the look on your face I don't think that knowledge comes from a book." Her fingertips brushed against his cheek then fell away again.

"I told you. I've been here before." In Pakistan, on the Siachen Glacier . . . under a landslide of rock and ice.

"You a mountain climber, West?"

"Definitely not." His life would be a hell of a lot easier if the bad guys agreed to stay under 4,000 feet.

"Then how?"

He couldn't do this. Purposely dredging up the memories and running through them begged for trouble. He stayed sane by forgetting. Blocked the bad and kept his mind clear.

Harlan and some of the others joked that the focus made him more machine than man. West could handle that. Machines survived. Machines didn't care if a slide of rock and ice crushed humans in front of him. Tore through friends and teammates, shredding clothing and skin. Machines didn't hear the screaming.

But he needed a clear head not only to keep them safe, but to keep up with her. "We are not playing twenty questions."

"You tell me and maybe I'll agree to give you the location of the secret encampment and not follow." She smiled as if she'd found the right argument.

Not a chance. Despite what she believed, they were not locked in some sort of negotiation. Little did she know that using his past as a bargaining chip was the exact wrong way to go. "Or I can tie you to a chair and leave without you. Maybe Javed will come find you, but maybe not."

Her face fell as all signs of light disappeared from it. "You're a dumbass."

And acted this way on purpose to shake some sense into her, which probably did make him a gigantic ass. "Not the first time I've heard that."

"Inside." She pointed toward the front of the house and started walking again.

Catching her a second time proved tougher because she had the sense to duck and weave. It took him two steps instead of one to get her turned around. "Excuse me?"

"We'll go in and I'll draw you a map," she explained.

"Just tell me."

"Go nine hundred steps and turn right. How's that?" Her gaze wandered over his face.

"Not great."

She shot him a gotcha smirk. "See, you need me. With all your fancy satellites and surveillance equipment, with your armed men on the ground, you can't find it."

True, and it pissed him off. If there really were weapons out there, someone had them stored to evade detection. He had no idea how they were moved without raising suspicion. Without Lexi's reporting, no one would know, which was why part of him hoped she'd gotten the facts wrong.

"Let's try that map." He guided her around back.

From his previous peek inside he didn't pick up any movement, but he saw a door and a room with few windows. He could barricade them in there until he got the information he needed or she talked him to death, whichever came first.

Her chin lifted. "I thought so."

"You didn't win." For some reason, he needed her to now that. Probably would make the next few hours easier if she at least pretended she understood the structure of command.

"Feels like it." She moved toward the door, looked determined to rush in and get herself killed. Not on his watch.

He slipped in front of her before she could reach it. "Stay here." He pointed at her, almost scolded when normally he would growl and threaten. "Lexi, I'm serious."

She answered by rolling her eyes. He took that as agreement and lifted his gun to go in.

The door creaked as he opened it. The usual humming sounds of a house were absent. No electricity meant no refrigerator or running appliances.

His footsteps echoed as he opened every door and checked behind everything he could inspect in the two-room place. At the back a kitchen. In the front a family room that ran the width of the house and included a section with a bed.

For Javed's sake, Lexi better not feel at home in that bed. West knew he shouldn't care, but he did.

"Have I told you I hate bossy men?" She whispered the words over his shoulder.

He had to fight from flinching. Not from her presence. He'd sensed that, but from the way she leaned her body against his back. Her fingers wrapped around his biceps and she pressed chest to thigh.

Then she was gone. She walked around him to the doorway to the front room. Her gaze traveled over the makeshift mattress on the floor and what looked like old newspapers stacked in the corner. Stood there not talking, resting her hands on her hips and highlighting every inch of that body.

Big talker or not, the woman was a temptation. But she might as well have had a flashing warning light above her head because there was no way he was going there.

He just had to remind himself that her personal life was none of his business. He had no right to want to rip this Javed guy apart. He decided to point that out. Maybe then he'd believe it. "Your taste in men is not my concern."

"Then why do you keep staring at my ass?" She glanced at him over her shoulder. "Hmm, nothing? No response to that?"

"I didn't." He'd glanced. There was a difference.

"Liar."

Whatever her agenda, he needed to shut this down. "The map?"

West looked around the room for a pen or paper.

Every time he turned or shifted, his attention zipped back to her.

"You're looking at it now." She brushed her hand over her ass, as if that particular body part needed more highlighting.

Sweet damn. "Only because you mentioned it." And because he had eyes and a dick that even now was paying attention when it should have been on leave.

"Is that also the explanation for looking at my mouth? For the way your eyes dip when you think I'm not watching." Her gaze traveled over him as she talked. "It's okay to admit you like how I look."

It absolutely was not. He didn't tell the last guy he extracted out of Syria that he smelled good, which he hadn't. The guy had been stuck in a cell, wallowing in feces and God knew what else. He needed to treat her the same way—as a job.

But he couldn't exactly deny he'd noticed her. "I'm not blind."

"Thank you."

Between the politeness and the smile, he needed to get his head back in the game. "The map?"

"We are in the middle of an adrenaline rush, guys are attacking and we're on the run." With each point she stepped closer to him. More like stalked, with hips swaying and shoulders back.

"Regular day at the office for me."

She circled around him, dragging a finger along his body. "Except for the staring."

He holstered the gun to keep from accidentally shooting both of them. "True."

After one full turn she stopped in front of him with her hands on his forearms. "We should just do it and be done."

Everything inside him froze. Came to a damn stop. "I'm going to need a definition of 'it.'"

He'd been tortured and buried alive, stabbed and shot. All in the same week. Yet only her and the mountain of ice looming nearby had the power to make him twitchy. He'd hated having one thing on that list. Now it looked as if he had two.

She smiled like she knew it would make him itch to move in. "I meant a kiss."

Hell, his mind had zoomed long past that. In the mental show playing in his head he had her pants off and her legs wrapped around him as he pushed into her up against the wall.

Not that he was thinking about it.

She leaned in and blew a whisper of breath across his ear. "Kissing. For now."

That was more like it. Sounded as if his mind wasn't the only one jumping to naked. But it still wasn't happening. "Bad idea."

She nodded. "Right."

The quick agreement, the face . . . one of them shoved him right into stupid territory. If he didn't kiss her now they'd both be screwed. It was going to be the only thing on his mind until he kicked it out.

"Fuck it."

His hands went to her waist and his mouth touched hers. Not sweet and quick. Not a kiss to say "There, now we're done." No, this one lingered, deepened. His lips touched hers and a fire raced through his blood. His arms wrapped tighter around her as he lifted her off the ground.

He intended to kiss her to quiet her down, to give tasting her a try and move on.

Huge fucking miscalculation.

When her fingers slipped into his hair, he almost lost it. Did for a second. Spun her around and pinned her body against the wall. Had one hand dipping down to catch her leg under the knee . . . then he sensed it. A small movement, the change in the air—something out of place. Wrong.

The visitor snuck up the side of the house. He was damn good. Way better than Raheel and almost as good as that Mossad agent Ward had disarmed and pinned to the floor a few weeks ago. Only a brief flash of movement and no sound.

West broke away. One hand went to his gun. The other went to her mouth. "Don't move."

He pushed her behind him, into the corner and against a cabinet. Without being told, she slid down, probably on instinct. The woman's sense for combating danger continued to impress him.

West was ready for battle. Would fire without any guilt.

Adrenaline pumped through him as his body readied for battle. He got the whole way to the back door before he lowered the gun.

"What?" Her harsh whisper carried across the small room.

This time he'd seen a shirt and the hair. "This isn't an enemy."

As West said the words, Josiah came through the front door. "I thought you saw me, mostly because you didn't shoot."

"You were making enough noise for even a novice to pick out your location." The comment wasn't true, but West was looking to stall, not win a debate.

Josiah looked from West to Lexi and back again. "Bad timing?"

Lexi stood up as she answered. "Yes."

"No," West said at the same time.

Josiah shook his head as he lowered his gun. "You Americans are never dull."

6

THIS WASN'T exactly how Lexi pictured the day going when she woke up this morning. Set a few broken bones, talk to hikers about general first aid, convince the one with a breathing issue to reconsider a climb up one of the world's deadliest mountains.

That was the usual stuff. Bandages, stitches, broken bones, and common sense climbing talk. As the season progressed, she'd have to worry about hypoxia and frostbite. Possibly deal with death. But today was supposed to be a normal day.

No one clued her in about armed men landing on her doorstep. Certainly no one warned her how she could lose all her father had built by doing what she believed to be the right thing.

And no one prepared her for West. Big and objectively scary, though that initial impression faded fast. Those hands and that kiss . . . yeah, forget dating studious guys. Her type might have just changed forever.

Josiah nodded toward the front door. "I can come back."

West still hadn't put his gun away. "Shut the fuck up."

Not the most flattering response to a kiss, but Lexi decided to stay quiet. If the big clench only affected her and not him, which she did not think was possible unless the guy had a "faking it" skill on his undercover agent résumé, fine.

"No one is going to believe this." Josiah shook his head as he leaned against the small table in the kitchen.

"No one is going to hear about this," West said in a voice that promised a whole lot of pain.

Josiah closed one eye as if he was thinking about it. "Is that accurate?"

"You want to die?"

She'd had just about enough of this nonsense. "I can hear you two. I am standing right in front of you."

They acted as if she had a horn growing out of her head. Sure, she might not be a supermodel, but she didn't have fangs or walk bent over with her knuckles dragging against the ground. West could calm down, and he'd be wise to do that soon.

Instead he had the nerve to frown at her. "I know."

For whatever reason, that simple answer struck a match and set her brain on fire. "Then maybe stop acting like kissing me is equal to the plague."

"Wait, you did kiss?" Josiah stood up and moved between West and Lexi. "While on assignment?"

West shoved Josiah right back down. "One more question and I bury your body at the base camp of K2."

From his smile, Josiah looked prepared to keep ribbing. "But I thought you hated the cold."

She'd been about to jump in again, maybe threaten to bang their heads together, when she heard that. The comment struck her as odd since it referenced a guy who kept talking about his knowledge of the area.

"Then why has he been up there before?" Her gaze went to West. "Care to answer that?"

"Has he?" Josiah asked in a voice filled with sarcasm.

Now she had no idea what was happening. Every time she thought she'd gained a bit more insight into West, something happened to slam the door shut again. The guy had her patience crumbling and her anger in free-fall.

"The map to the encampment, Lexi. Now."

And the ordering around thing had her back teeth slamming together. She was about to tell him when Josiah butted in.

"That's going to have to wait."

West opened his mouth, but she asked first. "Why?"

"I've lost contact."

"Fuck." West shook his head as he stared at the floor.

The guy had ample opportunity to lose his temper over the last few hours but hadn't. This was as close as he'd come, and he contained even this small blowup. Not bad for a guy she viewed as lethal and dangerous.

But since he reacted to Josiah's news, she guessed she should be in a full-fledged panic. Good thing she didn't really do that sort of thing very often. "I take it losing contact with whomever is a really bad thing."

West's expression went blank. "No, it happens all the time. Don't worry."

If that was his idea of consoling her, it needed work. Really, his people skills were about a D minus. Though it was kind of sweet that he tried. "Then why is your voice strained?"

Josiah balanced his palms on the table behind him. "I kind of like her."

"Spend some time with her."

She chose to ignore that shot from West. Maybe he got grumpy postkiss. She had the opposite reaction, so she could be tolerant for a few minutes. But she was pretty sure he'd use up her goodwill soon and looked at Josiah.

"Maybe I should go with you instead of West." Though the idea of separating from him made something shrivel inside her.

"Definitely not." West snapped out the response with a glare.

Josiah smiled. "Fascinating."

The glaring continued for a few more seconds, then West's shoulders relaxed. He put the gun away and his hands went to his hips. "What's the plan?"

"I do an emergency drop with the guys—"

"Who?" She winced after she interrupted. Now that they were finally talking about something other than the kiss, she should let them go back and forth. But there were so many blanks, and she'd never figure this out without pushing them around a bit.

If West was ticked off he hid it well. He shot her a quick glance. "The other members of his team."

"Two of them," Josiah said. "The fourth is on hold in Islamabad."

The way she counted, that meant five, but since Josiah actually answered questions and with him around West didn't change the subject—and she did not want either of those things to stop—the proper count could wait until later. "On hold for what?"

West shook his head. "Nothing."

They'd made a tiny bit of progress and then West did that. She guessed that was the more typical response for civilians for these two. "That thing where you guys talk in half sentences? It's annoying."

Josiah swallowed a smile before looking at West. "I'll connect with the team and headquarters. You hunker down here while I see if I can fix the communication problem."

The pieces started to come together in her head. The threats, the man at the clinic, Raheel showing up . . . not good. "Does this so-called problem have anything to do with the men you guys attacked?"

Josiah nodded. "Smart woman for a 'sort of' doctor."

About that . . . "I'm smart no matter what I do for a living."

West rolled his eyes. "No kidding, but some guidance on what you actually do in Pakistan would be helpful. Nurse, maybe?"

"No."

She searched her memory for the details she did provide. Not many. The idea of spilling her guts now, when West hadn't provided one crumb about who he was, ticked her off. So she went with an abbreviated, little information version. "My dad is the doctor. I work with him. There."

West's eyes narrowed. "There?"

She thought that explained enough, but from looking at their frowns maybe not. It was a sensitive subject for her, and West wasn't exactly coughing up details about his own life or his plans to get them out of this mess. She was happy to negotiate a settlement on this issue.

"You tell me about the last time you were in Pakistan and I'll talk about my life." She knew West would ignore her, but satisfaction surged through her at being able to say it. "Deal?"

"Draw the map." He ground the words out between clenched teeth.

"He says you don't need it." She pointed at Josiah. "Isn't he in charge?" Then the possibility hit her that she'd been reading the situation all wrong. She turned back to West. "Oh, God. You're not the leader, are you?"

Josiah laughed. "She looks horrified. More so than when we killed her attacker in front of her."

"I'm not denying it." Yeah, the idea of West leading a group of people made her question the group the government sent to find her and track down the weapons. He was strong and commanding but blended in and listened. She couldn't see him moving pieces around and sticking with an administrative job.

"A man came to the clinic and tried to hurt you. Your pal Raheel tried to drag you away."

"Who?" Josiah asked.

"Pakistani army." She figured she'd spill it all. "West here knocked him out."

West shrugged. "Went for the larynx so he'd have trouble talking for a few days."

"Wait." Josiah stood up straight again, as if leaning against the table made being in the guy's house worse. "You know two men in the Pakistani army?"

"I do live in Pakistan part of the year." Seemed obvious to her.

"If we could go back to my point." West stepped right in front of her. Those shoulders blocked everything else. "Don't you think, maybe, you have information that puts you in danger?"

"Possibly." It didn't take a medical degree or even a general knowledge of addition and subtraction to figure that one out. Maybe someone heard her relay the emergency message or saw her sneaking around the edges of the encampment.

West kept up that menacing stare. "Then 'maybe' you could follow orders."

"Smooth." Josiah said the word over a fake cough.

"She knows I'm right." West never broke eye contact with her as he said it.

As if that made it better. They acted like she wasn't even in the room. " 'She' can speak for herself."

"We have a lot of people roaming around and caravans of weapons. We don't have time to waste on finding the rest of the team," West said to Josiah, as if she hadn't spoken.

Leaving men behind. She was pretty sure every movie she'd ever seen said that was a bad move. "That's kind of bloodthirsty."

"No, he's right." Josiah waved her concerns off. "Or would be if the comm hadn't cut out. We're fighting blind, and I think that means we have company."

"What?" She wasn't sure exactly what to ask but knew his comment didn't sound good.

West answered. "More bad guys are coming."

She was starting to have some trouble telling all the players apart. "You're the good guys, right?"

He winked at her. "Count on it."

She pretty much was.

When Tasha called, Ward and Harlan answered. They walked into her office ten minutes after receiving the emergency command to find her standing by the window . . . or what would be the window if secure government offices could have those.

Instead, a painting hung there, and not a very good one. Looked like a countryside, and Ward couldn't imagine Tasha sitting still for two minutes to visit a place like that.

With the big desk and bookcases filled with binders, the room looked professional. Ward hated the office. It was fussy and orderly. There were rules and people

in suits. Not his thing at all. Not Tasha's either, but she
played the game and kept them all in business.

She turned and acknowledged them with a small
nod. Before anyone could say anything, she lifted a
slim file off the corner of her desk and handed it to
him. "You're going to Islamabad."

"Okay." From the flatness in her eyes and the chosen
location, Ward knew this wasn't going to be a fun trip.

"Why him?" Harlan scoffed and managed to make
it sound haughty and British. "No offense but we could
grab a guy off the street and have him shoot better."

"How could I be offended by that?" Ward wanted to
be but it was the truth. Having a stake driven through
his hand on his last job in the field messed up the muscles and confined him to a desk. Go figure.

"You're going, too." Tasha let out one of those sighs
that said she was not happy with how a meeting was
going. This time it was aimed at Harlan. "You were
stationed in Pakistan. You know the players and have
some old contacts. Use the plane ride to communicate
with them."

"About what exactly?" he asked.

"Your job is to find Josiah, extract this doctor's
daughter, and then come up with the strategy to track
those weapons and the person moving them."

Since that was exactly what they'd all been doing for
the last twenty hours, Ward suspected he had a schedule opening headed his way. "Am I serving drinks on
the plane?"

"You're watching Pearce. He'll be going with you."

That explained the look on her face.

"No fucking way." The words came out before Ward could think them through or contemplate how furious she would be about the accidental dress-down.

From the flat line of her mouth and stiff shoulders, Ward guessed the answer was pretty damn angry.

"Sorry." Harlan grabbed the file and paged through it. "I have to agree with Ward on this one."

Which never happened. It was enough to get Ward rethinking his initial response.

Not that Tasha was giving them a choice. She slid into the chair behind her desk as she issued her orders. "We need Pearce on this. He knows too much about West's location and assignment."

Ward hated that. "He could be guessing."

"It would be a damn good guess." She shook her head. "No, get him to talk. Let him think he's in charge."

Harlan was already shaking his head. "Too risky."

Very much so, but Ward understood her. He got how she thought, and this could work. "You want me to play him."

The corner of her mouth lifted but the small smile didn't reach her eyes. "Exactly."

Harlan wasn't done fighting. He went around the side of Tasha's desk and stood right next to her. "We can't give him what he wants. He's trained. We get him out and he'll run."

The plan formed in Ward's mind. It only took him a second to realize that, injury or not, he got the better part of this assignment. "Only if we want him to."

This time she did smile. Wide and sincere. "And don't bring him back unless it's in pieces or in a box."

"What about the intel he supposedly has?" Harlan asked, because those were the types of things he worried about.

"He's not worth it." She continued to look at Ward. "Bleed the information out of him then take him out."

Man, he loved this woman. "Yes, ma'am."

West and Josiah stood outside of Javed's house. They'd conducted a sweep, scanned the area before deciding they were alone.

Lexi waited inside, drawing her map. West had other worries now. Cutting the team's communication was no easy job. If someone was blocking signals, that meant they knew there was a team on the ground and in play. Which could cause the person at the encampment to move and try to hide the weapons.

They knew so little. Lexi provided some details in her initial reporting. West intended to get more out of her. But they had other problems to deal with.

"You need to run checks on Javed Gul and Raheel Najam." He wanted every detail on both of them. Lexi trusted them but that didn't mean he did. "Alleged Pakistani helicopter pilots."

Josiah's eyebrow rose. "You're doubting?"

"Raheel tried to take Lexi away. Made it sound like it was for her protection." That one smelled wrong. West would bet Raheel worked for someone in addition to the army. Someone who wanted Lexi to be quiet. "I'm not buying it."

"And you're neutral when it comes to her."

The tone annoyed West. He might suck at reading people but he understood sarcasm. You had to in Alliance or you'd be trounced daily. "I think you're trying to make a point."

Josiah leaned against the side of the house and stared out into the trees beyond. "Do I need to give you the talk?"

West thought they were already having one. "About?"

"Do not have sex with the asset." Josiah faced West then. "I mean, come on. I expect to give one of the other guys that speech, but you?"

West wasn't interested in the playboy lifestyle but he didn't like the suggestion he didn't know which end of a condom to use. "I have sex."

"On the job?"

Never. He'd never even been tempted . . . until Lexi. A few hours with her and his common sense took a hike. Fucking fickle thing.

"No, I generally spend my workday infiltrating hostiles' hiding places and grabbing them. Doing a lot of shooting." He played the enforcer and it worked for him. He'd been raised to come out fighting, but for Alliance the fighting had a bigger purpose and that made all the difference.

"I don't mean to sound like your father, but—"

"There's no way that could happen." West shut that line of thinking down as quickly as possible. Acer Brown had not been a man to give advice. Not good advice. His life centered on the Future of Tomorrow, the compound in a forgotten corner of Montana. A sex talk would have been a waste of his time.

Josiah had to know about his past. That's the way it worked. Harlan and Ward picked the teams, and the leaders of each—Josiah and Ford—had final say on each member. That meant reviewing files and back-grounds. That meant Josiah knew that he'd grown up in a doomsday cult.

After a few beats of silence Josiah spoke again. "The thing she said about you being here before . . ."

"You knew that." Another mark in the file. A Marine special ops assignment gone bad. They infiltrated then the avalanche came.

"Only Ward has the full file on that one." Josiah's eyes narrowed. "Is there anything I need to know that impacts what we're doing here now?"

The only thing that mattered. The only thing that West cared about. "I survived."

7

ALMOST TWO hours later Lexi sat at the small kitchen table and seriously considered plunking her head against it. Josiah had left almost immediately, and West spent the rest of the time since then questioning her about what she'd seen.

The size of the trucks. The markings. The men driving them. The weapons. The layout of the camp. Details spun around in her head. That's what happened when a guy made you repeat the same facts fifteen times.

He said it was something about clearing her mind and concentrating. She'd done that so much she needed migraine medicine.

He sat down across the table and put a cup of steaming liquid in front of her. She guessed tea since he'd been working over a small flame he lit under a hot plate of sorts he created. The guy was handy with or without free-flowing electricity.

The second she lifted her cup he started talking. "So . . ."

From his tone, she already knew this was going to end up in a bad place. "What?"

"Sort of doctor?" he asked from behind his glass of tea.

"A med tech." Thoroughly trained in the basics and accredited in specialized high altitude issues from a clinic in Switzerland. Not to mention the hours of service at her father's side.

But she didn't mention any of that because she wanted to see where West was going with this. And how likely he was to tick her off. She put the percent probability in the high nineties.

"Okay." He nodded. Didn't say anything else as he stretched his long legs out under the table and straddled hers.

"Are you judging?" Her dad did. The disappointment had been so evident when she left school. No matter what she'd accomplished since then had not been quite good enough.

Nice and slow West lowered his glass to the table. "What exactly?"

"I was in medical school, you know?" Her defenses rose. She tried to shove them back down but an angry burning heat swept through her and her fingers tightened on the cup.

"I didn't."

With all his background checks and access to who knew what sort of personal information, she found that hard to believe. "What?"

"Know much about you. I know plenty about your dad. Where he went to school. His record. His time here and in India." West ticked them off. "See, I expected to pick up your dad, not you."

"I find it hard to believe you didn't get a packet of intel about me."

"You were mentioned, but not the focus. You were off-limits unless something went wrong, so I wanted limited details. No need to split the attention if we weren't going to use you."

She hated that last sentence. "You mean 'need' me, right?"

He smiled. "Did you enjoy your recent trip to Paris?"

She had been half kidding about the packet of intel, but it sounded as if someone did spend some time tracking her location. "I was there for a few days. I needed a break from Skardu but came back early for climbing season and so my dad could leave for Everest."

If she'd still been away and her dad had been there, she might not have seen the caravans. She'd tried to reach him by satellite phone to talk about her concerns but couldn't. That meant falling back on the emergency protocol. He reminded her before every trip where to find the number he kept hidden and how to make the call.

The instructions were simple: call, type the code phrase, get the drop site, and pass the pouch. All she had to do was relay the facts in a few short, specially coded sentences and prepare for people to step in and handle the situation. The rest of what happened whirled around in her head until she couldn't make sense of it anymore.

Her dad would have wanted her to hand over the

information, then get on a plane back to the U.S. Not telling him was the only way to keep him from hiking back, and that couldn't happen. The expedition counted on him staying at base camp. He'd been paid a large sum of money to do just that, and the clinic needed the money for supplies.

And she thought she could handle it all—pass on the information then get back to work—until that stranger came to the clinic looking for her. Until West and Josiah stormed in. Who knew typing in a code and a few random words would lead to this sort of chaos in her life? None of it was supposed to trace back to her.

Something West said to her came rushing back. "You mean you would have tortured my dad, right?"

"Interrogate."

She had a feeling those were the same things to West. That side of him freaked her out a bit. Not her style at all, especially since she'd dedicated part of her life to helping people with injuries. Being with a guy who liked inflicting them struck her as odd. And the wild attraction made no sense at all.

"Back to med school." West leaned back in his chair, and the wood creaked under his weight. "You didn't like it?"

"I had to leave." Was basically escorted out and advised to try in-patient care. It was embarrassing and awful. She blocked those days and the memory of all those concerned faces as the people she knew looked at her with pity.

"That sounds like careful wording." West traced a fingertip over the side of the cup. "Do I want to know why?"

Two could play at the half-answers game. She shrugged her shoulders. "Things happened. Life throws crap at you and you pivot."

"Sure."

The look he gave her, open and understanding, filled her with cleansing warmth, and that made her wary. She expected smoldering and commanding from him. She could even handle annoying and dictatorial. But when he sat there, actually listening to her, acting as if he held onto every word, panic started beating at the base of her skull.

He needed him to be *that* guy. Protective and strong, hot and possibly willing to get sweaty with her to work off some of the energy buzzing around them. She could limit her interest in *that* guy. Keep the attraction on an informal and body-only level. A guy with more depth was nothing but a threat to her carefully crafted life.

She had to get up. Get some air or move or around . . . something. "I'll draw that map."

"Lexi?" That voice, so deep and inviting.

She spun around to face him again. Words rushed out of her, jamming in her throat with the need to get them out. "I didn't mean to call all this attention to Skardu and the clinic. I didn't think it through and realize what I said could lead to death."

"I know."

"All I wanted to do was run the clinic while my dad was away." To not screw up. To show everyone that she deserved to be here. That she had earned her place and didn't need babysitting.

"You did something better." West got up and stood in front of her.

"Get my butt in trouble and put the clinic in the position of potentially having to close." West didn't touch her but she could feel the heat radiate off him. She put a hand on his chest to connect with the hammering of his heart. "I'll probably get my dad kicked out of the region after all the time he's spent here."

She expected West to push her away or tell her to calm down.

He put his hand over hers. "That won't happen, Lexi."

But that was the ongoing threat. West kept talking about ushering her out of the area and putting her on a plane with men she didn't know. It didn't make sense that her father would be safe here and she wouldn't.

There was only one explanation, and it started a ball of fury bouncing around in her gut. "Because he has doctor skills and I don't?"

"Touchy." West threaded his fingers through hers and tugged her in a little closer. "For the record, my appreciation for med techs is pretty high. The important thing in an area like this is to be respected and competent."

This close, she could smell the outdoors on him. The

scent clung to him. His presence physically overpowered her. She now knew those arms could wrap around her and the tightness fill her with a sense of security, not worry.

"And you know that how?" The words came out breathy as she fought to push air into her lungs.

"People with your training, men who didn't go by the title of doctor, saved my life more than once." He let go of her hand long enough to drag the bottom edge of his thin black shirt and the one underneath up and over his stomach. "You can see some of the handiwork here."

All those muscles and no fat. Tanned skin, scarred with the marks of old wounds.

She skimmed her fingertips over what looked like more of a twelve-pack than a six-pack. Over bare skin. Across the jagged pucker of skin about four inches long. "A knife slice."

The injury brought back the harsh reality of the danger of his work, but the soft touch had her mind bouncing somewhere else. To the bed. To getting him naked.

He might be strong enough to lift a car, but his waist stayed trim. This was not a guy who bulked up until he looked more like a character than a man. No, he was firm and overwhelming but in the best way.

"And also here." He let his shirt drop back over his chest and winked at her as he put her palm against the bullet wound on his side. "And a few others I can't show you without stripping down."

"You're lucky to be alive."

He put his hand over hers and moved her palm until it slipped under his shirt to caress his chest. "I feel lucky right now."

"Don't do that."

His hand stilled. "What?"

God, she did not want the touching to end. Wrong interpretation there, so she rushed to correct it.

Her other hand slid under his shirt. Both palms toured his sexy chest now. "Be decent."

"You seem to look for things to get pissed off about. That one is just weird." But there was no heat in his voice as he lowered his head to kiss her hair.

"Do you know anything about women?" Because he was doing a damn fine job of seducing one. Right there, in a small house in the middle of nowhere with danger brewing around them.

His mouth went to her ear and the small dip behind it. "Almost nothing."

A shiver shook through her. She was amazed she could still stand. "You're telling me you're a virgin."

He lifted his head and smiled down at her. "Uh, no."

"I'm guessing you're the type to go from country to country, killing and sleeping around." She dropped a quick kiss on his chin. Loved the feel of the scruff under her mouth.

"Not at the same time."

"You're hysterical." But she had to admit that was kind of funny. She tried to imagine him juggling guns and lowering his zipper at the same time. Interesting mental image.

"For the record, I keep my mind on the job." That hot mouth traveled to her neck as he spoke. "I don't fool around with women or drugs or alcohol. I stay focused."

She could barely hear him. Her brain cells kept misfiring and her hands found his waist. "That sounds smart."

"Until you."

She buried her nose against his throat and inhaled. He made her feel so safe. So hot. "That's only because I piss you off all the time."

His hands smoothed down her back. "You do sometimes."

Maybe the guy needed some work on romancing a woman after all. "That's flattering."

With one hand he tipped her chin up and looked down at her. "But I meant in the way where I don't want to strangle you. You break my concentration just by walking across a room."

"So, I'm special." She actually didn't know what he was saying, but that intense stare held her mesmerized.

"I don't know what the hell you are." His palms framed her face now, one on each cheek. The move brought them in even closer. "Not yet."

"While we're being honest, you can kiss. Like, whoa and damn you can kiss." And it killed her not to stretch up on tiptoes and try it again. "That's why I assumed you had a lot of practice."

"Kissing."

Just hearing him say the world sent her stomach tumbling. "What?"

He stared at her mouth. "You mentioned it, now I'm thinking about it."

"We should do it." She let his shirt drop as she lifted her arms to wrap them around his neck.

"Is the 'it' still kissing?"

Only to start. "No."

"That would be really fucking dumb." But his hands tightened against her. One slipped down to the small of her back.

He doubted he even realized how he rubbed his palm over her. "True."

"I don't do dumb shit on the job. Ever. People die." His surprisingly gentle touch contrasted with the harsh words.

The breath hiccupped in her lungs when his hand landed . . . yeah, right on her ass. "I get that."

"You are a nuisance," he said, his hands pressing her lower half tighter against him. He shifted until she fit into the notch between his legs.

Then he rubbed his growing erection against her. She tried to fight the sharp inhale of breath but it escaped her throat. "Right back at ya."

"We need to stop now." The friction built as the rustling of their clothing echoed in the background.

"Absolutely." She couldn't *not* kiss him then.

Pushing against the back of his neck, she brought

his face closer. Her mouth covered his and heat raced through her for a second time. The touch of his lips freed something in her.

All those months of holding back and obeying every rule, trying not to upset anyone or risk getting in trouble in town. The control burst and need flowed everywhere. No other man had tempted her in more than a year, and now she knew that what she felt back then was pale and shallow compared to this.

The whip of desire had wrapped around her from the very beginning. He was Mr. Wrong in so many ways, but as the hours passed, everything about him seemed right.

"Lexi . . ." He growled her name as he lifted his head.

Maybe it was a survival instinct or a need for comfort mixed with the wild attraction. She didn't try to define it or figure it out, but she knew one thing to be true. "If I'm going to die out here, I want—"

He jerked back but not away from her. Just far enough to look down at her. "You will not die."

"You sound sure." And his determination calmed whatever kept jumping around in her stomach. His confidence fed hers.

"I will not allow it."

"I don't think it works that way." But she'd bet he believed it did. He could just will it and it would happen.

Both his hands slipped to her ass and pulled her in tight. "So that we're clear, anyone comes for you, they have to go through me. And, as you pointed out when we first met, I'm kind of big."

Everywhere. "You're pretty sexy, too."

A frown marred his forehead. "If you say so."

She gave in to the temptation to smooth her finger over those lines. "I do."

Something sparked behind his eyes as he wrapped his fingers around her wrist and tilted his head so he could kiss the inside. He lightly nibbled on her skin then licked the spot as he peeked up at her. "We're still not having sex."

The seduction wound its way around her and her knees buckled. "You're not interested?"

"You're saying you can't feel me?"

Already locked together, he shifted his hips from side to side. Maybe it was in circles. She was too busy trying to remember how to breathe to notice.

The voice . . . that body. "Oh."

He smiled. "Yeah, oh." It faded as soon as her fingers touched the waistband of his pants. "Lexi?"

"I can control myself." She unbuttoned the top. "Can you?"

"You are poking the beast."

Her fingers went to the zipper as her mouth traveled to his neck. She tasted him, nuzzled him. A smart woman would stop, lift her head and tell him what she wanted, but the need to keep touching drove her. She kissed that sexy dip at the bottom of his throat where his neck met his collarbone. So sexy.

"What are you going to do about it?" She whispered the question against his skin.

"This." With his palms on either side of her face, he lifted her head.

His mouth came down and the whirlwind of energy kicked up around them. This kiss bordered on a claiming. Deep and intense. His lips crossed over hers as his fingers caressed her skin.

His need pounded into her and whipped around the room. She didn't think it was possible but he deepened the kiss as he walked her backward. Her heel cracked against the wall and her shoulders balanced there.

She grabbed the edge of his shirts and stripped them over his head. She barely had time to study him, to brush her palms over him, before his hands went to her pants.

In a few efficient moves he had her fly open and the zipper down. His hand slipped under the elastic of her practical cotton underwear. Then he touched her. There. His fingertips danced over her, making her wet and bringing her hips off the wall.

"West . . ." She forgot the rest of what she was going to say. Forgot everything except the feel of his skin against hers.

Her hands traveled over him as she kissed him. She didn't want to break contact. Rubbing against him fueled her. She had to fight the urge to strip every last piece of clothing off him and push him onto the floor.

And she would have if his finger hadn't pushed inside her. If her brain still functioned.

"Can you . . ." Her brain kept blanking. When he made that circle with his finger, when he pressed a second inside her, her head dropped to his shoulder.

Need rode her and her lower body clenched. His fingers tightened in her hair as his voice rumbled against the space right above her ear. "Come for me."

"God, yes." The winding and pulsing built until her head fell back.

Her heart thumped hard enough for her to hear it in her ears. Sensations bombarded her and heat rolled through her. Through it all he kept up the steady rhythm of his fingers—in and out.

When he did it one last time, all the clenching broke loose. Her hips bucked and her breaths came out in pants. She tried to push the hair out of her face and get her muscles to work but her body turned to a pile of goo. All the tension seeped out but the tingly sensation lingered.

She closed her eyes and leaned into him, let him hold her up because she didn't have the strength to do it on her own. She felt him press a kiss against her head and she tried to say something but soon gave up. Talking could only mess this up.

More minutes passed until her brain finally rebooted. Now she could think, but standing still eluded her. Her body was too busy melting against him. "I thought we weren't having sex."

A laugh rumbled in his chest. "I never said we wouldn't fool around."

Fighting through the lethargy, she finally managed to lift her head. "Then I think there's only one thing left."

His eyes narrowed but the look of pure male satisfaction stayed. "What?"

Her hand slipped over the bulge in his pants. "Your turn."

A smile lit up his face. "I like your style, Alexis Palmer."

"Then get on the floor."

8

STRANGEST NIGHT of his life. Hot but frustrating because West only scratched half an itch. So good and mind-clearing but not smart. Anyone could have walked in and stabbed him in the back while he was on top of Lexi.

It started out pretty simple. Touch her. Ignore everything he knew to be smart and right and seize the moment. Give her release and watch her body move as it happened. An excellent form of self-torture that spun into something so damn fine when she put her mouth on him.

He spent the night switching between touching her and keeping watch. Somehow he kept his vow not to enter her, but he'd come close to saying "Fuck it" more than once.

But in the daze of the early morning sunshine, even the short stray from his objective—getting her to safety and locating that encampment . . . doing his damn job—struck him as a mistake. Tasting her only made him ache for more, and sex was not on the agenda. Or it shouldn't be.

Good thing it was cold out. Maybe that would take some of the heat out of him and prevent another round of kissing her all over again.

He made a second turn around the building. With each pass he moved outward, covering a larger swath of ground but keeping the house within his sights and within quick running distance, in case someone slipped through on the opposite side of the house.

Javed had picked well. The property sat in a small valley, surrounded by natural barriers and outlined with trees. The house was tucked away with a hill behind it, so that the only natural ingress came from the front. The guy was smart. Someone trained to think about what could happen. West could appreciate that.

He scanned the ground and the horizon as he looked for any signs of life. If someone came within two hundred feet of the structure, he wanted to know. Nothing could get to her.

The footprint in the dirt was the first clue that he wasn't being paranoid. He cleared his mind and reached for his knife, wanting the blade close by if he needed it. Gun ready and knife in his fist, he stalked. Keeping low, he followed the trail, knowing this could be intentional to lead him into a trap.

He listened for sounds as he ducked behind trees and rock ledges. Nothing struck him as out of place. But he knew prints, and the one he'd seen, clear and unaltered by the elements, had to be relatively fresh.

Then he heard it. The telltale sign of attack. That

giveaway most men did right before they launched. The inhale of one last breath. West had been trained to pick up the sound. Honed that skill so no one could get the jump on him.

He waited until the last possible moment to move. The attacker counted on surprise and, due to West's size, likely miscalculated his ability to shift. The guy would learn the hard way.

The air changed and West pivoted, turned on the ball of one foot and ducked down, leaning to the left side. The final footstep echoed as he heard the grunt above him. Shoes skidded and stones sprayed. West kept moving. He swung around, spinning and standing up, now behind the attacker. Just what he wanted.

The uniform registered just as West reached for the guy. He slammed an elbow right into that spot between his shoulder blades, sending the man falling. He hit his hands and knees with a thud.

Then West pounced. He had an arm around the guy's throat and his knife in his hand. The guy bucked. This one wasn't going down easy. The blade didn't seem to faze him and he never stopped kicking out, trying to throw West off him.

Using his weight advantage, West dug in. He punched the guy in the side four times in rapid succession as he used his legs to send the man crashing to his stomach. Once on the ground, his opponent didn't stand a chance. West dug a knee into his back and grabbed him by the neck while flashing the knife in his face.

"I dare you to move." He would slice if he had to, but he wanted to ask a few questions first.

"West, stop!" Lexi raced out of the house with her bare feet thumping on the ground and her hair flying behind her in the breeze.

She wore her pants and his shirt, which dwarfed her. Between the cold and the very real possibility that more men lingered out there, he needed her out of sight.

Anger rushed through him when he saw the wide-eyed fear in her eyes. "Go back in the house."

She kept coming. Ran straight for him as she shook her head and said something he couldn't quite make out. Before he could stop her, she straddled his back with her legs and started pulling on his shoulders. He was about to yell when her words got through to him.

"That's Javed." She said the phrase over and over.

At the sound of the name, West eased his hold. Adrenaline still shot through him but the need to strike and kill died down. He forced his arms to loosen and sat back, moving off the man and over to the side.

Javed came up in a rush. One arm back, he nailed West right in the jaw before falling back on his elbows in the dirt.

The shot rocked through West as his teeth clicked together. The guy had a good punch, and he hadn't prepared himself for it. He didn't see stars but his jaw did rattle a bit and he could taste blood in his mouth.

"Javed, what are you doing?" Lexi sounded appalled, as if this amounted to any sort of real violence.

This time West caught her, grabbed her leg before she could go after Javed. "Hold up."

"But he—"

"It's okay." He spit out a stream of blood. "I deserved that."

At least she wanted to protect both of them. Satisfaction soared through him. She'd been friends with Javed for some time and known him only one day. West didn't have a problem being on her protection priority list. It was misplaced, of course. He didn't need backup and could handle Javed without trouble, but the fact that she tried—yeah, that didn't suck.

Javed scrambled to his feet with a gun in his hand. "Who are you?"

The uniform registered in West's brain. Pakistani army. He just hoped Javed was on leave or checking the house, and not bringing the entire squadron with him.

West rubbed the back of his head as he stood up. "Put the gun down."

"I will shoot." Javed sounded pretty determined to do just that.

"Right." He'd never get the shot off. West would be in top of him, shoving a knife in his stomach before then.

Lexi moved between them. "West is with me."

West shoved her behind him. "Never step in front of a gun."

"I'm trying to help."

She acted as if she could stop a bullet by sheer will.

He made a mental note to lecture her on gun safety and the dangers of men pumped full of adrenaline later. "I told you to stay inside."

She made a face at him. Did nothing to even pretend he was in charge here. "When?"

"You may have been asleep at the time, but I thought that instruction would be obvious under the circumstances." The first rule in situations like this was pretty simple—don't get caught. Duck, run, lie, fight. Do not walk into the middle of two armed men locked in battle.

Seemed like they might need a lecture on that, too.

Javed's stance relaxed and the barrel of his gun tipped toward the ground. "You know each other?"

That was probably stretching it, but West went with it. "Sort of." Then he asked, "Are you on duty now?" The uniform and the realities of being who he was said yes. He didn't even ask Javed why he had a house here, away from his base. He'd get to that question soon though.

"Yes." Javed turned to Lexi. "You haven't been kidnapped?"

"What?" This time she shot Javed the screwed-up-lips expression. "No, I'm fine."

That explained the guns-blazing thing. Whatever rumor flew around in this place, they did not involve Lexi being part of a conspiracy or working undercover. That made life easier. They might be able to use that to their advantage at some point.

"Does she look like she's my captive?" West asked. Hell, she looked five seconds away from touching his gun and telling him to put it away, which was the ultimate no-no. Didn't matter what happened the night before. He would not tolerate that.

"Raheel said you'd been taken by a lunatic."

She snorted. "That might be a little strong, but—"

"I came back here to get some supplies and go look for you." Javed's voice rose the longer he talked. "You told me you saw strange trucks and then dead men were found in your clinic."

The tense mood combined with the explanation crept from worried neighbor status to something else. Something potentially problematic.

West stared at Javed, looking for any sign that what he felt for Lexi went beyond friendship. Javed could not play hero. Too risky.

"What do you know about the trucks?" he asked Javed.

"Nothing." Javed looked to Lexi. "You need to forget what you saw."

Interesting in a potentially shitty way.

Lexi made a strangled sound. "Javed, please."

The target kept moving. West started out thinking Javed's concerns centered on a kidnapping attempt, but now it sounded like he had knowledge of the trucks. That was pretty fucking bad news. If the weapons tied back to the Pakistani army, he would have to destroy the stash. Then all-out war would break out.

Javed looked at his hands. "I didn't tell anyone about the information Alexis provided."

West wanted to believe that but something about the delivery felt off. Javed knew how to fire a weapon and fight a battle. He was not as good at subterfuge, which worked to his advantage right now. "But?" he asked.

"I checked the area." Javed's head shot up again. "Something is happening."

"And you expect me to believe you didn't ask around or—"

"No."

Something else was at work here. West could feel it. "Is this an army mission?"

"No, but the general was there."

"Who?" Lexi asked.

"Everyone is looking for you." Javed focused all his attention on her. "The army has been mobilized."

Motherfucker. Last thing West needed was an entire army up his ass. He could take on a group of men without backup and come out fine. The idea of taking on the Pakistani army was a bit more daunting.

But seeing the panic in Lexi's eyes had West downplaying his concerns. "Let's get back to the general," he said.

She looked at Javed. "Wait, people think West—"

"Broke into the clinic, murdered the general and another man, injured others and took you and the drugs." Javed's gun was now aimed at the ground.

West took his relaxed stance and willingness to share information as Javed's way of saying he wasn't buying the story racing around town. While it would be easy to believe everything Javed said and have one person on their side, West knew Javed had a job to do. He followed his own code and sense of honor, and West wasn't sure yet where those would lead them.

But the only thing West wanted to hear about was this general and what he had to do with the clinic and the trucks.

Lexi jumped in. Even moved in closer to West. "He didn't hurt me or force me."

The shift had Javed's gaze wandering. He stared at the space between West and Lexi and watched both of their faces. "I can see that, yes."

West wasn't quite ready to play nice. Not after Javed dropped a pretty big piece of intel without connecting it to anything. "What general?"

"You don't even know who you killed?" Javed asked.

"No idea." But West was starting to put the pieces together. Lexi reports suspicious activity, then an army general visits her. "One was dead on the floor and the other was attacking Lexi, so I didn't ask too many questions."

"General Rashad Harif."

There was one fact that didn't fit, and West knew it was important. "He wasn't in uniform."

"There's some confusion about that." Javed shook his head. "He was dressed as a citizen. Didn't have any identification or weapons on him."

The one he didn't kill. West had no idea what that meant. Not yet. "Why would he go after Lexi?"

"I don't know."

West was pretty sure Javed did know. The look on his face. It passed quickly but it hinted at additional information. He decided now wasn't the time to dig for that. Not until Javed put the gun away.

"How is he related to the trucks?" He wanted to sit the guy down and rapid-fire questions at him, maybe kick in some intimidation, until he broke.

But Lexi stood there, all wide-eyed and uncharacteristically quiet. West had no idea what that meant so he tread carefully.

After a few seconds of hesitation, Javed answered. "I saw the general at the site."

That sounded like half a story. Javed held back, and West didn't blame him, but he needed the intel if he had any chance of finding the weapons and either destroying them or recovering them. "Anyone else?"

"Many men. Most not from here. Not Pakistani." Javed sneered. "American?"

"Possibly." West let it drop because he'd have to look for himself to be certain. Time to bring this to a close and get to the strategy stage. "There's some good news here."

Lexi eyed West. "What can possibly be good about this situation?"

"We might be able to preserve the clinic and your job if people think you're a victim."

"But you are a hunted man." This time Javed did put the gun away.

West took that as a good sign. "Well, there's that."

And the hunted part? That wasn't new. He had to avoid most of the former Soviet Union or risk immediate execution.

"Raheel wants your head." Javed smiled as he said it. Took a bit too much pleasure in passing that piece of news on.

West knew he should have shot Raheel when he had the chance. That's the last time he would watch out for Lexi's feelings first. "He can't have it."

"If they find you, they'll kill you." The amusement left Javed's face as he looked at Lexi. "If they figure out you two are together, you will likely be viewed as spies and both be executed. No one will remember or care about the good you've done here."

That was more than enough doom and gloom. The color had already left Lexi's face. Much more of this talk and she might stop breathing.

West tried to redirect her thoughts. "I hate that word."

Javed shook his head. "What?"

"Spies."

And just like that the color rushed back into her cheeks. "That's what you're upset about? His word choice?"

He shrugged. "It's a pet peeve."

"We are in grave danger."

That was not news to West. Really, it shouldn't be to her either, he thought. She continued to ignore the bravery it took to report the encampment. She'd risked everything. The fact that she didn't seem to realize that shook him. Even if they could make the victim story stick, she had a rude shock heading her way.

"Not to scare you, but we always were in danger." West lowered his head until he had full eye contact with her. "Have been since I met you."

"Don't blame this on me," she said, her anger fully back in place.

"Right now I'm blaming Pakistan." This country just kept kicking his ass. "Not my favorite place."

After a quick look around, Javed nodded toward the house. "We need to get inside."

"Then what?" Lexi asked.

"Good question." But West knew. He needed to get to that encampment, and now.

9

LEXI'S EYES started to cross. She wanted to blame the lack of sleep but she had no complaints about last night. Well, maybe one. West's stubborn insistence they go only so far and no further. Sure, the excuse about not being able to concentrate on keeping them safe while having sex made sense.

When the guy drove home a point, he tended to mention the possibility of dying several times. She had to admit that amounted to a compelling argument. But having him say no after she made it clear he had a definite green light didn't exactly give her a huge push of self-confidence in the sexuality department.

But that wasn't the reason her attention was fading. The constant talk about tactics did her in. She'd drawn the map and it matched the location Javed had seen. Now she had two grown men sitting at opposite ends of a table, staring at her . . . and not in a good way.

She lowered the glass of water and cradled it between her palms. "What?"

Javed leaned forward. "It was very dangerous for you to report this activity then stay in Pakistan."

West cleared his voice. "See?"

Now West acted friendly. She wasn't buying it after that scene outside. "Don't pretend you like Javed."

"He's growing on me."

Javed's eyes narrowed. "I'm what?"

"Forget it." West mumbled under his breath. Also said something about how he should become a vacation type of guy.

They acted as if they had all the time in the world. Forget that they kept tripping over men with guns or that West left the bed this morning to circle the house and play guard. He snuck out. Even kissed her on the forehead, which was just about the sweetest thing ever.

She'd been warm and happy and thinking about dragging him back down on the floor when he started checking his weapons. With each look, each click of this or that, the lethal warrior persona snapped into place. Before her eyes he morphed from sexy bed partner to armed and deadly.

The change should have terrified her, but it didn't. For a woman who always struggled with confidence, who had to drop out of medical school after a breakdown, seeing West so sure and clear appealed to her. He was everything she wasn't, and right now that's what she needed.

"You should have flown out of here when you had the chance," he said. "That's my point. A version of the point I've been making since we met."

Amazing how she could be thinking positive thoughts about him, get all warm and fuzzy, and then he opened his mouth. Part of what made him strong and so devastating to her also made him demanding and a tad assy sometimes. She didn't love that.

Javed turned to West. "I can take her in with me. Say I found her, that she got away."

Her friend made her sound like a lost puppy. Not exactly how she liked to think of herself.

"Not with a dead general and no viable suspect," West said. "If your superiors get her, they will interrogate her." His mouth fell into a flat line. "No."

And they were off to planning again. The men seemed to think they could handle her life without talking to her.

She tried to let them know what she thought of that. Loaded her voice with sarcasm. "For the record, I'm not a fan of the potential torture part. You know, in case I get a say in my life. Which, clearly, you two think I don't."

"You have the wrong government," Javed said. "If you want torture you should go back to the U.S."

"We are not going to have a battle tactics discussion or argue about which country scores better on the humanity scale." West plunked his glass down on the table as he sat back in his chair. "And she stays with me."

Javed started shaking his head before West finished the sentence. "She can't go to the encampment."

She'd had enough. She could stitch up a wound and treat frostbite. She could not tolerate two men bickering about her. She'd found her limit and hit it.

Now to let them know.

She snapped her fingers until they both looked at her. "You two see me, right?"

Javed nodded. "Yes."

"She's not really asking." West looked ready to laugh. "She'd scolding. She does that."

This time she put the brakes on before they launched into a new round of pretend-Lexi-isn't-in-the-room. "We're talking about my life, my safety. I decide where I go."

Javed shook his head. "That's not the case."

"While it would be interesting to hear Javed argue with you about women's rights, I happen to agree." West spun his glass around, letting it clank against the table as he looked at her "You're coming with me until my communication is restored and I can pass you off to my team."

That comment had Javed sitting up straighter in his chair. "Team? There are others?"

"No." West kept spinning that glass.

"You just said—"

"Stop." She broke in to keep Javed from launching into an informal interrogation. Not that West would answer a single question. She also used the time to prove a point . . . and grab the glass before her head exploded. "I will not be passed off."

He moved the glass out of snatching range. "I thought I was clear."

She had no idea when that would have been. "Apparently not."

"You're. With. Me." West's voice grew louder with each word.

Admittedly the delivery needed work, but she didn't hate that idea. Hell, she'd lobbied for it, so she didn't argue. For now.

Javed's gaze switched to Lexi then back to West. "I can get you part of the way there but then you're on your own. We'll leave as soon as the sun starts to set."

West nodded. "Fine."

"I'll get the truck and the gear you'll need and be back." Javed got up and halfway to the front door.

"Alone." West turned in his chair and faced the other man. "I mean it, Javed. No one knows about this or me or what's really happening with Lexi. Not even Raheel."

"You are not my superior." Javed's voice stayed firm but he didn't show any outward signs that the comments annoyed him.

Still, Lexi sensed a battle brewing. She was about to step in when West piped up again.

"I will kill you. Do you understand me?" West's voice stayed deadly low. "I don't care about your uniform or what country we're in. You have two seconds to convince me you're going to obey."

She winced. Clearly West skipped the day his group taught diplomacy and tact.

Javed's jaw tightened. "I am not—"

"Look, this isn't a pissing contest." West matched Javed's attack stance with one of his own. "It's about keeping Lexi alive, and I will do whatever I have to do to make sure that happens."

Javed glanced over West's head and directly at her as tension buzzed around them. "Then I'll agree."

"Good." West didn't bother to hide his satisfaction on getting his way. "Then I don't have to shoot you."

After a few more hours of prep West stared out the front door and waited. Javed had dropped off food and additional weapons with ammunition. He was about to head out again to get the truck but stood out on the grass and dirt talking to Lexi.

West still didn't trust Javed, but he trusted the way he looked at Lexi. She meant something to him. Maybe nothing sexual, but the concern was right there on his face and in the way he pleaded for her to remain behind. West heard every word, as well as Lexi's stubborn refusal to concede.

He had to admit that Javed's solution did tempt him. If he thought he could stash her in a building or even under one and keep her safe for the next few hours, he would have. But Javed's latest verbal update spoke of a house-to-house search, which meant the safest place for her now was by his side. He could protect her and, if it came down to it, put on whatever show he needed to make it clear she was a victim and not an accomplice.

His assignment from Alliance focused on the weapons and recon, but the secondary job was about getting the doctor out of country. As far as West was concerned, that duty extended to Lexi since she made the call to report the weapons sighting.

He danced around the meaning behind the orders to make it work, but that didn't bother him. He'd never been a follow-the-rules guy anyway. And there was no way he would leave Pakistan or this Earth without knowing he did everything possible to protect her.

That was the job . . . and in this case something else pushed him. Something he couldn't define. Attraction maybe, but he doubted it. He'd rescued pretty women before. But this woman, with her sharp responses and hot kissable mouth, got to him. Those eyes that turned sad when she thought he wasn't looking. The fierce determination even though she had to be terrified. The trust she placed in him, even as she fought it. The mix of tough and vulnerable packaged in that sexy shell had him thinking things he should not be thinking while stuck in the middle of Pakistan with hostiles on his tail.

After a brief touch of Javed's arm, Lexi started back to the house. She glanced up, looked at West, and her footing faltered, but then she moved forward again.

He met her at the door and opened it for her. He promised himself not to pry, because there was no way he could justify the questions being any of his damn business, but then she passed within inches of him. "You sure there was never anything between you two?"

She stopped and looked up. "You mean like there was with us last night?"

As if he needed a reminder. Hell, just looking at her

made the blood pound in his veins. "Yeah, anything like that."

"No, you're the only one I've . . . done that with while in Pakistan."

The way she stumbled over the words had him biting back a smile. He could describe every inch of her skin. Give a complete play-by-play on how her thighs tightened against his shoulders as he lay between them. Could but wouldn't because her cheeks had already turned a rosy red.

But that didn't mean he couldn't nudge her a bit. "Done 'that'?"

"What?"

"You can say the actual words." He leaned down until his mouth hovered over hers. "I'm a big boy."

"What are you talking about?"

Man, he'd been hoping she'd give him an opening like that. "I touched you. Went down on you. Licked you. Kissed you. Tasted every inch or you then went back for more." He hesitated for a few beats. "You blew me. Your mouth on my—"

Her head snapped back. "Aren't you chatty all of a sudden?"

He turned and with a hand on her back brought her farther inside and closed the door behind them. With every step forward he took, she retreated. The doorway got in her way and she jammed up against the frame.

He put a hand on the wall next to her head and leaned in. "Do the words embarrass you?"

"I'm not a child." The only honest reaction came in the way she twisted her hands together.

His gaze bounced down to her fingers then back up again. "Then what's the problem?"

She pushed at his chest then. Shoved until he moved, and ducked her way out of his confining stance. "You're trying to make me feel ashamed or naïve or something. I don't like it."

"Whoa." He caught her elbow at the last second, stopping her dramatic exit, and spun her around to face him. "Listen—"

"And I hate when you order me around." But she didn't try to shake off his hold or swear or hit him.

He decided that was a good sign and tried to explain. Not something he usually did. He'd act out of instinct and training, and would deal with the fallout later. This emotional bullshit wasn't for him, which was evident by the way he sucked at it. "I was trying to take your mind off tonight."

"What?" Her expression suggested he'd grown two extra heads.

Maybe downplaying only made things worse. Hell, he didn't know. This was not his area of expertise. Shooting shit, yes. Talking to women and easing their fears or whatever? God no.

He loosened his grip on her arm and slipped his fingers through hers instead. "You need to be realistic. This is balls-out dangerous. I would never let you go with me if I thought I had a choice or if I believed you'd be safe if caught walking around Skardu."

With her free hand she played with the zipper on his slim jacket. "People think I'm a kidnapping victim."

"With a general dead you're a suspect." And he knew she understood that. This was about working it out in her mind and finding a way through it, and he could give her a second or two to figure it out, but not much more.

"I didn't know he was a general."

"The army won't care. They'll want to know why he was in the clinic and what happened, and if they don't like the answers, they'll try to get you to give others."

She flattened her hand against his chest and leaned in, balancing her head under his chin. "Every part of that sounds horrible."

"Worse than that." This part was so important that he wanted to watch her as he spoke, but he couldn't move her. Holding her felt too good to stop, even for this. "So, if we're seen, or taken, you act like my prisoner. Show hate and fear. Scream for help. Spit on me. I want to see your best acting."

Her head shot up. "They'll kill you."

He had to shift to avoid being knocked in the chin. "They'll grab you and that will buy time so my team can rescue you."

"You'll still be dead," she said in a near whisper.

Her mouth dropped open as her hands went to his biceps. Fingers dug into his skin through the fabric of his shirt and jacket. The pleading was right there in her eyes.

He had to glance away for a second. Something

about her knocked him sideways. "That's not important."

"Do you have a death wish?"

She had it exactly wrong. "No."

"You act like killing doesn't matter. Like it doesn't
bother you or touch you." Her hands dropped away and
she moved away and started to pace.

"That's not true."

Back and forth, right in front of him. She walked
and mumbled. She got to the farthest point away from
him then turned on her heel and came back. "You don't
even blink when you strangle a guy or whip out that
knife to stab one."

He refused to apologize. The work he did had to be
done. He stepped up when others couldn't. It wasn't as if
one more thing haunting him would matter that much.

But now wasn't the time. She didn't need sharing.
She needed a bodyguard, and he willingly stepped into
that role. Into whatever role she wanted.

Pushing away the drawn look on her face and how
much he wanted her, he focused on the job ahead. "We
need to get ready."

His footsteps tapped against the floor and echoed in
the small structure as he walked into the kitchen. One
final check and they'd be ready. He'd walk her through
every step and over the contingencies he'd planned for.

A second later her footsteps sounded behind him.
He could feel her standing there. Almost sense the
anger flowing through her.

She grabbed his arm and walked around him until she stood in front of him. "You can touch me everywhere but not carry on a simple conversation?"

Those hours, the loss of control. He couldn't think of either right now. Not and get the job done.

He shook his head. Tried to shake off every distraction. "None of this is relevant to the next few hours."

"Must be nice to be able to compartmentalize like that." She shoved at his shoulder then did it again. "To lock all those emotions away."

The machine thing. He'd refined it until it became second nature. Here he thought they'd done all this talking to the point where he needed to pull back on what he revealed, and she still found him to be more machine than man.

When he didn't say anything, she made a noise and walked away. Kept going until she got to the family room and only stopped at the front door. She fidgeted. Wrapped her arms around her waist.

They stood not more than twenty feet apart, and the distance between stretched for miles. He didn't know how to bridge the gap or make her understand. He had never cared how someone viewed him before. He went in, did the work, and walked away, trying to leave it on the floor behind him. He carried the marks but he didn't break.

There was no way he could fall down now or ever. That wasn't who he was or how he acted, and that had always been good enough for everyone. Until her.

Thoughts and ideas bombarded his brain. All those memories he kept blocked flooded through him. He wanted to storm out and refocus.

But the longer he watched her stand there, all stiff and facing into the darkening night, something changed. The hard shell around him cracked. For once he wanted to explain, if only a horrible fucking moment of his life. To let someone in.

"I was last here in 2012." The words clogged his throat but he spit them out. "Close to Skardu. In Gyari on an undercover operation. Was with my men, following orders."

She pivoted so slow that it felt as if it took her a month to finish. "You got caught?"

"Not the way you think." A flash of cold hit him from out of nowhere. He'd been wearing his thin hiking jacket for three days. It fit like a shirt, and he had one of those on underneath. The same one she wore earlier now skimmed his skin.

What hit him now wasn't a breeze or the inevitable temperature drop that came with night. No, this was a bitterness that seeped into his bones. A gift from his imagination. He relived the numbing cold as if he were buried in snow right now.

She shook her head as though trying to ferret out what he was saying. "West . . ."

"We were doing recon in and around the Siachen Glacier. Checking on intel that pointed to Pakistan making headway in the ongoing battle thanks to a new weapon." There were limits on what he could say, and he'd already stepped over the line.

A top-secret mission behind the lines. He and his team snuck in to observe the war between India and Pakistan being played out 18,000 feet in the air. The highest battleground on Earth and the location of every fucking nightmare he'd ever had in his adult life.

Throughout his career, military and with Alliance, he'd killed and narrowly escaped death several times. Survived gunshots, being gassed, and blown up. He'd describe that as the easy stuff.

He once lay in the mud while Chechen commandos walked the fields around him describing how they planned to skin him. Another time he purposely got caught by rebels in the Sudan who were hell-bent on killing women and children. Survived the knives and the torture just so he could take them down from the inside. But nothing came close to the horror of being in this area three years ago when a piece of the mountain came down.

The color left her face. "The avalanche."

He let out a relieved breath. She knew. Not a surprise since anyone who lived and worked in the area knew. The devastation had touched so many, and the memory of how quickly life could end stayed with them.

There was no way to prepare for the next time. Even though locals and climbers talked about an angry mountain and ascribed emotions and feelings to it, the thing wasn't human. The height, the location, the unpredictable weather. So many factors and so little control.

He didn't even realize they'd both moved until they met in the middle. "Some argue it was a landslide. A slick brought on by rain that sent ice and rocks cascading down on top of us."

He could see it. Hear the roar and remember the raging panic.

"Avalanche or landslide, it doesn't matter. It wiped out a Pakistani army camp, buried hundreds alive, including my team." Every last one of them. Eight men gone in a flash, some buried alive and others ripped to pieces and strewn all over the side of the mountain."

"What about you?"

He knew what she wanted to know, and didn't make her work for it. "I volunteered for the riskiest part of the mission. Crawling closer to the glacier to stake out each country's respective position while searching Pakistani ground for weapons. I assumed going in that it was a one-way mission. I'd get the location, use code to radio it back, but never make it out."

"You went in expecting to die."

The confusion was right there on her face. He got it. Normal people didn't walk into danger thinking they wouldn't come out. Most Marines did. He certainly did. "Yeah, but I didn't. Being on the way to the glacier put me off track for the slide."

She exhaled, long and loud. "You weren't buried."

"I was but I didn't get plunged under like the others.

If you're a foot or less under the slide you have a chance of digging your way out."

She put her hand on his chest in a light but reassuring gesture. "Which you, of course, did."

"We'd had avalanche training before they left. Real basic stuff. Something that seemed like a waste of time because in a battle of man versus mountain, the mountain wins. But the training helped."

She spread her hand on his chest. "I'm sure your survival instinct proved to be the difference."

The military counselor he was forced to see said the same thing. West didn't believe it back then. He put some stock in it now.

His hand covered hers because it just felt right to touch her then. "I knew to dig out a small air pocket so I could breathe, and kept one arm raised so I would know which was up. The small shovel I carried with me helped do the rest."

Never mind that he wrenched his arm out of the socket and fractured it in two places. That was nothing compared to the collapsed lung and broken ribs, neither of which made his rescue attempts of the others all that easy or successful.

"That sounds so horrifying."

"No, seeing blood sprayed over the white snow, knowing my men were either in pieces or buried deep without receivers or any way to locate them . . . that was horrifying."

She pulled their joint hands and rested them against her chest. "I'm so sorry."

Any other time being touched while remembering those days would set him off and have him yanking away. With her, warmth spread through him and he grabbed on. "No one comes to rescue you when you're where you're not allowed to be."

"Your men?"

"Died." It took him a full year to be able to say the word. Not one of them walked out with him, and he couldn't take them home. "I stripped off anything that would identify them and buried the bodies I could find."

Actually stood there, freezing and in blinding pain, half wrecked with grief and in shock, and dug with his hands. He'd known that if found, their bodies would be used as propaganda or as an excuse to start or escalate a fight with the U.S. He couldn't allow either.

But he'd left men behind. Two. He remembered their names and their faces. Broke his vow after days of digging and dodging the Pakistani army, all while not eating and having no warmth or place to sleep other than the killing snow.

He refused to make that choice again. He should have stayed and dug until his hands were raw. He owed his men that.

That was the day he became a machine.

He inhaled, forcing out the words left inside him. "So, no. I don't welcome death, but I don't run from it either. I have a job."

She lifted their joint hands to her mouth and kissed the back of his hand. "A horrible one."

The warmth of her fingers provided a strange comfort. "One that's twice stuck me in this hellhole."

She shook her head, and her hair fell around her shoulders. "Why would you ever come back here, where all those memories linger?"

"Technically, for your dad and the information we thought he provided. In reality, for you." Looking at her now, seeing the warmth in her eyes and touching her fingers, he knew one simple truth—he'd walk into Hell for her, and for him this place came close.

"We have to leave." She jerked away from him and looked around the room. "Get you out of Pakistan."

No one had ever told him to walk away before. He knew this was about her concern for his sanity. He should have been offended, but he wasn't. "Hey, in a race of me against the Siachen Glacier, I'm ahead."

She turned back with an expression filled with fury. "Don't be flippant. Not now."

"Okay."

She moved fast as she grabbed the bag he'd already loaded and started pawing through it. She was this vibrating ball of energy and looked two seconds away from spinning out of control.

"I can't believe your idiot boss and that so-called team of yours sent you here," she said as she threw one item after another out of the bag.

Well, this was new. He waited for the anger to hit him but it didn't. Having a woman want to protect him didn't suck.

"Lexi, listen to me." He caught her shoulders before she undid all of his work and put them off schedule. "I don't run away from an assignment."

She waved a hand at him. "Let the rest of your team do it. Didn't Josiah say there were four others?"

That didn't sit right with West at all. "Do you think that's who I am? That I pass off the danger, so I can stay safe?"

"Is it wrong that I don't want you to get hurt? That I want you to be that guy this one time?" She practically yelled the question.

"Yeah, that guy sucks."

She shrugged out of his hold and grabbed a jacket. Almost dislocated a shoulder putting it on. "That's the point. I want to figure out who you are, and I can't do that if you're dead."

His mood bounced from concerned to humbled. Watching her amounted to pure entertainment. He didn't dare laugh. He didn't find it funny. More like sexy and flattering as hell.

The only way he knew to calm her down was to stay even-keeled and try to talk her down off whatever emotional high buzzed through her. He went for an uncomplicated list. "We're going to get the intel, get out and be fine."

"You can't promise that." She continued to stew and bounce and shift her weight around.

But she looked so damn cute in the oversized jacket. Javed found her a smaller size but it still dwarfed her.

This time West did smile. "I have an incentive."

She frowned at him. "What?"

"Once we get somewhere safe I'm going to be all over you."

She blinked several times. "West, I'm serious."

"So am I." He touched her then. Put his arms around her waist and pulled her in close. "Inside you."

"Oh."

His mouth found her neck. "Should I describe what's going to happen. Use every dirty word I know?"

"Like?"

"I can talk about how I intend to fuck you." But it would be more than that. She wasn't an easy and for-gettable lay. He knew that already.

She turned her head and kissed him. Her mouth lin-gered over his as her fingertips danced over his skin.

It took another minute before she lifted her head, and even then she balanced her cheek against his. "If you break this promise, I'm going to take that knife and stab you."

And she would. He loved that about her. "Fair enough."

10

LEXI HAD done some risky things in her life but this blew them all away.

After her breakdown, she'd received a leave of absence from school. The facility her father found for her to "recuperate" only increased her anxiety. She left the hospital—and that's what it was, no matter how many pretty words her father used to call it something else—early, after two weeks, and against the doctor's advice. She'd walked in voluntarily, and they couldn't hold her no matter how much influence her father tried to bring down on everyone, including her.

But she couldn't go back to medical school. She'd failed. Flamed out, and everyone knew. So she walked away from it and a career focused on helping people. Afterward, she never expected the call to hit her so hard, but it did.

She opted for specialized training everyone told her was a waste of time. The kind that would make her useful to her father. Relocated to Pakistan at a time when being an American woman in that country could be problematic.

It all worked out until the one night she snuck around, following mysterious trucks, then made the call that brought West and his team running. Everything snowballed from there. The danger. How she rolled around naked with West, a man she barely knew but instinctively trusted. Now this. Riding in the back of an army vehicle to some covert area that was so dangerous there wasn't even a word strong enough to describe it.

Javed all but promised they'd be caught and killed as he got into the driver's seat back at his house. That now seemed like it happened hours ago.

At least the modified Jeep looked the part, with the camouflage paint. A large metal bar separated the front from the back, but nothing covered them as they rumbled over uneven terrain, sending her bouncing around on the hard bench seat. Watching West didn't help. He sat across from her, switching his gaze back and forth from the dust kicking up behind them to the open road ahead.

They stayed off-road, however, and moved slowly. A large hill blocked their sight lines to the right, and West had complained to Javed about this route choice because of it. In addition, Pakistani army roadblocks set up to look for her and the general's killer limited their options, so they spanned the miles in darkness and with only the parking lights on to guide their way.

"The temperature has dropped dramatically." Lexi had to force her teeth from chattering just to get that sentence out.

"Which is why I'm wondering where the cold weather

gear is," West said without looking at her. "I'm guessing Javed forgot it."

She wore an oversized army jacket that Javed scrounged from somewhere, but the cold wind blew right through it. West insisted she wear his gloves. They helped but she still had to tuck her hands in her armpits to keep the circulation going. She had no idea how he sat there in that thin black jacket with bare hands and a bare head.

"Too obvious to wear that," Javed shouted over his shoulder while the Jeep's wheel shimmied back and forth in his hands. "If you were caught it would trace back to me."

West blew on his hands. "So?"

"Alexis would not be able to act the victim." Javed looked over his shoulder for a second, then his gaze went back to the route he created as he drove.

Lexi didn't see how those two things related to each other but she wanted the conversation over. She was already sorry she'd said anything at all. That would teach her to think the weather was a safe topic.

"At least it's not winter," she said. They would literally be blocks of ice riding in an open Jeep if it were a few months later.

West traded hand-blowing for rubbing his palms up and down on his legs. "That will be a huge comfort when you freeze to death."

"Hey." She stretched her leg and tapped her foot against his boot. "It's fine, so ease up."

His gaze shot to her and his mouth opened. Whatever he saw on her face or picked up in the air had his jaw closing and him nodding instead.

Between the strain around Javed's mouth and the anger vibrating in West's voice, Lexi knew that both men had hit the end of their patience. They were snapping at each other. Maybe that's how men handled these things. She wasn't conversant enough on the typical alpha man to know.

Without warning, West shifted in his seat. He had his gun out as he went up on one knee on the bench. "Do you hear that?"

"What?" But Javed slowed the Jeep down.

Now both men looked around, scanning the area. She didn't hear or see anything out of the ordinary. Just the knock of her heart crashing against her rib cage. Fear pinged around inside her as tension whipped around the vehicle.

Her mood tended to switch to match West's, and right now he was up and stiff, with his gun aimed. Him being on high alert sent wave after wave of anxiety crashing through her. She tried to slow her breathing and focus.

"West, what is it?" Those coping tools she learned so long ago came rushing back to her. She needed facts or she'd panic.

She could face this. Could survive.

He held out a hand toward her. "Duck down. Sit on the floor. Head between your knees and arms over your head."

They were going to crash. He didn't say it but she knew.

She'd just started to drop when she heard it. The roar of an engine off to her right in the still darkness. Javed continued to drive. He and West talked back and forth but she couldn't hear them.

Then headlights flashed in front of them from the right. It was as if a vehicle appeared out of the middle of the rock wall. She assumed that meant the rock wall had ended but her brain lagged behind what she was seeing. So unexpected. So terrifying.

"Stop the Jeep." West gave Javed the order before glancing over at her. "Get down," he said again.

She wanted to. She should. But the danger paralyzed her. She watched it like she would a movie, from a distance and unattached.

For a second she thought they got lucky. The lights moved away from them in the quiet night, highlighting the miles of open and unused land. She held her breath, but then the truck or car or whatever it was swung around. Tires screeched and the lights swung in a wide arc and headed right for them.

West looked down at Javed. "Hit the gas."

"No, no." Javed yelled something else in his language as their Jeep sped up. Plumes of dirt billowed around them and pebbles kicked up and pinged the side of the vehicle. One nailed her in the arm and she bit back a scream.

"Do not blink, Javed." West balanced on his arms. "Keep going. Faster."

She watched in horror as a truck with floodlights barreled toward them. West didn't flinch, but Javed shifted in his seat and shouted. He'd rattle off a few words in rapid succession then shake his head.

They were playing a deadly game of chicken and Javed didn't appear to have the stomach for it. West must have known because he jumped into the front seat and pointed, giving orders as he reached back to push her head down.

She balanced on her knees, ignoring how the hard floor bruised her skin. With her shoulder braced against the back of Javed's seat, she waited. Part of her wanted to shut her eyes and block out the nightmare. But she needed to see and be ready.

West would throw his body in front of hers. She knew that without asking. He'd made it clear his job was to gather evidence and get her to safety.

She heard the revving of an engine. A banging noise came next, and both West and Javed crouched down. Gunfire. Had to be. As soon as she thought it, the Jeep slowed down.

"Javed, no." West grabbed the wheel and slid over, almost on top of him.

The headlights of the other vehicle were still there. The Jeep swung from side to side over the bumpy land and the truck kept coming. Shots rang out and West fired back. The headlights cast most of the area in shadow.

The noise and chaos raged around her. She held her hands over her ears but watched every second. The

need to pull West to the back with her nearly overwhelmed her. She wanted him protected, not this huge
target only thirty feet away from the oncoming truck.

A figure hung out of the side of the truck ahead.
They were within twenty feet apart now. West shouted
something as he pushed on the back of Javed's head.

"Lexi, down!" West screamed out his orders as he
pulled the steering wheel hard to one side.

The Jeep went into a slide. Brakes squealed and
gunshots rang out. She closed her eyes for a second
then opened them again. The world spun around her
and the Jeep wobbled. She saw lights and then darkness in front of her before the Jeep tipped.

Bangs and thuds sounded as her body went into
freefall. She felt a hard slam and a jolt then she turned
weightless. She flew through the air and crashed back
down again.

Lexi's head slammed into something metal and her
legs twisted underneath her. She smelled smoke and
gasoline. Voices ran together and she tried to pick out
West's. When she opened her eyes again, two men
stood over her. Neither looked familiar but she recognized the Pakistani army uniforms.

A groan came from the front seat, and one of the
uniformed men shifted to look. Javed sat up, rubbing
his shoulder. Blood spilled from a cut in his head, and
even in the dim light she could see the haziness in his
eyes. A concussion maybe.

But all of her attention went to the deathly quiet

from West's side. He was slumped over and hanging down. The steering wheel stopped him from rolling on top of Javed, but she could see the blood. On his head. Matted in his hair.

The second guard, or whatever he was, poked West with his gun. He didn't move.

Every bone and muscle inside her shook. Waves of nausea crashed through her. She had to bite back the bile rushing up her throat to keep from throwing up.

Meanwhile, the other uniformed man pulled Javed out of the Jeep. Yanked on his arm and dragged him. Javed fell in a heap on the ground and the man yelled something at him. Javed yelled back and the two of them carried on a shouting match, back and forth. She caught a word or two.

The man with the gun kept asking Javed why they were there and why he hadn't turned her in. The other man paced around the back of the Jeep toward her. She knew her turn would come next and hoped her legs would carry her.

"Get up." He said the words in clipped English, then nodded as if he wanted her to crawl out of the Jeep.

Shaking and swallowing and trying to concentrate to pick up any sign of life coming from West, she put her palms under her and pushed up. Her shoulders trembled and she couldn't hold her weight. When her chest fell he grabbed her hair and pulled her head back.

She tried to breathe and make her legs work. Anything to stall for time and keep his fury in check.

"Okay." She held her hands up. It took her two more tries to stumble to her knees.

He grabbed her arm and twisted. A cry escaped her lips and then she heard the bang. A loud crack by her ear that had her ducking. When she lifted her head again she saw the bullet hole in the guy's forehead and the second his body held before it dropped.

She shifted around as West came up over the steering wheel firing. He hit the other armed man in the shoulder but the man didn't go down. He took a step back and then his arm came up and West stood right in the man's line of fire. She was about to call out some kind of warning when the guy's head flew back and his body fell.

Her gaze flipped back to West's arm and the gun in it. Even with blood running down the side of his face he looked deadly calm.

"You okay?" His voice sounded hoarse as he focused his intense stare at her.

Relief pounded her hard enough to steal her breath. Her shoulders fell and what little energy she had ran from her body. All she could do was nod.

"Lexi?" He barked out her name. "Talk to me."

She swallowed a few times as she managed to get her legs under her. "You're bleeding."

"No big deal. Head wounds bleed when they're not serious." West used his chin to gesture toward Javed. "Check him."

In the next breath, West started moving. He winced as he pulled his legs out from under the crushed dash-

board. One then the other. He kept his arm bent at an
odd angle as he slid to the ground. Without a word he
headed for the truck.

He looked ready to drop. He might think he was invincible but she knew better. She had enough medical
training to know he needed attention.

Fresh panic soared through her as she called after
him, "Where are you going?"

"To make sure I got them all."

It was sick and probably really wrong, but she sat
there and prayed he did, too.

West made one last round of the truck and the direction from where it came. Nothing. Looked like he
stopped the threat. Good, because now he had time to
kill Javed.

Forget the thumping in his arm. Forget the blood
dripping off his forehead. He was on a mission.

By the time he got back to the Jeep, Javed was leaning against the sidelined vehicle while Lexi checked
his head. She had a bag open and her medical kit out.
With who she was and what she did for a living, the
scene made sense. But seeing her touch Javed sent
anger raging like a wildfire through West.

The truck headlights lit their immediate surroundings, but the rest of the area lingered in darkness. Still,
he could see her hovering over Javed. That was about
to end.

West allowed himself two seconds to block out

Javed and drink in the sight of her. She moved around without limping and he hadn't spied any blood on her. The lack of injury was the only reason he hadn't killed Javed already.

He switched from walking to stalking and had his hands on Javed's shirt a few steps later. "Who did you tell?"

West pulled Javed off the truck and shook him as hard as he could. The guy's head could fall off for all he cared. So long as he gave up the names of the people he told about this mission to the encampment.

Lexi jumped to life. She pulled on West's arms. Or tried. "West, stop it."

He ignored her. He had to. Coincidences set off his inner alarms. He didn't believe for a second a truck just happened to be hidden behind that rock wall. Driving there, waiting.

West's body slammed Javed's back against the Jeep. With it turned on its side it was a weird position, probably injured the guy's spine, and West did not give a shit.

When Javed started squirming, West put a hand around his throat. "I told you not to talk to anyone. I warned you I would kill you and I wasn't kidding."

Javed's eyes were wide and full of fear. He started to shake his head but West held him still, daring him to lie.

"I didn't," he choked out.

"Then someone saw you, which I find hard to believe. I've seen your tracking skills. You're a fucking professional." He lifted Javed just enough to get some air under him and slam him back down. "How does someone get the drop on you?"

Javed kicked out and clawed at West's hand. He did not cower or give up. "I fly helicopters."

Then West had to fight off two of them—Javed shifting all around and Lexi slapping at his arm to get him to ease his grip on Javed. Neither of them fazed West. Javed had talked to someone, and that could have gotten Lexi killed. It was the only fact that mattered right now.

"West, stop." She was screaming in his ear.

"Not yet." He never stopped looking at Javed. He needed the man to see the hate in his eyes and know just how far this could go if he didn't start talking. "You're in the Pakistani army. I know you can be lethal when you need to be."

"I told you everyone is looking for Alexis." He looked in her direction.

"So, what, that was just a regular search party?" West butted in before Javed could answer. "No way."

"I'm serious," Lexi said, grabbing his arm with both of her hands and yanking. "No more."

As far as he was concerned, she could draw a gun and it wouldn't stop him. He wanted answers. This country had fucked him over once, and he'd be damned if he let it happen again. "Your friend here knows more than he's telling."

She leaned in until her hair fell between the men's

bodies and her face swam in front of West's. "Yes, he *is* my friend. I don't want him hurt."

West pretended he hadn't heard the second sentence. "He's about to be your sliced-up friend."

"You don't scare me." Javed spat out. He sounded tough but had gone pale, and every line of his body shouted fear.

West recognized the signs. He'd forced information out of more than one man while working for Alliance. Shot, stabbed, blew up, set on fire. He did what had to be done and he would here, too.

"Javed, tell him." Lexi put her hand against the truck. "Whatever West needs to know, just say it."

She'd probably be able to get Javed to cough up something, but West didn't like her that close to the guy. He preferred his intimidation and pain method.

"Who is Raheel working for?" he asked. There it was. The blip. The brief expression that gave Javed away. West went in for the kill. "You're protecting him. Talk."

"He has not done anything wrong." But Javed didn't sound like he believed it.

That fast West felt the advantage shift to him. "I think you're missing the word 'yet' in that sentence."

Lexi's pleading continued but she changed the target. "Javed, please."

The swing served West. With her on his side, he had a shot of convincing Javed. And he was desperate for this to work because what he would do to Javed—

and he'd do it without regret—was not something he wanted Lexi to see.

Right now she saw him as a man. A few seconds of watching him using his fists and a blade to convince Javed, and she'd see him for what he truly was. The machine behind the man.

Javed looked at Lexi with eyes wide and full of panic. "He will kill Raheel."

"He already had the chance to do that and didn't," she said.

West was done negotiating. "You have three seconds."

"Just say it." Lexi's harsh whisper echoed in the darkness.

West had a better way. "One . . ."

Javed kept shaking his head. "There is nothing."

"Two . . ."

Lexi put her hand on her friend's shoulder. "Javed, do it.

Time to inflict some pain, to show Javed that when he threatened, he meant it. "Three."

"Stop." Javed held up a hand as soon as West's hand tightened on his throat.

"Talk." West loosened his grip again. Much tighter and he'd damage Javed's larynx and the guy wouldn't be talking for weeks.

"Raheel had been working with the general who was killed in the clinic. On a secret assignment." The words rushed out of Javed now. There was no holding back or chest puffing to show his lack of fear.

Just as West expected. "Which was?"

"Whatever he saw upset him, and he wanted out."
Javed held up both hands. "That's all I know."

Not a lot to go on but it made sense. Whatever Lexi
had seen concerned the army and was possibly sanctioned. That fact made this assignment a complete
fuck-up.

Yes, Alliance needed to know what was happening,
but walking into the middle of a sanctioned Pakistani
government battle plan promised disaster. Alliance
needed more men on the ground to make that kind
of operation work, and even they might struggle with
odds that sounded like five against a brigade, or whatever they were dealing with here.

Which was why he needed more intel. If this wasn't
sanctioned and Pakistan had a rogue general or two,
everyone would want this shut down now.

"Where was Raheel going to take Lexi?" West
asked. He heard a sharp inhale and knew that Lexi had
just realized how close she'd come to having something
truly awful happen to her.

"He wouldn't hurt her."

West wasn't sure he bought that, but he did think
Javed did. With some reluctance, he let the other man
go and backed away. "I'm not taking that chance."

Javed reached for his gun. "You cannot kill me."

Unfortunately the guy was right, but not for the reasons he thought. Even he needed a reason to shoot a
man. He didn't have one here.

West held up Javed's weapon, the same one he'd lifted when he tackled the guy. "You say Lexi is your friend? Prove it."

Javed frowned as he smoothed down the front of his uniform. "Meaning?"

"Your job is to go back to your superiors and explain this accident. You tell them I jumped these two, got command of the truck and rammed you."

"Will they believe him?" Lexi asked.

"The bullets in these two are mine, from my gun." West held Javed's weapon out to him. "They won't trace to Javed."

Some of the tension left her face. "You did that as cover. You're protecting him."

For now, but he would turn in a second if needed. "So he can protect you."

"You'll be an even bigger target," she said.

"That doesn't bother me." And it didn't. To West, if someone wanted you dead, they wanted you dead. *Really* wanting it didn't change much.

Lexi half smiled, but the expression looked strained. "Anyone else think we just keep getting deeper into trouble?"

West held his arms out at the destruction around them. "Welcome to my world."

11

WARD STOOD just outside the cell holding Pearce. They'd landed in Islamabad less than an hour ago and traveled straight to this location. Secret and underground, with cells built into the wall and sealed off with floor-to-ceiling metal doors.

The only way Ward could see Pearce was on the two-way camera or the two-by-two pane of bulletproof glass in the center of the door. Talking was limited on Ward's side. Pearce had his microphone on. Ward knew because Pearce spent his time humming. Ward shut his side off, effectively cutting off all communication but the staring.

This was the kind of place no one talked about in White House briefing reports. The existence of this facility was on a need-to-know basis, and not knowing gave the higher-ups deniability.

The guard who traveled with them stood in the hall with two Marines and a half-dozen Defense contractor specialists. Only Ward walked into the small room in front of the cell and waited for one of the few other cleared people to walk in. One of his men.

A buzz sounded and the locks opened with a clunk. In stepped Michael Shelby, blondish hair and blue eyes. A midwestern farm-boy type. Which was exactly what he was before he joined the Army, and then Alliance plucked him out to join Delta team under Josiah.

Quiet, and the most private of Alliance members, Mike could sweet-talk and charm. He could also slit your throat while pouring you a beer. You'd hit the ground before he stood up straight again.

He'd stayed behind in Islamabad to run point for those Delta members in the field and work contacts on the ground. Now he got to help babysit Pearce.

Ward turned parallel to the window in the cell door, refusing to step into a corner and hide. Let Pearce watch. Let him see freedom, taste it and not have it.

Mike shook Ward's outstretched hand. "Have a good trip here?"

Pearce stepped up to the window and his voice crackled through the speakers. "Michael Shelby. A man with so many secrets."

"Totally enjoyable," Ward said. "Pearce talked for almost all twenty-one solid hours of it. I almost shot him twice."

"Should have." Mike smiled as he crossed his arms in font of him.

Pearce shifted his gaze to Mike and didn't let up. "Would you like to talk about your new apartment? Or is it a condo? Did you buy a place to bury your secrets?"

There it was again. Pearce would drop one piece of

information. Find the thing that tickled a person's curiosity. Ward knew it came from some training course and that Pearce had honed the skill over time. That didn't make it any less effective.

"What is he talking about?" Ward asked, knowing even if there was something to tell, Mike would never say it.

"Who the hell knows?" Mike didn't show an ounce of recognition. No reaction at all.

Talk about excellent training. Ward would put his guys up against anyone in any military or intelligence agency anywhere.

"Get me to Skardu." Pearce acted as if he gave orders.

Ward added that to the list of reasons to hate the guy.

"Shame we can't keep him in there all the time." Mike glanced at Pearce then. Looked and dismissed. "Let him be someone else's lifetime problem."

Ward would explain the one-way nature of the trip to Mike later. "You checked in with Harlan?"

They talked half in code. Intercoms malfunctioned. Hell, Pearce could read lips. Ward wasn't taking any chances. He trusted his people and that was about it.

"Yes, and I'm still working on my project." Mike stopped for a few beats before speaking again. "Josiah is trying to meet up with West."

In the span of ten seconds Mike had delivered a full report. Harlan in the field, Josiah couldn't find West at either of the arranged meet-up points, and their internal comm still malfunctioned. None of that qualified as good news.

Mike nodded. "Josiah and Harlan are going to meet."

They had to regroup. Pakistan was a big country with a lot of places to hide. Caves and houses. They had assets here but they had way more enemies. And then there was West's past dealings with the place. So many ways for this mission to go sideways and that didn't include Pearce's presence, which was a total wild card.

"In the meantime, we get him." Ward nodded in Pearce's general direction.

"Why is he here?" Mike smiled. "Which is really my way of asking why we haven't killed him yet."

Ward liked where Mike's mind was on this. "He insists he can help."

Pearce stood right in front of the camera wagging his finger back and forth. "Tick tock."

Mike watched on the monitor. "That's annoying."

"I seriously considered throwing him out of the plane." Ward was only half kidding.

"No loss."

"West is running out of time. So is the pretty woman with him." Pearce's voice sounded muffled through the speakers, but the singsongy warnings were clear.

Mike didn't even spare Alliance's nemesis a glance. "Shut up."

"He can't hear you," Ward pointed out.

"Can he see me?" Mike held up his middle finger first to the window in the door then to the camera on this side of the glass.

Ward laughed for the first time in days. "Feel better?"

"Not really."

Pearce shook his head. "West survived an avalanche, so I bet he thinks he can survive his search for the weapons."

This time Mike angled his body when he spoke. He no longer faced the camera or door head on. "How does he know this shit? It's fucking spooky."

Sometimes they forgot the men they hunted had the same training. In Pearce's case, being career CIA in a life undercover, he knew all the tricks. Right now, Alliance was mobilized to find Pearce's old partner, Benton. He'd proven to be even more tricky and elusive than Pearce ever was. It made Benton's true identity even more of a question mark.

But the immediate problem was Pearce and his intel and his ability to move and acquire information from a lockdown facility with no visitors. None of that should have happened. "I had a lot of time to think about that on the way here."

"And?"

Ward hated this part. "Tasha and Bravo team are tearing apart the lockdown facility back in Virginia now. We'll find the guard who's working for Pearce."

Mike closed his eyes. "Jesus."

"There's no other explanation." Ward hated the idea of a traitor, but it was the explanation that fit. Despite all the security checks, some rotten ones slipped through. Even the good ones, when offered enough cash or the right promises, could turn. "He has someone on the inside."

"So what is he talking about now with West?" Mike actually lowered his voice as if someone could listen in. "How does he know where he is and what's happening?"

Sounded to Ward that Pearce had them all paranoid and chasing their tails. There was a reason the CIA asked him to help set up Alliance way back when it started, and Pearce still acted like a legitimate covert asset. Everyone fell for the act and relied on his record. They'd ushered the enemy in and shown him the plans to everything. It made sense that he'd pick and remember stray bits of personal information. Just enough to have them doubting.

Until he knew if there was a leak, Ward decided, he would downplay it all. "He's guessing. Trying to get us worried about West and trick us into making a dumb move."

Pearce tapped the camera. "I wonder what's worse—"

Mike swore under his breath. "Really, that is annoying as hell."

"—being buried alive or being stalked like an animal." Pearce shook his head. "Almost makes me feel bad for West, good little killing machine that he is."

Mike scoffed. "Very poetic."

"Not at all overly dramatic," Ward said at the same time.

"We'll know soon because the men watching West's every move are getting bored. They've cut him off by taking away his communication with you. Now he's being led right to slaughter," Pearce continued on an exaggerated sigh. "They're tracking him and the woman and are about to start killing."

The corners of Mike's mouth fell. "What the hell?"

"Fuck it." Ward leaned over and hit the speaker button on his side. "You want to talk so badly, go ahead."

Pearce laughed. "I thought that would get your attention."

"I hate to ruin your fun but West is out of Skardu and in debrief." Ward lied his ass off and sold it. If someone hooked him up to a polygraph, he'd beat it.

"We both know that's not true. Lucky for West, I'll talk again when I'm on the ground in Skardu." Pearce tapped his wrist as if he were wearing a watch, which he wasn't. "But I'd hurry because West is getting very close to the line."

Ward decided to play along. "What line?"

"The one he can't cross and still live." Then Pearce turned his back to the camera.

Mike watched Pearce move then broke off to look at Ward. "Is he messing with us?"

"I don't want to wait and find out." Ward knew the second the reality of the situation hit Mike. His shoulders fell and his expression morphed from frustrated with a side of bored to pissed off.

No one threatened an Alliance member. Pearce had done just that.

"Shit." Mike's fingers went to the end of his gun where it rested on his hip. "This is just shit."

Ward knew the feeling. "Exactly."

Lexi twitched at every little sound. They'd stolen the truck from the dead soldiers after West decided that story would be the easiest for Javed to sell. Took it then ditched it. Only temporarily, but they couldn't exactly drive it into the secret encampment. Even she knew that much.

The truck sat in a garage and they walked. They stood what felt like miles away from their target. She couldn't see anything from their perch on a small incline. Some figures moving around. A stray truck. Nothing that made sense or justified the big secrecy play or all the armed men chasing her.

"This is as close as we're getting," West said as he looked through his fancy high-powered binoculars. He let them fall again. "God damn, I wish I could stash you somewhere."

"I'm not a sweater." She'd been ordered around, manhandled, and shot at. It was official, she was tired of all of it.

He glanced at her. "Okay."

Even loading equipment for this run became one more chance to argue. She couldn't believe she'd had to insist that she wash the blood out of West's hair and stitch the gunshot wound across the top of his ear. The man was the very definition of stubborn.

"Let's get what you need, then get out." She didn't even know what that was or what it would entail, but the advice to leave town started sounding good to her.

"It's not that simple."

It wasn't for her either. The climbers needed the clinic, and locals depended on it. She couldn't help either group if she were dead. It was as if West's warnings finally sunk in. No way was she admitting that to him.

He took something out, small and square. She lifted up on the balls of her feet to get a better look at it over his shoulder. When that did't work, she stepped in front of him to examine it. "What is this?"

"Nothing."

He shrugged at her. If they survived the next few hours she was setting down a new rule: no shrugging. There would be others but it was a place to start.

And she knew enough about him to know a one-word clipped answer meant something. "You are not taking photos."

"Yeah, I am."

Forget jokes about a death wish. "You're going to get caught and killed."

"It's a risk."

He said those things and they tore through her. Ripped her stomach right apart and had her gasping for breath. They lived in a dangerous part of a dangerous world, but she fully expected to walk out of this alive. His determination that this could be the end for him played with her confidence. Had her emotions ping-ponging inside of her.

"I'm not willing to take it." Chalk it up to adrenaline or the daze that kept clouding her mind, but she hated when he treated his life as disposable. Even after a short time he'd come to mean something to her. But she couldn't fight for him alone. She needed his help.

"We're far enough away." Both his words and tone dismissed her concerns. He was too busy looking up to notice any reaction or measure his comment. "Can you climb?"

The words scrambled in her head. "I don't even understand the question."

"The tree." He pointed up.

Tall, with the lowest branch well over her head. No thanks.

She didn't freeze with fear at the thought of heights but she didn't like them either. "Are you kidding?"

"People don't think to look up, even trained military officers."

She wanted to brush off the comment as interesting discussion but she knew better. He'd been thinking and planning the entire time. That's what he did. He developed contingencies and didn't panic. That was a part of him she didn't get at all.

And that was the hiding place he picked? "Where will you be?"

"Out there." He nodded in the direction of the encampment and all the men walking around down there. "From above you'll be able to see me."

"No." It was the only word she could force out.

"Yes."

From his determined expression, she knew he'd ride this battle into oblivion. He wasn't really asking her or seeking input. He issued orders, and she'd become the subject of one in his head.

Fine. He wanted stubborn, she'd show him stubborn.

She held out her hand. "Give me a gun."

He looked from her face to her palm then back around again. With each pass his frown grew more severe and unforgiving. "Can you shoot?"

She had no idea. It looked easy on television but she doubted it was really just a matter of lifting the barrel and firing. "I need a sixty-second lesson."

"It doesn't work that way."

She was counting on that. Maybe if he feared for her safety he would turn back. She would use anything to keep him alive and on his feet. The idea of him being hurt threatened to drive her to her knees.

So did the prospect of being left alone without a weapon when more men stumbled by. "We're losing time."

He took a small gun out of the utility pocket on his pants. He pointed to different features on it. "Trigger. Keep your finger off it unless you plan to fire."

"What about the safety?" People always talked about that on cop shows. Since that's where she got all her legal and police information, she went with it.

"Consider what I just told you to be the safety." He flipped the gun over in his palm and pointed it toward a bush about ten feet away. "Here's the sight. Aim at the tree. Hit the branches."

"The sound." Gunfire would bring people. They hid on a hill, far away from anything. The idea of purposely bringing men running made no sense at all.

"No one will hear from here." He nodded at the bush again. "Do it."

She picked it up and pulled the trigger, but not until she'd opened one eye then the other, trying to aim the right way. The shot went wide. Brushed by leaves on a small tree outside the informal shooting area.

She lowered the weapon as the anxious feeling inside her bubbled over. "Huh."

"Good news is any man coming after you will be wider than that tree." West kept talking. "Do not be a martyr. Shoot only if there is no other option. If they walk under you, stay quiet and don't move."

The advice made sense in the abstract. In reality she feared she'd fall down in front of anyone who walked by. Already it took all of her willpower not to grab onto West's pants leg and scream until he took her out of there.

With the gun in her pocket, she held out her palm again. "A knife."

He glared at her open fist. "Why?"

"I can probably stab easier than I can aim."

"That is exactly wrong." He held her wrist in one

hand and gently tucked her fingers into a fist with the other. "It's harder to kill a person close up."

"Why?" It didn't require aiming or a unique skill set. To her it made sense to have a knife. She could throw it or jump out at someone with it.

"You can feel him breathing."

All the thoughts racing through her head stumbled to a halt. She wanted this to be some sort of game so that the risks weren't real and the bodies weren't dead. But that wasn't reality.

She came crashing back down. "I'm sorry you said that."

He didn't respond at first. Just leaned over and kissed her on the cheek. Lingered as his fingers touched her hair. Right before he broke contact he tucked a closed pocketknife into her front pants pocket.

"Please be careful." The whisper of his voice blew over her.

"How often do you usually say please?" Emotion clogged her throat, but she managed to ask.

His palm cupped her face and his eyes searched hers. "Never."

Her breath hiccupped inside her chest. "Maybe there's hope for you yet."

12

WEST LET the night air clear his head. Thoughts of Lexi clogged up the strategies and tactics swimming around in there. He needed to stay focused.

He'd never had to give himself a mental shake or deliver an unspoken lecture on appropriate behavior on the job before. It was her. She made him do things, think things, that couldn't happen. Hell, just stroking her hair quieted the demons dancing around inside him.

What the fuck was that about?

He'd cut himself off from emotion for so long that when it hit him now it knocked him sideways. Had him spinning and placing her safety above all else. With her, he morphed back to the guy he was before the mountain fell. Someone who stayed on mission but never lost sight of the human toll. With her, those machine parts crumbled and the man stepped out again.

With emotions came pain and regret. It all flooded back on him and he hated it. Yet, he couldn't stop watching her, thinking about what it would be like to be in a hotel in London or walking around in Paris. Something not fraught with danger.

She opened a door in him, and the more time they spent together the harder it became to slam it shut.

But he needed every brain cell working on the current problem. He'd hiked about two miles out and back, ducking from search vehicles and lying flat on the ground as armed men passed. He saw the encampment tucked into the side of a mountain. Also figured out that it hid something much larger.

Whatever weapons and whoever was holding them hid behind the beige-draped makeshift building. People went in and out, disappeared into the rocks. Caves were the only explanation.

West knew all about the series of tunnels running through significant portions of Pakistan. There was no map and no easy way to navigate it as an outsider. In other words, the perfect place to hide something you should not have.

He zigzagged on his jog back to Lexi. He didn't use the same path, in case someone tracked him or spotted anything out of order. The new trail took him an extra quarter mile out of his way, but that's how recon worked.

But as he jogged something inside him began to twist. He couldn't shake the sensation that something had gone wrong. If he let his mind wander to the horror show of Lexi being taken and hurt, he'd buckle. No matter how many times the images flashed through his mind he blinked them out again.

He ran faster.

The swift movement created noise. His footsteps

fell louder than normal. He knew he needed to keep it down, stay covert, but a strange panic drove him.

He circled around an outcropping of rocks and passed a stack of abandoned building supplies. He could make out the outline in the distance of the tree where Lexi should be. Still a long way off. Good thing he could run pretty damn fast.

That's when he heard the shuffling. Clothing rustling. Shoes falling against the dirt.

He hit the ground on his stomach. With his palms pressed in front of him, he rushed to get his bearings and distinguish one noise from another. The cold breeze moved the grasses and whistled around him. But he had heard a person. More than one.

He lay there, not moving. He slowed his breathing as he ran through a mental list of his weapons and calculated how quickly he could reach each one. The inventory always worked. Within seconds his mind worked like a computer, assessing and analyzing without emotion. One of the few valuable skills he picked up from his doomsday cult father.

The minutes ticked by and the night settled in. There were a few hours before daylight, but not many. He needed to be out and have Lexi somewhere safe by then.

Footsteps sounded around him. Not near his makeshift hiding place. A few feet closer and he'd jump up. He could handle and take down a group. It was the wave of men behind this one that was the question. His ammunition would run out and he'd leave Lexi vulnerable.

So he bided his time. Instead of fighting before a battle came to him, he waited. He stayed on the defensive, which made a nerve in his cheek tic. He much preferred offense.

When the quiet pulsed and long minutes had passed without noise or movement, he pushed his chest up a fraction. Nothing. He hit his feet in a squat and stayed there, low and out of sight. Something kept him in place. The way the air moved or the leaves blew.

He reached for his gun.

Thundering footsteps broke through the silence off to his left and had him spinning on his heel. A thin beam of light clicked on and then off. As quickly as the noises exploded they faded again, but now he knew. There were people out there. Question was, how many and if any of them had found Lexi's hiding place.

He could wait them out. He'd sit for hours if needed.

But that wasn't necessary. They did what human nature dictated. They attacked too soon and without thinking it through. They didn't know exactly where he was or they would have begun firing. They went with an ambush, probably thinking to force him into a run. West almost smiled over the rookie mistake.

A shadow came toward him. West watched it come, seeing if others followed and how many he'd have to go through to fight his way out of the dark. One shout and a runner. That was it.

He held until the last second then stood up with the knife in one hand and went right for the neck. Stabbing, he put his weight behind it and was rewarded with the telltale gagging sound. The guy dropped to his knees, and West knocked him over while he tried to make out what attacker number two was yelling about.

Back on his stomach and crawling on the ground, he heard a name shouted and a panicked call from the other man. The first guy couldn't answer. He was too busy bleeding out in the dirt.

All the chattering gave the second guy's position away. He used a boulder for cover. Smart move but not quite clever enough. West made it to the opposite side of the hiding place without being discovered. He froze, trying to pick up the man's exact location.

Then West heard it. A radio. This guy was talking to others, which meant the whole army might come down on them soon. That moved up his attack timetable. He pushed up and took off. Pivoted around the boulder and shot the guy in the temple before he could finish relaying his current position.

The radio squawked and West knew the word would go out. He had to move, and the radio was coming with him.

Just as he stood up, he felt the shift in the wind. The human kind. He reached for his gun but one already pressed against the back of his head.

A man screamed an order in his ear. West couldn't make out the order over the mix of fury and fear in the guy's voice. The attacker might have the advantaged position, but West knew he was still in charge here.

Except if he wasn't careful, this guy might shoot him by accident.

West lifted his hands. "It's okay."

"On your knees."

Seemed like the guy did speak some English. Not knowing what he'd heard or seen, West tried to throw him off. "Climber."

"What?"

"I'm a climber." It was a cover he could sell at this time of the year. It didn't explain the gun or the blood, but the darkness should hide both.

The guy punched him in that space right between his shoulder blades. "No."

That fucker hurt. West bent forward.

The guy started a one-handed pat-down. "On your knees."

West didn't see a choice. He had to shoot this one. The question was how to duck without getting a bullet in his head from a lucky shot. He'd just decided to fall to the side then come up shooting when he heard another voice.

"Put the gun down."

No, no, no. It was Lexi. This was a damn nightmare.

The other man didn't hesitate. He turned and grabbed the gun, twisted Lexi's arm until she doubled over and lost her grip.

She let out a yelp. "No!"

That's all the diversion West needed. He slipped his knife out and slid it right into the back of the man's neck.

Blood spurted, but he didn't make a sound. Just dropped in a whoosh as if every bone had been removed.

Lexi stood over the body with her hands at her sides and her eyes glazed with horror. West expected her to pass out or throw up. Either made sense to him. She spent her life supporting life and he kept taking it front of her.

"Lexi?"

She shook her head. Didn't make a sound.

Staring at the body couldn't be good for whatever was zipping around in her head. Putting the knife away, West stepped toward her. They needed to move but he had to make sure she could.

Almost afraid to touch her, he hesitated. Once he figured out a way to soothe her, he'd try that. "Are you okay?"

Her eyes finally focused as her stare switched from the body to him. Then she launched herself into his arms. Fell against his chest and her hands went into his hair.

"You're okay." She whispered so softly that it sounded more like a breath than a word.

"What?"

Her mouth found his cheek then his chin. "Thank God you're okay."

She feared for his safety? The idea floored him. He couldn't remember the last time anyone cared about him.

"I was worried about you," he said. "You were supposed to stay in that tree, out of harm's way."

She pulled back but didn't break contact. Her hands rested on his forearms. "I saw them move in on your position. Then the third one broke off and got behind you."

A fact West still didn't quite believe. "We need to leave in case there's a fourth man around here somewhere."

Her next words stopped him.

She held his jacket in a death grip. "You should know I plan on kissing you when we get wherever we're going. Like, the knee-buckling, can't-get-our-clothes-off-fast-enough type."

Forget safe and smart and careful. Fuck the rules. He was taking her up on that. "Then let's get moving."

Ward sat on a conference room table with his feet on the chair below. He wasn't even sure what this facility was used for, probably didn't want to know. But Alliance had a cell for Pearce and office space in the conference room thanks to whatever group operated this place.

Mike and Josiah milled around the room. The rest of Delta team took off with Harlan. Josiah had tried to make contact but West was still in the wind with the doctor's daughter. Josiah had filled them in on what he'd seen and heard and his impression of Lexi. But Ward worried about West. No check-in but no reports of his capture either.

Losing contact with West made Ward want to beat

someone to death, preferably Pearce. "You can't even pinpoint a last location for West?"

"Not one that would help. It's too old and West is too smart to walk around in the open." Josiah stopped pacing and stood in front of the monitor carrying the feed from Pearce's cell. "What does he know?"

"We're not sure." Too much, but maybe nothing. Pearce had contacts here and the job that made him a traitor was about stolen weapons. Could be he was tied to whatever was going on in Pakistan. Maybe even in charge of it. "He wants to go to Skardu."

"Pearce *wants* to be in Pakistan?" Mike asked.

"He's involved with all of this somehow. It traces back to him. Has to." Josiah stood there, shaking his head as he watched Pearce sit on his bed and stare at the ceiling. "The references to West can't be a coincidence."

Mike clicked on a key and the camera flipped positions inside Pearce's cell. "Did Bravo locate the guard who helped him?"

That had been the most interesting piece of intel from Tasha. Leave it to Ford and Bravo team to ferret out the truth. They had the guard on his knees and begging for forgiveness almost immediately. "One of them."

Mike stopped his mindless wandering around the room. "What does that mean?"

"The guard fessed up and admitted to having a wife . . . and a girlfriend, which is why he needed to accept Pearce's money offer. Apparently the guard's wife watches the money pretty closely." And buying a condo and jewelry for one woman while paying the mortgage with another was problematic.

"Who is the number two?" Mike asked.

Ward decided to show them. "Here." He pushed Josiah out of the way and started typing. The GPS immediately located the guard they brought with them from Virginia. Ward pointed to the feed showing him sitting in a room eating a sandwich. "Him."

"One of the guards the CIA handed us?" Josiah didn't rein it in. He let out a string of profanities that could make hardened Marines blush.

Ward felt the same way. "Convenient, right? I'm guessing he and Pearce have a history."

"This is why we need to only use Alliance members. No matter what part of the assignment. Hell, I'll drive a bus if I have to, but no more outside help." Mike stopped long enough to swear like he usually did in situations like this. "This shit doesn't happen when we keep everything internal."

"I agree and I'm on it." Ward had already made that clear to Tasha in his venting phone call. Alliance might be connected with the CIA and MI6 tangentially, but no more sharing.

There was a reason Alliance had been formed. They didn't play have-to-be-nice with others, didn't follow the same rules as the CIA, and no one he brought on was a fucking traitor. He didn't hire Pearce. That was someone else's responsibility, and Ward insisted he handle all hires from now on as a result. He'd handle the guard situation, too.

"Happy we understand each other." Mike put a thigh on the edge of the table and half leaned into the computer. "Why didn't Pearce make a move on the plane?"

"Too many guards." Flying with a contingent felt like overkill at first. Now the move to keep security surrounding Pearce at all times seemed smart. Score one for Tasha.

"Bigger question." Mike seethed with anger. It practically poured out of his pores. "Why is the crooked guard still working here?"

"I wanted to see if I can catch him in the act. Figure out how he's communicating with Pearce and make sure we've rounded up all the Pearce-friendly players." The guard and Pearce had to talk sometime or have a code. Nothing in the old security logs from back in Virginia suggested Pearce had talked with anyone.

Josiah continued to stare at the camera as he rubbed his fingers over his chin. "I think we should stay out of this guard's way and let him do whatever he plans to do for Pearce."

Mike's eyes narrowed. "Care to say why?"

"If the plan is to break Pearce out of here, I say we let him." Josiah smiled. "Pearce could lead us to the weapons and possibly to West."

The idea took hold. Ward wished he'd come up with it first. "You mean follow him."

Mike held up a hand. "Or Pearce could run in the

other direction and we'll lose him forever. I am not answering to Tasha for that."

"Me neither," Ward said, "which is why Pearce getting away is never going to happen." He would walk through glass to get Pearce. Letting him go, losing him . . . He'd shoot the bastard in the back first.

Mike looked at Josiah. "So, you're saying—"

"See if the guard breaks Pearce out, then we follow." Josiah sounded so sure.

Ward admired the spirit and tried to ignore just how many things could go wrong. Pearce's ego could trip him up. And there was no way Ward would leave West and the woman behind. Not on his watch.

Yeah, the way he figured it, this might be more than the best choice. It could be the *only* choice. "It's time for Pearce to escape."

Mike laughed. "The guys out there watching over him are not going to like this. We've got Marines and contractors on site, and we don't control them. This is their playground."

"They'll like it when we find a stash of weapons and let them take credit for it all." Ward said it because he didn't care who got the glory so long as he got West back and Pearce went down.

13

TWENTY MINUTES later they stumbled across a truck, just where West predicted it would be. He'd spotted it on his hunt and tagged it in his memory . . . or so he said. At this point he could insist they walk to India and Lexi would have agreed.

As she watched, he opened the hood. She held a flashlight while he tooled around, moving wires and clipping this and that. She had no idea what he was doing but the engine turned over a second later. "You know how to hot-wire a truck."

"Start one without keys. Fix an engine. Wire it to go off like a bomb." He closed the hood and flashed her a smile. "That can't be a surprise to you."

No, his skills seemed endless at this point. She hadn't had any doubts about his ability to shoot and protect from the beginning. He didn't disappoint in that regard. It was everything else. He could control his temper and calm her down. He reasoned things through and always had a contingency.

He was the guy you wanted on your side. But his

mere presence didn't lessen the danger. If life were fair, the books would balance that way, but no.

He helped her get up to the footstep then she slid into the passenger side. She missed the Jeep but this came close to being a tank. West insisted it wasn't and that a rocket launcher would blow it up. Not exactly news she needed to have now that she was inside it.

She waited until he jumped inside to point out the obvious. "Once we get it moving we still have to get through roadblocks and around roaming guards."

He shot her a look, and that smile hadn't faded. "You sound negative."

"I just watched you kill three guys in two seconds." She tried to put that out of her head but her hands kept shaking. Even now she rubbed them together to keep from flying apart.

She'd seen death. Men and women came off that mountain in pieces. For many, climbing K2 was a dream that turned into a nightmare. Sherpas and guides lost. Climbers who trained for a lifetime swept away as part of the serac broke off or the storms moved in. Lost fingers and toes. Bodies in bags while other people fell and were never recovered.

It all touched her. But high elevation climbers had certain expectations and understandings of what could happen. Everyone knew the risks, and K2 had a reputation for being the deadliest mountain.

That was different from watching a man collapse at her feet or seeing the blood run out of a body and being grateful instead of rushing in to help.

West had put the truck in gear. The vehicle idled as he shifted in his seat to face her. "Are you okay?"

"Of course not." She wasn't naïve, but she wasn't heartless either.

Men were dying because of choices she made. The right choices, yes, but the lives were still lost and someone somewhere would mourn them. The least she could do was take two seconds and give a crap. Maybe throw up a little.

She expected West to lecture her about life and death or good and bad. A man like him had a code for this sort of thing. Probably had a speech prepared that he could whip out and deliver.

Instead, he nodded. "That's probably healthy."

Not what she expected, but then he'd been a surprise from the beginning. No pretense. No macho bullshit. He just acted without apology.

And somehow she stayed on her feet through it all. That might have been the biggest surprise. "If my old doctors could see me now."

He reached his arm across the back of the seat and his fingers toyed with the ends of her hair. "What doctors?"

She hadn't meant to say anything. Whatever he thought of her would change if she went one step further. It always did, which was why she didn't tell anyone. The few friends she had back home, she'd had forever. They lived through those dark days with her and never mentioned them in their limited communications back and forth.

He didn't push or insist. He put the truck back in gear and started moving. They rode in silence over divots and holes that had her bouncing around in her seat. Neither of them talked, yet the silence remained comfortable. Still, she could almost see his mind working. He constantly scanned the area, and every now and then his gaze would fall on her for a second, linger then move away.

She sighed. "Just say it."

He didn't pretend to be confused. "We've got nothing but time here, Lexi. The sun is coming up and we need to spend most of the daylight in hiding."

The comment raised a whole bunch of questions in her mind. "Where?"

"Storage facility, basically an overgrown garage."

That struck her as random. "Are you guessing or do you know where one is?"

He likely knew the area from surveillance shots, and those were taken when there wasn't a manhunt under way. Not something she could think about for even a few seconds without her nerves fraying and fear spiraling through her.

They would kill him. The Pakistani army might hold him long enough to make an example of him, but he would die, and not easy. She didn't blame anyone for that reality. West was sneaking around their country without permission. If the roles were reversed he'd capture the suspects . . . yeah, that's what she'd become. A suspect.

"Javed told me about a site." West hitched his thumb toward the bag in the back. "I have a lock on me—"

"Of course you do." The man was prepared for everything.

"—and we can use it for added protection in case soldiers come by. Them getting through a lock will give us time."

"To escape?" For her only. He didn't say it but she knew.

That's what he did, put his body in front of hers. It was sexy and scary and a whole bunch of others things. She just wished he'd stop pointing it out in both subtle and obvious ways.

He shrugged. "What else?"

She wasn't buying that at all. She also didn't get when Javed had become a valued resource. "I thought you didn't trust Javed."

"I don't trust many people."

She focused on the sun rising and the rocky landscape in front of them as West dodged this rock and that tree on the road he forged.

But she wanted to know, so she tortured herself and asked, "What about me?"

He glanced over at her and kept looking until she met his gaze. "You, I trust."

The quick response threw her for a second. "Really?"

"Total trust."

The words sounded like a vow, and for some reason she believed them. She'd been fed lies by guys trying to get her into bed or, in the climbing community, trying to get close to her semifamous father. But this from West came off as genuine. Maybe it was his ultimate skill, making her believe the impossible, but she bought it.

She needed more. "Why?"

"I have no idea."

She probably should have been offended, but she laughed. Leave it to West to throw her off guard. "Now that's honest."

After the slow slog, all done on the lookout for new attackers, they arrived at a hill. The truck crested and on the other side, in a valley, sat a garage between two overhanging trees. Javed might call this a shed but the space was bigger. Looked like it could house a few of these larger trucks.

There was a road leading off to the left. Lexi guessed that it led around and back toward town. She didn't really want to find out and hoped the trail stayed clear.

West hit the brakes and the truck shuddered to a stop. "We'll go slow, watch for any workers lingering around here. If I tell you to duck, you duck. Got it?"

He sure did like to give orders. She decided, after so little sleep and so much danger, she'd obey. "Yes, sir."

Some of the tension left his face. "I probably like you saying that way more than I should."

That made two of them.

She balled her hands into tight fists and brushed them up and down her lap. "That sounds naughty."

"I certainly hope so since I was imagining you saying it while naked."

Before she could say anything, the truck started to

move. It rolled down the other side of the hill toward the garage. West downshifted and the gears squeaked. They bounced as they rode over rough terrain.

But no one came out to greet them. That's what mattered. The welcome committee she feared never showed up. At least not yet.

"Do you want to tell me about those doctors now?" The question came out of nowhere. He asked while his gaze stayed locked on the area in front of him.

This wasn't the time, and this topic was not even a little relevant. She opened her mouth to tell him so but a different thought popped into her head. "I'm not sick."

She needed him to know that. Wanted him to see her as something other than a liability.

"Happy to hear that." The gears screeched as he guided them down the steep hill. The tires slid and the truck seemed to pitch forward.

She dug her fingernails into the side of the door. "I'm not crazy either."

The truck thudded as it took to the air then crashed down on the ground again. "No. I know mentally ill and you're not it."

The words soothed her. Her past didn't embarrass her but she did worry that it defined her. That people could see the weakness on her face. She'd spent her entire adult life running from that possibility.

One last crunching bump and they reached the bottom of the hill. West drove around to the far side of the garage and stopped in front of the door. Lexi knew they were here to hide, and the timing was wrong but she suddenly needed to tell him. To see his reaction and figure out if she'd read him right or wrong.

Before she could work up the nerve, however, he pulled on the door handle and jumped out of the truck. There was a clicking sound as each section of the garage door rolled to the side, revealing a dark room inside. Then he was back inside the cabin.

When they rolled to a stop again the truck idled in the middle of the garage. She waited until he shut off the engine to start talking. "When I was in medical school my mom died in a car crash."

He sat back in his seat and faced her. "I'm sorry."

"I was driving."

"Oh, shit." His arm slipped across the back of the seat again. This time his hand dipped under her hair and he massaged the back of her neck.

She faced forward because looking at him would break her concentration, and she needed all of her strength to get this out. "No one said it, but everyone blamed me. And they should have. We were arguing and I lost focus."

Silence filled the car. She looked over at him, expecting to see judgment or pity in his expression. Those were the two options she usually got. But he just sat there with his fingers rubbing her aching muscles.

The quiet support spurred her on. "Anyway, I went back to school and tried to fit in. To act as if everything was normal."

"But it wasn't."

"No." She remembered those days and the numbness that flooded her, turning the world gray. Her father's flat voice on the phone.

Then the paranoia set in. She didn't want to leave her room, and when she did she felt eyes on her all the time. The staring sent her running back to the safety of her bed. She'd rock and hum. She didn't realize how many days had passed or that she'd locked the door to her room until her father stormed in with the landlord, a police officer, and a bunch of other men.

West slipped a strand of her hair around his finger. "So, you dropped out."

"Not exactly." Failing out of school would have been a failure to her father, but she took it one step further. "I had a mental breakdown. Agreed to go to a facility for a while and then I never went back to med school."

He didn't even flinch. He sat there, nodding and listening. "Understandable."

"How so?" Maybe he could explain it to her. Before that day her life had run so smoothly. School and activities. She'd overhear the occasional fight as her mother complained about what she called Dad's wanderlust. Then her mother was gone and Lexi's brain shut down.

"You were a kid."

She'd love to take that out, but she couldn't. "It wasn't that long ago. I was twenty-one."

"And you felt guilty. You lost your mom. Your dad was grieving." West made a humming sound. "Add in the pressures of medical school and something had to break. Seems pretty human to me."

"You don't break." She'd barely seen him bend.

"If I break, people die."

She wanted to lean into him. To close her eyes and enjoy the touch of his hand. Maybe run her palm over his leg. Anything to drink in his warmth. "That makes you strong. You have this laser focus."

He gave her a quick look before returning his gaze to the road. "Lexi, I've been shoved to the edge. Those long hours trying to dig my friends out of the ice, the days when I was sure I was going to die . . ." He didn't say anything for what felt like minutes. The silence ticked on. "They changed me."

His admission stopped the ball of anxiety that had been bouncing around in her stomach. Since the minute she met him she viewed him as unbreakable. She couldn't wrap her mind around any other version. "But you face death without blinking."

"Now. I learned to."

"You're invincible." It sounded stupid when she said it, but in her head that's how she felt.

"I'm a man. A fucking tough one, way deadlier and competent in danger than most, but still a man." His hand stilled against her neck. "Is that what this is about? You think you're weak or incapable or something?"

"My dad does. He never says it, of course. He just treats me like I'm going to shatter." He'd made a life out of being in dangerous places and helping climbers and others who thrived on adrenaline. People who were the exact opposite of her.

Some time in therapy helped her see her choices now stemmed from what happened then. The need to show she could take it, whatever "it" might be.

"He's probably afraid of losing you."

"Years have passed and he refuses to see me as whole again."

West shook his head. "That's his thing, not yours."

West made it sound so simple. She knew from experience it wasn't.

She twisted her hands together tight enough to make her knuckles ache. "Meaning?"

"You risked your safety to track trucks and call in reinforcements. You faced me down with a gun and threatened to blow my balls off."

God, did she really say that? "I didn't."

"Trust me, I remember those types of threats." His hand shifted to her shoulder. "My point is, you are not weak. Human, yes. But I like that about you. It's easy to lose your humanity in this job. To always see the worst, but you remind me good is out there."

Guilt smacked into her. She'd pinned him as a killing machine and stuck him in that box even though every tough decision showed him to be a decent man. "You are human."

"My point is, you are strong in ways you don't realize." He shot her a heated look. "Most men shrink away from me, but you don't let me get away with shit."

"Do you like that, too?"

"It's sexy as hell."

Acceptance. She didn't realize she'd been craving it or missed it until West handed it to her. The words to form the right reply jammed up inside her. She had no idea what to say or how to say it. A simple thank-you seemed insufficient.

She cleared her throat and said the only thing that jumped into her head. "We'll be locked in there all day."

She thought she saw West's lips twitch in a smile, but he held it back. Probably a good thing.

"Yes. Javed said it's an outpost for specialized training, but with everyone mobilized to hunt us down, he doesn't think anyone will be out here. Even then, not until late afternoon."

"So, we'll be safe now." New possibilities rumbled around in her head. Things that had nothing to do with her past or the danger that swirled around them.

He moved back over to his seat and put a hand on the door handle. "For a while."

Before he could open the door and jump out, she said the one thing that had been playing in her mind since he came back from his look at the encampment. "You should know I don't go back on my promises."

The intensity of his stare switched to white hot. "I remember a promise about a kiss."

"It's going to happen." She wanted it more than she'd ever wanted anything.

He nodded. "You bet your sweet ass it is."

"Well?"

"Let me lock the door."

14

ANOTHER HALF hour passed. West locked the door and checked the building. Despite the need revving inside him, he didn't ignore his usual safety procedures.

He'd crawled up into the loft space. The faint scent of gasoline still hit him, but he shoved the loosened ceiling board and created an opening to the roof. Not the most romantic spot for foreplay ever, but he had to know she was safe.

"What are you doing up there?" She stood about twenty feet below him on the garage floor.

Satisfied she could fit through the opening, he balanced the boards on the beams again. "Making an escape hatch."

"I don't even know what to ask next."

He climbed down the cross beams and jumped the last few feet to land in front of her. "If anyone storms in here, you climb up and out as fast as you can and without being seen. There are lower hanging tree branches. Grab one and hide up there until Josiah or someone from my team comes to get you."

She crossed her arms in front of her. "And where will you be during all of this?"

"Creating a diversion." He thought that would be obvious, but then she didn't have the training he did.

"In other words, dying."

She was really stuck on that point. "I do win some battles, you know."

He walked around her to the bags he'd grabbed out of the back. Crouching down, he did another informal inventory. They had additional weapons and ammo. A few cold weather supplies and food basics. Javed had provided enough to set them up for the night, maybe two, but no more.

Footsteps thudded against the floor. She walked over and stood right in front of him. "If I climb up there, you are climbing with me."

He glanced up and saw shoes and her legs. The tour ended at the grim line of her face. Looked like he wouldn't be able to laugh this off. "We're not arguing about this."

And there was no way he was agreeing to whatever contingency plan she'd devised. He knew the best way to ensure her safety might be to sacrifice his. He was fine with that.

"West, I'm serious."

"Me, too." Time for a diversion.

He stood up. This close, his body skimmed her as he rose. He ended with his arms around her waist and her body hugged tight against his. "I can think of better things to do with our few minutes of open time."

Not needing another second to think about his next move, West leaned down. He caught her sharp inhale of breath as his mouth covered hers. Sealed up tight in this building with warning bells ready to ring if some-one came by, he felt safe touching her.

His hands roamed over her trim body and his lips covered hers. The kiss went deep fast. Heat rolled over him and his common sense took a sharp nosedive. He couldn't get close enough. The need drove through him rough and sharp. He had to lift his head to bring his mind back into focus.

She glanced over at the open gym bag on the floor. "Any chance you have a condom in that bag?"

He should say no and limit this to kissing. Locks or not, they were not safe. All of his training pointed to walking away. If they got through the next twenty-four hours they could reassess . . . ah, fuck it. "One."

Her eyebrow lifted and amusement filled her voice. "You brought birth control with you?"

West wasn't sure how to answer that without sound-ing like a dick. He went with a shortcut version of the truth: "It's part of the 'go' kit."

"You have a kit?"

It also included supplies for convincing people to talk, but he kept that gem to himself. Talking torture tended not to charm the ladies. "They teach you that in spy school."

"Funny how you throw out that word when you want to avoid a question."

Maybe humor would help get this conversation back on track. "You mean teach?"

"So, this happens a lot on your assignments? You need to reach for a condom." She stared down at the bag as if trying to search through it without touching it.

So much for humor. "If you're asking if I bed a woman on every job, the answer is no."

The idea of that made his dick shrivel. On assignments, he thought about the briefings and the breakdown of duties for the team. Usually that meant him using force. For him, sex and violence didn't generally mix.

He understood the punch of adrenaline. He'd run that high before, but putting down a gun to pick up a condom wasn't really the way he operated.

Since she kept staring and not talking, he tried to narrow his answer down. "It's never happened, actually."

"Hard to believe, coming from a guy with an emergency condom."

West didn't see how this moment could go worse. Emotionally stepping away seemed like the only solution. "We don't have to have sex."

"I know."

"Okay." But, really, she could have at least fought him a little bit. He knew the attraction moved both ways. He'd find her staring at him, and the way she worried about his safety and tried to keep him safe.

He let his hands drop then because holding her felt weird. Good, excellent even, but ill-timed. It was hard to think about kissing her when she was busy wondering how many assets he'd screwed.

He put a few feet in between them. Almost fell over
the damn bag while doing it. He bent down to move it
out of the middle of the open space not sucked up by
the truck.

"What if I want to?" Her question came from right
behind him.

He turned and nearly fell over. Him, the guy who
once snuck up on a higher-up in the Taliban and slit his
throat before the man could call out to the two body-
guards in the room.

She steadied him, then left her hands on his chest.
The light touch ignited a firestorm inside him. Common
sense battled with need until the need to be inside her
overwhelmed his need to keep watch.

The lower half of his body sparked to life. His brain
took a few extra minutes to catch up. "The way this
conversation is going, I'm afraid to answer that."

"Let's try this again." Her hands went to his shoulders
as she balanced her body against his. "Do you make it a
habit of sleeping with the women you're rescuing?"

Easy one. "No."

"Women you're questioning?"

Those were often the same thing, but he didn't point
that out after her earlier panic about being interrogated.
"No."

"I'm just the lucky one?"

She stuck. She mattered. Little time had passed but
she'd wound her way through his defenses. She was not
the battlefield sex type, but neither was he. He couldn't
explain why he wanted her so much, but he did.

And forget fighting it. She just had to say the word. He said, "I'll do whatever you want here."

She stepped back. "Find it."

They were either experiencing a mixed message problem or he'd lost all ability to read a situation from one minute to the next. "What?"

She rolled her eyes and somehow managed to look sexy doing it. "The condom."

That was the word he'd been waiting for. "Done."

West set a speed record tearing through the bag and coming up with the small packet. Satisfaction soared across his face. Lexi half expected him to throw her over his shoulder and take her on the truck's hood.

Not that she would hate that.

When he stood back up again, every line of his body was pulled taut. Tension thrummed off him. He held the packet between two fingers, right in front of her face. "Here."

"So romantic."

He winced. "Sorry."

She was pretty sure they could do better than a few thrusts and grunts. But he was not in a position to get them there. The burning in his eyes clued her in. He'd pushed right to the edge and was ready to go.

She took the condom and folded it in her hand. Her arms wrapped around his neck. "Tell me what you want."

Those strong hands went to her waist. "You."

The man could not be more specific than that. But she gave it a try. "How?"

"On the ground, against the wall, in the truck bed. I don't care so long as you're naked with me inside you." There was a soft growl to his voice as he said it. The promise went from his tone to the spark in his eyes.

Her heart did a little spin. She tried to downplay how happy the comment made her and how it sent a kick of life through her . . . and failed.

But she could not get lost in the moment. Not fully. "The danger?"

His fingers tightened on her hips. "I can handle it."

Interesting. "How?"

"I'll keep my pants on."

His sweet talk needed some work but she knew the comment came from the right place. No matter what, he'd protect her. She couldn't ask for more than that.

She leaned in until her mouth brushed over his ear. "Do it."

A shiver. She felt it under her hands as it moved through him. She was going to say something but his mouth covered hers and the ability to do anything but feel abandoned her. Sensation bombarded her. Want and need, hunger and desperation.

She felt as if she'd waited for this moment forever. Never mind that she didn't know him two days ago. In a way, she'd been in a holding pattern. She talked herself into wanting one type of guy—safe for her. But she needed the thrill. The guy who loved quiet but wouldn't hesitate to spar with her.

He backed them up to the wall he'd climbed earlier.

One dip and he grabbed a blanket out of the bag and threw it over his shoulder. "Up."

He had to be kidding. Her legs barely held her when she stood on the ground. "We could—"

"I'll guide you."

She had a feeling there would be a lot of that over the next few minutes. Diving in now made sense to her.

She turned in his arms and started to climb. With each step his hand would brush against her. At first almost impossible to detect. A brief moment of contact, then his hand was gone. The higher she went, the more he touched. And when he cupped her ass, she flew up those last two ladder steps.

The loft had just enough clearance for her to stand. That likely meant he would be bent over. Preferably, lying down.

As if he heard her, he stepped onto the loft. Without a word he spread out his blanket and dropped to his knees. With a hand in hers, he tugged and her body fell. She ended up straddling his thighs with her chest pressed against his.

So many moves and all of them taking them right where she wanted to be. "Impressive."

He ran his palm up and down her back. "I told you, I have many skills."

Apparently seducing the panties right off a woman was one of them. "Show me."

The room spun. When she opened her eyes again he loomed over her. He balanced his weight on one elbow as he bent down and traced her collarbone with the tip of his tongue. She didn't know that part of her was even sensitive until her nerve endings burst to life.

"You have too many clothes on." He pulled down the zipper to her jacket and pushed it off her shoulders.

Next came the sweater. He pushed it up far enough to kiss her bare stomach. The light touch had her inhaling. When he repeated the kiss, she relaxed into him.

She thought to grab his shoulders and drag him up her body, but he was already moving. His mouth traveled over her. Everywhere his fingers touched, his lips followed. He burned a trail from her chest to the area between her thighs.

He kissed her through layers of clothing, rubbed his cheek against her in the most sensual caress she'd ever experienced. When he hummed, she felt it to her core. Her hips lifted off the blanket and her fingers slipped into his hair. She knew what she wanted and used her body to ask for it.

Forming tiny circles, he pressed the heel of his hand over her zipper. An ache formed deep inside her. Heat built and an inner clenching took hold. A flush covered her body as she fought the urge to rip off her pants and drag him even closer.

Her hand fell to the blanket beside her and her fist opened. The condom lay there. West picked it up and put the corner between his teeth. Then his hands went to work.

The sound of her zipper screeched through the room as he dragged it down. His fingers slipped under the elastic of her underwear. With one swift swoop, he had her bare to the knees, then the pants and panties were gone.

"I thought we were keeping them on." Not that she missed the clothing one bit. She just wanted him to take a turn.

"Only the few essential ones."

She thought about the top she still wore and the way he seemed satisfied to leave the material balled up against her breasts. The way his fingers lingered over her as he reeled her in. "Are you afraid I'll freeze to death?"

"Not happening on my watch. I'll make it my personal responsibility to keep you nice and warm." He used a gentle touch to move her legs, bending them at the knee and putting her feet flat against the blanket. His shoulders touched her inner thighs as he lay between them.

Before she could drag in enough air to breathe, his mouth was on her. Licking and sucking. Warm breath brushed over her. The intimate kissing had her hips lifting off the blanket and her heels digging into the loft floor. When his fingers joined his mouth, she almost begged him to end it. The seductive torture had her both relaxed and on edge. The tight coil inside her had her panting with the need for release.

His thumb flicked over her, and her shoulders came off the floor. "West."

He looked up the long line of her body. His mouth didn't move from her except to utter one word. "Soon."

"Now." Her need reduced her vocabulary to one-syllable grunts.

Much more of this and she'd lock her legs around his hips and turn him over. The idea of climbing on top of him, sliding all over him, appealed to her. She was about to try it when she heard his zipper. One hand stayed on her as his finger slipped inside. The other opened his fly.

Thank God.

Her palms traveled over his shoulders, loving the hard angles of his body. She tried to turn to the side and reach down his back but he held her steady beneath him. She settled for bending forward and kissing his hair. Soft and gentle, letting her inhale his scent as she offered him her body.

The move set him off. He lifted his shoulders and she saw a flash of determination in those eyes before his hands went to the waistband of his pants. She wanted to help but the energy spinning up inside of her exhausted her. She lay there, watching every delicious inch of him as he peeled the pants down and dropped his boxer briefs past his knees.

When he lifted his head again, she knew every part of him came in at an impressive size. She had to touch him then. Her hand went to his erection. She wrapped her hand around his hardness, thick and long in her palm.

As his finger danced inside of her, she caressed him, pumping her hand up and down. She wanted more but didn't want him to stop using that hand on her. Her eyes closed and her head dropped forward. She wanted to concentrate on giving him pleasure but all she could do was drink it all in.

He reached over and she spied the condom wrapper lying next to her arm. She didn't know when he took it out or put it on. She was just grateful he did.

One time, maybe over and done.

But with the condom on and his hands pressing on the inside of her thighs she wanted to forget any restrictions. That was her last thought as he pushed inside of her. The friction fueled her. She felt every delicious inch as he entered her.

Her inner muscles clamped down on him and heat smacked into her in waves. Her body went wild.

The push and pull as he entered her then retreated. The spinning deep within her that sped up as she ground her heel into the back of his thigh. In and out. A steady rhythm and harder thrusts.

He had a haze blanketing her mind and her body on fire. She clamped her thighs tighter against him, trying to quench the hunger for him. She could feel him inside her, around her. It was a sensual assault unlike anything she'd experienced before.

He plunged and their bodies slid on the blanket. Despite the stinging cold, sweat formed on the back of her neck. She could see it gather on his forehead.

His muscles tightened as he held his body over hers. Tiny groans escaped her lips as he hit that spot that sent her head flying back.

Everything inside her clenched and tightened one

last time as the orgasm hit. Slammed right into her as her breath whooshed out. Her fingernails dug into his shoulders as she fell open. His head dipped and warm breath blew over her cheek. She could hear his grunts and feel his body shift over her.

She came. The spooling inside her ripped. She bucked and held him as the sensations crashed through her. Her head dropped forward then back. She couldn't focus and didn't want to.

Her haze cleared as his shoulders began to tremble. Her orgasm had touched off his. It held him in its grip now. With every push his hands tightened on her and he wrapped her closer. By the time he collapsed against her chest, the tension spinning around them had wound up to near screaming. Then it blinked out.

With his mouth buried in her neck, he cuddled closer to her. The sound of their rough breathing filled the air. She tried to hold him but couldn't drum up the energy. It drained away to pool in her belly.

Her insides tingled as the thickness in the air evened out. She took advantage of the quiet to touch him. Her fingertips danced over his shoulders. She tried to think of something to say.

He beat her to it. "I can't believe I only have one condom."

She hadn't been thinking that before. It was all she'd think about now.

15

Ward hated the idea of letting Pearce go. The plan was the right one, but losing touch with the man, even for a second, pissed Ward off. They'd planted a tracer on him through his food, and Mike and Josiah would be up his ass the entire time. Harlan stood ready to take Pearce out sniper style, if needed. Ward liked that last part of the plan best, so long as he had West back first.

The afternoon hours ticked by until they hit go time. The guards changed and the pieces clicked into place. In two minutes the Marines would muster for a briefing, and the contractors were out chasing a wild lead Ward had planted about a missing truckload of rocket launchers.

With a nod, Josiah got up and Ward followed. He called to Mike over his shoulder, "We'll be back in ten."

"I'll be sitting here watching our prisoner sit on his bed. My life is exciting." Mike stared at Pearce in the monitor.

Pearce stared back.

The plan depended on a few simple facts. The first

being the dirty guard, Tom something—Ward didn't
bother to learn his name because the guy would be
dead or in lock-up within the next few hours—would
make a move at the clearest time, and that was now.
Ward also counted on Tom not wanting to draw attention with a noisy takedown of Mike that would bring
the Marines running.

Mike was one of the biggest wild cards in the plan.
He generally reacted on instinct, and this time he'd
have to fail. Josiah would watch from a safe distance,
ready to break in if Mike got in trouble, but Mike was
pissed off he had to lose this round, fake or not.

That was one of the things Ward loved about the
men of Alliance. They rarely got on the wrong side of
being injured.

The mental countdown began. Josiah and Ward
looked on from the closed circuit in one of the meeting
rooms as Tom walked down the hall. He watched his
steps and looked around before opening the door to the
anteroom outside of Pearce's cell.

With a swipe of the security card, Tom was inside. The
name and photo came up on the screen in front of Ward.
It was not Tom's. He'd either picked at random or targeted
some sergeant and would let him take the fall. This Tom
guy was all class. When he sold out he didn't half-ass it.

"Annoying as hell, but smart to steal someone else's
credentials for this." Josiah pulled his gun, clearly
ready to rush in to rescue Mike if needed. "But not
smart enough to disable the cameras."

"Hard to, when he doesn't know they're there." Truth was, the entire place was wired. The commanding general shared the layout with Ward, but Ward only showed Tom part of the setup. It let them run this scam now.

Mike sat with his feet up on the table and his back to the door. Something he would never do. He stayed on alert always, and protecting their backs was second nature to Alliance members. But Tom wouldn't know that. He'd be too wrapped up in making this grab happen to reason through the clues in front of him.

Mike glanced over his shoulder at Tom. "Hey, man. You need something?"

The guard hesitated. Just a second. Stood by the door holding it open until he finally let it slide shut. "Where is everyone?"

"Ward and Josiah will be back in a few minutes."

Ward smiled at the delivery, calm and convincing. Mike also handed Tom a deadline within which to act. Go or walk away. For a second Ward wasn't sure which way Tom would go. Then Tom wrapped his arm around Mike's neck and tightened his elbow around his throat.

Mike's body jerked as the band came down. Those long legs kicked out. He knew how to break the hold, but he didn't. He struggled and squirmed and then dropped down.

Tom pushed him off the side of the chair to the floor. "Easy work."

"Too easy, maybe," Josiah said from their watching station. "Is Mike really out?"

Ward doubted it. Mike could hold on longer than that. "I told him to go fast so he didn't pass out."

Josiah laughed. "This shit must be killing him."

"He wanted to just shoot Tom and Pearce and be done. Probably would have if he didn't like having West alive and around." Ward liked that about Mike. He'd encounter a threat and destroy it. That shoot-first attitude served him well in the military and now with Alliance.

Tom stepped over Mike's still body and around to the computer monitor. The security codes for the lock changed three times a day. Earlier, Ward made sure that Tom saw the handoff, then left the file in his locked top desk drawer instead of burning it as he usually would.

The key was to make the situation just hard enough to be a struggle for Tom but not impossible. Have him sneak around and run risks. Run into enough roadblocks so he didn't become suspicious.

They seemed to be walking that fine line, but Ward wasn't ready to celebrate just yet.

After another swipe of the security card and more keystrokes, the lock opened. Tom pulled the door open and Pearce stepped out, tall and regal and looking every inch the British university professor he once pretended to be. The glasses were a nice touch. Ward didn't even know for sure if Pearce needed them.

But Pearce being Pearce, he didn't race out to safety. Tom stood at the door to the hallway keeping watch and gesturing for them to go. Pearce ignored the frantic movements and walked around Mike's body.

Josiah stood up. "Shit."

Yeah, Ward didn't like it either. Tom might not be schooled in covert strategies and tactics, but Pearce was. He pressed his foot against Mike's side. He crouched down, just outside their line of vision. Part of his body was obscured and Ward couldn't see what was happening.

Josiah had his gun in his hand and walked to the door. "I'm going in."

Ward understood. Mike was his man and part of Delta team. That made him Josiah's responsibility. "Hold."

Josiah's expression turned to steel. "Pearce will kill him."

"No, he won't. He wants me to see my failure." This was a game of cat and mouse, and Pearce believed he was about to win. He would love that and think it handed Ward a huge defeat. Little did the guy know.

Pearce stood up again and looked around. Could be he hunted for a camera. He'd never find it. The commanding general described it as a black speck on the wall. Every room had one, and none of his men or the contractors knew.

Agitated and shifting his weight around, Tom came over to stand beside Pearce. Taking out his gun, Tom aimed it at Mike.

Anxiety jolted through Ward. Mike had a protective vest but that wouldn't do anything for him if he got shot in the head.

"Ward, I'm going in." Josiah swore under his breath. "I'll torture the truth out of Pearce somehow."

Not going to happen. Pearce knew every trick. Hell, he'd taught interrogation at the CIA's training facility. Breaking him would be hard if not impossible.

"Wait." Ward hated to say the word.

Pearce's hand shot out and he touched Tom's arm, lowering the weapon. Pearce turned and walked to the main door, gesturing for Tom to lead. Then they moved into the hallway. They had a minute to get out before Marines poured out of the main briefing room. For someone else that could be a problem, so could the security system, armed guards, and the fence surrounding the property. Not Pearce.

When Mike jumped to his feet and looked into the hidden camera, Ward's breathing evened out again. Then Mike gave them the finger, and the tension tightening Ward's muscles eased.

"This will work," Josiah said, more to the room in general than as part of a conversation.

Ward wanted to be convinced, so he went along. "It has to."

Lexi's legs still wobbled. The man might only have had one condom and one shot but he used it well. Right now he prowled around the inside of the garage, clearly uncomfortable about being pinned down.

She watched, fascinated by the way he moved. That build, rugged and large, should slow him down. Instead he moved with the grace of a predator. Sort of like a lion playing with its prey.

The sex had been wild. Open and free, no holding back. He touched her and tasted her. Plunged inside of her without handing her some "this means nothing" speech or flipping into the mode where only his needs mattered.

He took her to the edge of reason and shoved her off. Afterward he comforted her. A few minutes of holding her before declaring it time to get back to work. Maybe she should have been offended by the abrupt turn in emotions, but she wasn't. This, protecting and being prepared for the next attack, was second nature to him. She knew him enough to know that.

She liked that side of him and refused to blame him for not being more cuddly. They were in the middle of a war zone, after all.

But they had hours to kill, and sitting on the floor trying to keep warm was not her idea of the best way to spend them. She'd changed into a heavier sweater, and the boots she wore sat a few feet away. She needed them on because she knew West wanted her battle ready at all times.

Grabbing the shoelace, she pulled the right boot closer to her. "My dad wanted me to be a doctor. Was yours a military guy?"

The idle conversation seemed like a good way to fill the hours. It ranked higher than him listening to the army radio he picked off one of the dead attackers or watching him try to communicate with his team.

Plus, she wanted to know more. They'd been thrown into this high intensity situation. She knew that accounted for some of the blinding attraction to the guy but there was something else there. He was so solid and clear on what he did and why. He didn't question, and since she'd spent a lifetime questioning her every move and decision, she loved his approach.

And she liked him. Too much. She'd closed her eyes for a second after the sex and fantasies started spinning in her head. She saw herself with West and not in Pakistan. In a big bed, acting like normal people acted who weren't being gunned down.

She could imagine it so easily. He wasn't the pay-ten-bucks-for-coffee guy, but that wasn't her thing either. He appreciated quiet. And if the way they lit up the blanket was any indication, he'd appreciate a few more rounds of naked touching with her.

"Definitely not," he said into the quiet.

She'd almost forgotten what she asked but the "definitely" intrigued her. "What did he do?"

"Dad collected weapons as he waited for the end of the world." West turned around to face her after dropping that line.

She laughed but West didn't. That sobered her right up. "Wait, you're serious?"

"He believed the end was coming and that we had to be prepared. Shooting, foraging for food. Survivalist training." West balanced on the balls of his feet in front of her. "I had it all long before I went into the military."

"But that's crazy." Then she remembered he'd said something about being able to recognize crazy. "How did you get away?"

"Someone shot him and the State stepped in." He offered the fact then stopped talking.

That food bar he gave her churned in her stomach, threatening to come back up again. "It wasn't you, right?"

He frowned. "What?"

Her gaze traveled over his hair and face then dropped down to his arm. He had that thin black jacket on again but she'd stripped the shirt off him postsex to caress those muscled arms. "You didn't shoot him, right?"

"No."

She blew out a relieved breath. Not because she'd think less of him but because that would be a huge burden to carry. She knew guilt and she knew fear, and no one should be saddled with either.

Her mind spun with a million questions, all of them nosy and probably inappropriate. She wanted to know how old he was and if he'd witnessed the horror. She couldn't imagine how that would plague a person.

But those questions would take time to coax out of him, and the rough answers might throw him off when they both needed him at top efficiency. So she went with what she thought would be the least offensive. "Do you ever think about him?"

"I carry reminders."

She had no idea what that meant. "Emotional?"

"These." He lifted one arm then the other.

She'd seen the tattoo bands around his upper arms. Not just on one side but on both. She didn't know the right name to describe them. Tattoos were not her usual thing. His stuck out because of the print. Not flowers or a vine. "Barbed wire."

"They are a reminder."

She traced her finger over the one on his left arm. "Of what exactly?"

"A time when I was bound to a man determined to cause death and destruction. How sick I felt. How desperate I was." West pinned her with his intense gaze. "It will never happen again."

Memories bombarded her. Between this time and the time at Javed's house she'd seen a lot of West's body. The scars. His warrior wounds. But he had something else. Something that didn't fit with how she viewed him.

"I saw the marks or the other tattoo or whatever it is." On his back. Just over his right shoulder. A series of lines and crossed-out marks. A count-off of sorts.

His hand went to his shoulder then dropped again. "A tattoo."

"You keep track of the men you've killed. That's what it is, I'm guessing. A sort of scorecard." As someone who tried to save lives, she tried to block out the human toll behind those lines.

His expression went blank. "Is that what you really think?"

"Am I wrong?" She sort of wanted to be. To her there was a difference between fighting for what was right and liking the kill. She prayed he fell into the former category. Every piece of evidence suggested he did, but her radar could be off and that scared her to death.

He turned to the side. Looked like he was going to say something, then he froze. "What is that?"

She followed his gaze to her shoe. She'd known this lecture was coming but wasn't about to let him derail her. "My boot. No big deal."

"This." He grabbed the boot and showed the side. "Fuck."

Looked like dirt to her, or a pebble. Either way, nothing to worry about and not a reason for the kick of rage he aimed at her "What do you think it is?"

"It's a tracking device."

Panic filled her brain as she shot to her feet. "That can't be"

He turned the boot over then lifted her leg and examined the other one. "When we found the other one I asked you if anyone had touched you."

"Right." She remembered the questions and her confusion.

"The boot, Lexi."

"No one . . ." Then she remembered. The life drained out of her. "The guy at the clinic was going to bind my legs to the chair, grabbed them, then didn't."

West swore. "That explains the how. The question now is who's watching."

She knew he was thinking Javed but she didn't know how that was possible. She'd had these boots on since the clinic. Then fear hit her full force. Forget who planted it. A tracker meant they were being followed despite all the fancy backtracking and covering. "You mean someone knows we're here?"

"Possibly." He stood up and looked around.

She now knew that tone. "So definitely. That's what you really mean."

He ripped the dot off her boot and held the shoe out to her as he nodded toward the loft. "Climb up."

Terror washed through every cell and she nearly buckled. "West—"

"Now."

He peeked out through two slats in the wall, the same sliver of light he'd been checking since they got there. This time his head dropped. He swore and kept swearing. "I hate this fucking country."

She knew he wasn't talking about the people, but she didn't know what was happening to send him off now.

"Come out, West." A man's voice all singsongy and far too happy filtered in. "And bring the pretty woman."

Everything inside her froze. "Who is that?"

West grabbed his gun. "A man I should have killed months ago."

16

THIS WAS a fucking nightmare. West blinked, hoping to push the image out of his mind, but Pearce still stood there. He had some guy that looked vaguely familiar with him. West would worry about that later. Right now his concern was how Pearce got the whole way to Pakistan and what that meant about the security of Alliance and the people who worked there.

His mind shot to his other major concern. He looked at Lexi. "Get ready to get up on the roof."

She shook her head. Stood there holding her boot and disagreed. "He's right out front. He'll see me."

"I'll create a diversion." Shooting Pearce's sidekick in the forehead should do it, West thought. He would fire through the entire Pakistani army if that's what it took to get her out safely.

"West, you're not thinking." She came closer and put a hand on his arm. "There could be others out there. If this guy, whoever he is, found us. Others probably did, too."

He tried to remember the last time someone questioned his concentration and thinking. Yeah, never. He let her get away with it because she could do pretty much whatever she wanted. But the tremble moving through her suggested she wasn't nearly as unmoved by this as she appeared.

He wanted to touch her but couldn't. He needed all of his focus and energy to get through the next few minutes with Pearce and whatever wave came after him.

West looked at his protective vest. It lay on the ground next to where she was sitting. He'd left it off earlier because once he touched her, really touched her, he hit a tipping point. Her safety passed the job as the most important thing he did out there. That meant he needed her alive more than he needed to finish this, so the vest went to her. No arguments.

"Grab that and get in it." He pointed, and she picked it up without question. "This guy is dangerous. Serious dangerous, Lexi."

"So are you." She slipped the vest over his shoulders and stood there while he fastened it.

She had a point, but . . . "He trained people like me. This is a pretty even match, except for how pissed off I am that he's still breathing. That gives me an edge."

She peeked over his shoulder and through the opening between the slats. "But he's not with you?"

"He's a traitor and a disgrace."

"That seems harsh." Pearce's voice sounded from the other side of the door.

West pushed Lexi behind him as a piece of the wall

gave way. The other man came in first. He had a retired military look to him. Tom . . . something. A CIA guy. "You're working with Pearce?"

"Drop your weapons." Tom issued the order.

West ignored it because that just was not going to happen. "Pearce. I see you're still a gigantic pain in the ass."

Months in a secret locked-down facility hadn't had much of an impact. Pearce was still tall and lean and, if West guessed right, able to strangle another human without using more than one arm.

"You should thank me." Pearce held his hands together in front of him.

This should be good. West could hardly wait to hear Pearce's newest bit of self-delusion. "For?"

"Not barging in a few hours ago." Pearce hesitated as if waiting for that blow to land. "I let you and your lady friend have some alone time before you died."

The color ran out of Lexi's cheeks. "Oh my God."

West knew where her mind went. Flipping through memories of her being half naked. Of him inside her. All while Pearce and possibly his buddies watched.

Now he had a new reason to kill the motherfucker.

"I'm Jake Pearce, by the way." Pearce tried to shift around West's frame and held a hand out to Lexi. "And you are?"

She ignored it. "None of your business."

Pearce laughed and leaned in with a man-to-man gleam in his eye. "She's perfect for you."

"Fuck you." West thought that covered everything.

"There's no need for an introduction. I am quite familiar with Alexis Palmer and her work in Skardu." Pearce made a tsk-tsking sound. "I think you've been nosy and caused some trouble for people I work with. That's a shame."

The comment grabbed West's attention. He knew Pearce didn't accidentally drop the information. Pearce didn't do anything by accident. It was a calculated remark. He was either showing off or letting them know that the end was coming.

West wanted to know which, so he played along. "The weapons stockpile is you?"

Pearce sighed. "You underestimate me."

Wrong. "I don't waste a second thinking about you."

"I bet Ward is thinking about me right now. And Mike." Pearce glanced over at his bodyguard or whatever the hell the guy with the weapons strapped to his chest was supposed to be. "It's a shame I didn't let you kill him."

"You're telling me you escaped Alliance." West couldn't come up with any scenario where that was possible.

Even if Pearce got out of the cell, he'd have to get past all the security and the team. Ward would nail him with a bullet and Tasha might take the guy down with her bare hands. And that was in another country. He'd somehow spanned continents and made it here.

Not fucking possible.

Pearce held his hands out palms up. "You guys are not as unbeatable as you think."

West didn't accept that either. "We caught you."

"And then you lost me."

That piece stabbed at West. He couldn't get his mind to accept it. "Maybe I should just shoot you and be done with it."

The idea was so tempting. Which was probably why Pearce made it clear he had an interest in the weapons or something to do with them. That made it harder for West to take him down without procuring the intel he needed.

"If you try to come near me, Tom here will gut your pretty girlfriend." Pearce put a hand behind his ear. "No comment to that?"

West couldn't look at Lexi, didn't even glance in her direction. But he was proud of her. She stood there, not panicking or begging for anything from Pearce. She'd shifted a few inches closer to him but their bodies still didn't touch.

But he wanted Pearce's mind off Lexi and back on him. "What do you want?"

"You have her well trained, but I have to say this is a surprise. You seemed like the type to stick to hookers. Can't really see you with a former mental patient."

Sounded like Pearce was running through the handbook, trying to humiliate her. West refused to play. "What's in the caves?"

Pearce nodded. "I knew you'd figure that part out. I told Benton to eliminate you when he had the chance."

Motherfucker. That name. Alliance's nemesis. The enemy of most countries. The man who dealt in bodies and weapons and kept his face out of the limelight as he skulked around from country to country wreaking havoc.

Pearce could only be considered skilled and lethal and, as West saw it, delusional in his belief that the intelligence community owed him something and deserved to be punished. But Benton was the goddamn king of death.

West didn't let the kicking in his gut show. "Benton is here."

Pearce smiled. "He's my partner. He's been my partner for years."

Two peas in a sick and twisted pod. "He didn't do much to rescue you from jail." West threw out his own poking words. Pearce wasn't the only one with the interrogation handbook.

"I didn't need someone to rescue me." For the first time, Pearce moved. He shifted his weight and crossed his arms in front of him. "We're a lot alike in that way."

That didn't even deserve a response.

Lexi delivered one. "You just like hearing yourself talk."

The comment had Pearce focusing on her again. "Did West tell you about his bad daddy."

"Yes." Her tone stayed flat as she stood there with one boot on and the other swinging from her hand.

Pearce took a step toward her. "Did he tell you about yours?"

West shoved him back. "Shut up, Pearce."

But Lexi didn't let it drop, as West had hoped she would. "What are you talking about?"

"Why do you think your daddy had the codes to call in his concerns and have them telegraphed to Alliance? Only the really bad shit gets through to them. The intel has to be trustworthy." Pearce walked over to stand next to his bodyguard. "They're not exactly on speed dial, but I think you're smart enough to know that."

As if mesmerized, Lexi followed Pearce. "What are you saying?"

West grabbed her arm and brought her back even with him. He wanted to shove her behind him but had to keep his control in check. "Nothing. Ignore him."

"To use Hollywood jargon," Pearce said, "your daddy is a spy."

Her mouth dropped open. "I don't—"

"He is not." That was more than enough of that. West needed them back on track and not talking about Lexi's dad and his supposed ties with the CIA. Alex Palmer used his position to funnel information to the right people. He was a sometime asset, not a spy.

"I guess we can debate his title," Pearce said.

West didn't care about that or dwell on it. If the doctor wanted to put his life at risk to relay information, fine. That was his business, and it was his job to fill in Lexi. "What's the plan here, Pearce?"

"Simple."

West inhaled, trying to rein in the need to smash this guy to the ground. "Enlighten me."

"I take you to Benton and we make an example of you." Pearce nodded at his bodyguard.

West saw it coming. He quickly threw his body to the side and took the bullet meant for Lexi. It ripped through his shoulder, slamming him into her. Her scream echoed in his ear and the burning sensation seared through him. "Damn it."

"West." Lexi's arms came around him.

He would not fall over. Refused to even wince. He didn't want to scare Lexi or give Pearce the satisfaction.

"I'm fine." The bloodstain on his shirt grew larger and his shoulder went numb. He could shoot from either hand, so that wasn't the problem. The issue was the loss of blood. Unchecked, it would slow him down, or worse.

If he passed out, she was done. And if he shot now he could start a firestorm and she'd end up as a collateral.

"So predictable," Pearce said. "You can always count on West to go in for the save." He clapped his hand on Tom's shoulder. "Grab the girl and West will follow."

"He needs help!" Lexi shouted.

Pearce shrugged. "It's a shame you didn't stay in medical school, then."

Ward, Mike, and Josiah watched the scene unfold. Harlan and the other members of Delta were staked out

in positions all over the area and within a mile, ready
to follow no matter which direction Pearce used to exit.
But Pearce was not Ward's main concern right now.
Yes, the mission came first. Always. But he needed to
see West walk out of this showdown.

From their position they could see Pearce and Tom
standing in the doorway. Mostly a side and back view.
Then the gunshot rang out. It took all of Ward's strength
to hold Josiah back. He was kicking and swearing and
only settled down when Mike added his body to Ward's
human shield.

Josiah shrugged out of the hold in a rage. "We need
to move."

Ward had a load of patience but it faded the longer
he stayed on the ground in Pakistan. "Not yet."

Not that he wanted to hang around. His heart hammered in his chest as he waited to see what unfolded
in that garage. The minutes ticked by, with each one
seeming to take hours.

Then four figures walked out. West cradled his arm
and Lexi walked by his side, bent in close and talking
to him as she touched his shoulder. Pearce and Tom
followed.

"West is alive." Josiah bent over and blew out a long
breath.

A shot of relief burst through Ward. Finally, some
good news. It was too soon to celebrate but they'd made
it through this first piece of this risky mission. "Yeah."

"Let's get him," Mike said.

Ward put a restraining hand across his chest. "We follow."

"No way, man." Mike shook his head as his mouth flattened. "They just shot West."

"We let this ride." Ward stood alone against two furious glares. Josiah's face flushed with fury and Mike looked ten seconds away from ignoring orders and shooting his way out of the situation.

"West—"

"Is strong." Ward said the words and knew they were true, but the guy was human and sometimes they forgot that and took his survival ability for granted. Ward didn't want to miscalculate and do that here.

"If anything happens to him . . ."

Ward knew a threat lingered right there on the tip of Josiah's tongue. He decided to let the Delta team leader say it. "What?"

"We don't leave men behind," Mike said, looking every bit as homicidal as Josiah.

"And we're not going to." Ward made that vow and meant it. He'd risk his messed up hand and go in himself to pull West out, if needed.

17

LEXI'S HANDS shook as she patched up West's shoulder. She'd had to peel off his blood-soaked jacket. Red blotches stained the dark gray shirt underneath and covered the sleeve. Everywhere she looked she saw splashes of red, up his neck and on her hands.

She had no idea how he continued to sit there without keeling over. He should have passed out or at least been dizzy. Instead, he half sat, half leaned against a wooden table set up in the middle of a cave.

The dim lighting didn't give much away but she saw the rough rocky walls and what looked like a piece of metal fence set up at the far end with a trough of water in front of it. She didn't know what happened in this room but she knew it had to be awful. Which likely explained West's stubborn refusal to so much as close his eyes.

She admired the bravery, especially as her insides jumbled and her stomach rolled. But she feared his strength would make the men in the room go after him even harder.

He reached up and slid his hand over hers. "It's going to be okay."

With her frazzled nerves, she didn't notice how the bandage she held to his shoulder jumped around wildly until he touched her. "You need help," she said.

"Baby, trust me," he said in a gruff voice.

The endearment. The comfort of his voice. They meant so much, but they didn't stop the mix of rage and terror racing through her.

She had training, but bullet wounds were not her specialty. On the way to the cave he'd been kicked and punched. Whenever Pearce had threatened her, West stood there and took the beating.

He did exactly what he promised—he put his body in front of hers. She knew that he focused on staying alive long enough for his team to burst in. That's how his plans worked. When chaos broke out, he stalled to find time to get her to safety.

This from a man who insisted he'd lost his humanity.

"I'll get you out of here." His voice dropped to a whisper.

She heard pain and a small break before the last word. "You need to save your strength."

"It's too late for that." Pearce walked up behind her with his bodyguard at his side. "We need to get West ready before he meets Benton."

She'd had so many names and so many people thrown at her. Separating them out became harder each day. Now she had a new player. "Who is Benton?"

West lifted his hand to touch her face but it dropped against his lap again without making contact. "Lexi, no."

"Benton is a very powerful man. Someone you don't cross, and unfortunately for West, he is very upset with Alliance." Pearce put his hand by West's neck and squeezed. "Right?"

West's jaw snapped shut but he didn't make a sound as the color drained from his face.

"Benton once had a deal for the sale of some toxin, and Alliance got in the way. West here played a rather large role in ending that venture." Pearce moved around the table, picking up the unused bandages and looking at the supplies she used to sew up the wound. "Now Benton has a new operation, but West is going to pay for messing up the old one."

"That's their job." She assumed that was true about Alliance. She'd seen West in action, and Josiah to a lesser degree. They didn't sit around. If there was a deadly toxin on the loose, they'd hunt it down and destroy everything to get to it.

"This was a very lucrative deal." Pearce acted as if he were delivering a lecture.

Her hand hesitated over the needle she used on West. "But they caught you. Stopped you."

"Aren't you enterprising?" Pearce reached over and grabbed the needle and small scissors. "Or very stupid."

"You should be in jail now." Lexi had more to say but cut herself off when West pressed his leg against hers.

"Your man here might pretend to be one of the good

guys," Pearce said, "but he had no problem storing me underground in a tiny cell, taking away my rights and my life." As he talked, a bit of his controlled facade broke. Anger seethed under the surface and seemed to bubble out.

West faced Pearce head on. "I'd do it again except for the part where I let you live. That was a mistake."

A nerve jumped in Pearce's cheek as he visibly wrestled his anger back down. "Which is why we stopped here first. See, I can't have you running around, getting in the way."

Something about that line had Lexi's head pounding. "What is this place?"

"You should be comfortable here, what with all the medical tools." Pearce walked over to that rusted piece of fence sticking up in the room for no good reason. He reached behind it and pulled out a metal box. Putting it on the floor, he opened the top, showing off piles of ordinary tools. "Now, normally I'd use these to get West to cough up some information."

She looked at the wrench and the hammer and her stomach flopped. "You're sick."

"Yet you're sleeping with West and he uses the same tactics you think are so sick." When Pearce stood back up, he held the hammer in his hand. In a few deliberate steps he stood in front of West again. "He's an expert with them . . . aren't you?"

"Fuck you." West spit out blood and hit Pearce's shoes.

Fear battled with adrenaline inside her. She wanted

to grab the tools and throw them at Pearce one by one. She looked at West and wanted to believe he sat up a little straighter than before, but the fact was, he remained doubled over. Even though the blood flow had stopped, red still covered his torso.

"The game is simple." Pearce wound up and hit West right in the biceps with the hammer.

Lexi heard West's sharp intake of breath and lunged for the weapon. "Don't touch him."

"I hurt him, you fix him and we start all over again, until we get to the one time when we can't revive him." Pearce pulled his arm back again. "This will be fun."

Before he got off a second hit or made contact, West reached over with his uninjured arm and grabbed the man's fist. "You want to go up against me? Do it. With only one arm I will tear you apart."

From his intense glare, Lexi believed him. West was no longer bent over double. He sat up straight with his head back. Those eyes glistened with rage.

The tension ratcheted up. Tom stepped forward, but Pearce kept him back with a shake of his head.

West had upped the stakes, dared Pearce to knock him out. She could not watch and did the only thing she could think of to swing the attention back to her. "I won't do it. I won't stitch him up over and over again."

In truth, she'd throw her body over his if she had to. He'd spent the last few days rescuing and protecting her. Now she would do it for him. Somehow. Despite being smaller and not as strong, her will rose up.

No one would touch West. Not when she was so desperate to explore the sudden and shocking depth of her feelings for him.

Pearce gestured toward the stack of bloody towels and bandages piled up right near her hand. "Then he'll bleed out."

"Leave her out of this." West shot her a wide-eyed look that telegraphed his desire for her to stay quiet so he could use his body as a punching bag. Then he turned back to Pearce. "You want me, you have me."

Pearce exhaled, all dramatic and serious. His ego and confidence appeared to be firmly back in check. "Your girlfriend has been causing trouble around town, but then I think you know that. Maybe that's why you like her so much. Who could tell with you."

West's words of warning came rushing back to her. He'd insisted she was brave for reporting the weapons. Now she knew it touched off a series of events that brought them to this horrible place. "I didn't mean—"

Pearce's head whipped around toward her. "Benton wants to see you, too."

He delivered the ominous statement then motioned for the bodyguard to step forward. Tom pressed down hard on West's wounded shoulder and impassively watched his knees give out.

West fell to the floor, but he didn't stay there. Finding a store of strength she didn't know anyone could have, he came up and lunged for the bodyguard's gun. She heard Pearce shout for Tom and then an arm slipped around her neck. The point of a knife danced in front of her eyes.

"I will kill her." Pearce shouted the ugly promise. The noise pinged off the solid walls.

The words sliced through her and a new shot of panic exploded inside her, threatening to send her to her knees. She grabbed for Pearce's arm and tried to ease the pressure against her windpipe. If she folded or cried out, West would give up. He'd sacrifice his life for hers. Every step he'd made since he met her made that clear.

Looking at Pearce, West stopped moving and held up his good hand. Tom wrenched it behind his back and marched him to that damn piece of fence.

She watched in horror as Tom tied up West with what looked like sharp wire. Blood trickled down West's arms and his feet dangled above the ground. He was suspended and vulnerable, without a way to defend himself. His face tightened with pain as every movement caused the bindings to rip into his skin.

The arm around her neck vanished and she lost her footing. She stumbled, grabbing onto the edge of the table. All the sharp tools were gone. Pearce had left her with bandages and little else.

She glanced up in time to see him douse West with a bucket of what looked like water. Then he reached for a wire at the end of a rod. It buzzed and snapped.

One look at the water dripping from West's hair and the current in Pearce's hands and she started gagging. Pearce would not make this easy.

"Lexi, close your eyes." West stared at her as he gave the order.

"That's sweet but she's going to hear your screams and see all the blood." Pearce laughed. "She will watch every second as I set you on fire from the inside out and your body jumps around in response. She will watch or I will inflict even more pain on you."

West was going to die.

Right there in a cave in Pakistan. Led here by her. Only hours after he held her and kissed her. After he entered her with such aching need that she forgot about every man and every love that came before.

"Please don't do this." Her whispered plea did not affect Pearce.

He shook his head as he inched closer to West, prolonging the agony. "She's too good for you, West."

Giving it one last try, she ran up to Pearce and grabbed his arm. Tom was on her a second later, pulling her back. Yanking her arms behind her as he dragged her away from Pearce but still within viewing range of the sickness to come.

"We'll leave and not say anything." She was willing to promise anything.

"You don't know West, then. He will hunt me until he kills me." Pearce turned back to West.

He got too close. West nailed him in the face with a wad of bloody spit. "Go to hell."

Without any fanfare or even saying a word, Pearce pulled a tissue out of his pocket and wiped his face.

"He's been called a machine but he's really more of an animal. Definitely not human."

Before she could respond, Pearce touched the end of the rod to the fence holding West. She heard a zapping sound and West's body jerked and flinched. He didn't yell but he threw his head back and tightened his jaw. She felt the jolt run through her in sympathy and had to fight back the tears of helplessness she felt at not being able to stop this madness or get him down.

"Really, unless you need a killing machine, you could do better. Well, could have." Pearce went to a small box connected to the rod in his hand and turned the voltage dial. "I'm not sure you'll get a chance later."

"Why would I help you if you just plan to kill me?" She talked fast, trying to keep the attention on her and off West.

"I'm betting you won't be able to stand seeing me tear West apart socket by socket."

"We barely know each other," West said.

A new pain shot through Lexi. He spoke about her in a dismissive tone, with disdain. She suspected this was part of his plan. Make her appear irrelevant and potentially prolong her life. She knew it. She got it. But right there at the end, when all seemed lost, she wanted to hear other words from him.

"Really? Because from what I could see on that blanket—"

The chains and bindings rattled as West made a move toward Pearce. "Shut up."

"That sort of thing is not received well in this country. A young woman sleeping around," Pearce said, talking right over West's outburst. "And West here, with his need to protect and willingness to use his skills to track and kill. Not so tough now."

She tried to move into Pearce's line of vision again, but Tom kept a tight hold on her arms. "What do you want?" she asked.

"Revenge."

"Take the weapons and go."

"Spunk. Nice." Pearce smiled at West. "You chose well."

"She means nothing." This time he sounded even clearer.

Pearce lifted the rod again. "We'll see."

Ward gathered Harlan, Josiah, and Mike a half mile away from the encampment and the series of caves behind it. The other two team members were miles away, keeping the Pakistani army away from this location.

Not that there was any debate here. He'd let Pearce go. That decision rested with him, which meant he would be the one to get West out. And he had a feeling they needed to hurry.

Ward spread the map over the open back gate of the military truck Josiah had borrowed. "I'll be bait."

"No." Harlan shook his head. "Tasha will kill me."

No question she wasn't going to take any of this well. She was not a woman who handled being cut out of the loop. With the communications blackout, that's exactly what had happened. Ward half expected to look up and see her, finding out she'd commandeered a military flight and came to find them all, which was why he needed to move fast.

"You're needed to run point," Harlan said. "No one does that better."

They'd spent almost a year all but comparing dick sizes as they argued about how to run the men and operations in Alliance. Now Harlan pulled out the you're-the-leader bullshit. "Interesting time to tell me that."

Harlan shrugged. "They aren't expecting me."

"Pearce knows you're in Pakistan," Mike said.

"Enough." Ward knew that if he let it, this conversation would rage for days. This was what happened when you mixed a group of alpha guys and tried to keep them all from running straight into fire. He looked to Mike. "You and Harlan plan a diversion, and make it fucking good. I want every piece of garbage in those caves to come running."

Josiah made a strangled noise. Probably meant he was trying not to yell. "But not until West, Lexi, and the weapons are out."

Ward nodded. "Josiah and I go in."

"You're going to just walk into an armed camp full of weapons and gunmen and secrets people want to keep hidden?" Mike said. "If we really don't think this is government sanctioned, then some of those men are rogue Pakistani military. Not guys you fuck with." He scoffed as he said it.

"He's not going." Josiah put a hand over the map. "I am."

Ward refused to battle this out. In the absence of Tasha, his word ruled. "Josiah—"

"You have limited use of one hand and Pearce knows that. They are going to kill you." Harlan held up both hands. "What don't you get about that?"

Ward understood every word. Had weighed the risks and decided he could handle them. He didn't have a fucking death wish. Tasha waited at home and he wanted to be there.

But he had to get out of here first. "They can try to take me out but it's not going to happen."

Josiah looked from one leader to the other and his expression changed. The tension pulling across his forehead eased. "We need to synchronize this to the second."

"We still don't have our communication up and running. They're blocking it from here." Mike glanced around. "Somehow."

All good points, but none of it qualified as new information. The same factors had been in place a half hour ago when Ward decided on this course. "We'll set hard times to move since we can't have a countdown and ongoing chatter in the comm."

Mike's eyes narrowed. "And if you're not out before we light this place up?"

That one was easy. Ward always had that contingency ready. "Run like hell."

18

WEST COULDN'T BREATHE.

He sat on the floor of a cell deep inside the cavern of caves. The area consisted of little more than an indentation in the rock wall. The space allowed just enough room for him to sit on the floor with his legs stretched out in front of him with Lexi beside him.

There wasn't a door. He'd had to squeeze through the opening, and now his captors or the guards or whomever was in charge around here walked around outside. The setup made it tough to plan an escape. So did the pain ripping through him with each exhale.

Every time he inhaled he heard a whistle and his ears felt clogged, as if he were trapped underwater. He'd taken quite a beating. Good thing he wasn't a screamer and had undergone days of intense torture training in preparation for this sort of thing. And he'd lived through this before.

But every drop of blood, every grunt, had registered on Lexi's face. Pearce made her watch, fix a dislocated shoulder, set bones and bandage him up for the second then the third rounds. The sick fuck.

He also tortured her by saying they'd stop for a few minutes then start again. By the time they left the room West thought of as the pain dungeon her hands shook as she wiped the blood from his fresh wounds. He vowed Pearce would pay for throwing her equilibrium off like that.

The entire Alliance wanted Pearce dead, but he had dibs on that job. He'd use a knife. Twist it in and watch the life drain from him. Just thinking about gutting Pearce kept the pain of what West thought might be bruised ribs at bay. The adrenaline kicking through him did the rest to fight off the aftermath of the shock treatments.

Lexi slipped her hand over his knee. With a gentle touch, she lifted his palm and cradled it in both of hers. "You really know how to show a girl a good time."

Her spunk resurfaced and that eased some of his pain. "Wait until you see what I have in mind for our third date."

She put her head on his shoulder. "I hope it's a movie. Something slow and kind of boring."

"I don't do boring." But, man, that sounded good right now.

"You know I'm on to you."

He closed his eyes. Just for a second. "Meaning?"

"You lied to me."

He almost missed the accusation because of the cathartic touching. Then the word registered and his brain jump-started again.

He could be tagged with many faults. He'd done a lot of terrible things in his life in the name of patriotism and the common good. No regrets, but he remembered them all, and outright lying to Lexi was not on his list.

"When?" he asked, wondering if one knock too many had put his memory on the fritz.

"The tattoo on your upper back."

The memory of that conversation came rushing back to him. She'd broached the topic, one he didn't discuss ever. If she'd hit on the truth he would have admitted to it. But she concluded he liked death. Maybe that was fair in light of who he was and what he did.

People could tag him with many sins. "Someone who loved to kill" wasn't one of them. For some reason, he had hoped she would be the one person to see that.

"It's a tattoo." He tried to shrug but the move had him gasping. "No big deal."

She traced her finger over his thigh. "It's not a scorecard."

Well shit. "I don't know what you're talking about." But he did. She'd used that word and been wrong. Now it looked like she knew that.

"You do." She looked at his shoulder then frowned. She whipped a new bandage out of nowhere and went to work on his shoulder for what seemed like the hundredth time.

The poking and prodding had the wound ticking again. "Ouch."

"You pretend to be this killing machine, but—"

"Lexi, you need to understand that's what I am." How he felt about the serious import of death didn't change the fact that he was good at taking lives. He didn't debate. He made a decision or followed orders and moved. "Trained by my father, honed by the military, and used with perfect precision by Alliance. That's my role."

Her hands froze in midair and she frowned at him. The look suggested she thought he was either clueless or not that bright. "Your self-assigned role."

He didn't deny it because he really couldn't. Sniper skills and world-class patience separated him from some of the others on the team. He wanted to stay and be an essential player, which meant he needed to show that *they* needed him. "I'm good at it."

"Then why do you have the marks?" Her hands fell back on her lap.

He looked at her joined fingers and noticed they'd turned pink from all the scrubbing to remove the blood. "To keep track of kills."

"It's penance." What little fresh air moved through these twisty caves seemed to be sucked out of the room. "What, no response?"

God, she got it, but she did understand. He'd made himself get the marks. People died, many of them in covert operations. That meant dying without people knowing how you really lived. It was important to West that someone take notice since no one would ever apologize for the deaths he carried out. He picked the only way he knew how to do it—a pinch of pain and an indelible mark.

"The tattoo is a reminder." To carry around a bit of his humanity to carry him through those days when he felt it all slip away.

"Because despite the training and your tough words," she said, "killing matters to you. It leaves a mark."

"Right. So I leave a mark." But she needed to understand one very important point about who he was under everything else. "And while that's true, I don't feel guilty for doing my job."

"But it touches you. You like to pretend the death around you is normal and not a big deal, but it is." This time her hand went to his chin. She rubbed her fingers over the scruff.

Pretty words but she was treating him like the man she wished he was. The man he knew he could never really be.

He leaned his head against the hard wall behind him. "You're giving me more credit than you should."

"The man I've seen wouldn't hunt another human for fun."

He knew men like that and they made him sick. When the operative became emboldened and began to make life and death decisions based on something other than the terms of the job, the operative needed to go.

"It gets in the blood." And here was the bottom line. "Lexi, I know it feels real, but you don't actually know me."

"I want to."

He loved that she didn't try to correct him, but it was time for some harsh truths and a bit of fantasy. "If I live through this, I go back to work. Get on a plane and leave, and you can't know where to."

He had to push the words out. The idea of walking away from her made his gut clench. Only a few days and his life mixed with hers to the point where separating them proved difficult. Not that he really wanted to anyway.

True, leaving and not looking back was the smart thing. It was the thing he *would* do. But as Pearce had touched the rod to him that last time, West let his mind wander to another place. One that didn't exist but where he could be with Lexi and without all the other bullshit and baggage plowing them under.

"Is that what you want?" She shifted until she faced him, instead of the far wall. "For me to go away?"

The affirmative response lingered right there. West tried to choke it out but couldn't. "I don't know."

"Know this." With her fingers under his chin, she moved his head. Her mouth came down on his in a heated kiss filled with longing and a touch of sadness. "I don't want to go anywhere without you."

Pearce popped up at the entrance to the closed-in area. "I hate to break up your final hours together."

At the sound of his voice, Lexi broke away from West. She immediately regretted the lack of his touch. Heat warmed her when she sat close and hands wandered. A cold chill returned whenever they separated. Maybe it operated as a metaphor. All she knew was that being with him, taking care of him, helping him see the man she saw, became for her an all-encompassing goal.

"You've done enough." She mumbled the response because she was feeling hollow and grumbly.

"Look at the good side, West. I'm saving you time and heartache because she isn't your type." Pearce motioned for them to stand up. "Despite the shaky start and the repeated failures, she's actually quite lovely. Much stronger than the type of woman I thought you'd prefer."

West didn't move. "I'm going to fucking kill you."

"From what I can see, you can't even stand."

They were only prolonging the inevitable. Whatever Pearce had planned—and from the smirk, it was something big—he needed to unleash it on them. The waiting tore her apart. She could deal with the terror pounding her every second if Pearce didn't toy with her.

"What do you want now?" she asked, not bothering to act as submissive and willing to deal with this insanity.

"Your attendance." Pearce leaned in and grabbed for her leg.

That fast, West shifted. He got to his knees without a visible struggle and put his body in front of hers. "Do not touch her."

Pearce watched it all without any outward reaction. "You're coming, too."

Knowing this could blow into a full-fledged battle, Lexi rushed to cool things down again. She slid along the wall as she stood. The move put her right behind West. "You've made your point."

"I actually haven't, which is why you're both still alive."

"Attendance?" West asked as his body continued to block hers.

"Benton has been waiting for you. It's time for you to see what we have here and how close you came to uncovering it, only to fail again." Pearce nodded at her. "Help him up."

She waited until he turned around to slip her arm around West's waist. "He sure does talk a lot."

"Do not engage," West whispered back.

"How can you walk?" She whispered the question, sure that West didn't want Pearce hearing the real answer.

He lifted some of his weight off her shoulders and his steps fell surer. "I'm fine."

Doubts smashed into her. For a second she wondered how much was an act. West wouldn't be one to show weakness, but she wouldn't put it past him to pretend to be worse off than he was to gain an advantage.

But then her mind shot back to that fence and the electricity. No, West might put on a good show, but he was injured. And he needed her to be something she generally wasn't—strong.

People scurried around from one section of the caves to another as Pearce guided West and Lexi through the tunnels. There was an elaborate transit system and tracks that allowed for some sort of vehicle to get in and out without trouble. They turned the corner and passed a stockpile of something. Crates lined the walls.

Lexi looked at the writing on the outside but couldn't pick out the language. "What is all this?"

"An aerosol spray of death. Well, the delivery mechanism for it." Pearce stopped long enough to lift the lid off one of the crates. He brushed his finger over a tube about eight inches in length.

She had no idea what she was looking at. West stared at the contents as if trying to mentally catalog exactly what he saw.

"It's brilliant, really." Pearce spun the canister around in his hand. "We weaponize a toxin based on the chemical structure of the one West and his friends at Alliance stole from me, and then it goes in these, which go in those." He pointed at crates stacked on the other side of the area.

"Toxin you stole from a government lab," West said, piping up for the first time since they left the cell. "I'm betting the delivery system is government-issue and stolen as well."

Pearce stopped moving around and faced West. "So, only the government can make weapons these days? That seems unfair."

"You're a demented asshole."

Pearce continued talking as if West hadn't spoken. "We've figured out a way to launch it and disseminate it over a town or a city. Five minutes to create small-scale Armageddon, and by small scale I mean tens of thousands of people, maybe more."

The words sunk in. Pearce talked about annihilation as if it were a code word in a video game. "You've lost your goddamned mind."

He shrugged. "Think of it as capitalism."

Lexi let her fingers tangle with West's as they

walked. Not overtly holding hands, but brushing up against each other in silence. "I thought this was about revenge."

"He likes to say that and insist the CIA and the US and Ward and my bosses and everyone else screwed him, but this is about old-fashioned greed." West rested a hand on his hip, looking as if he regained strength with each passing minute. "His pension wasn't high enough and he's throwing a tantrum."

"You can't tweak me, West." Pearce returned the canister to the crate and shut the lid.

"Don't plan to."

Satisfaction poured off of Pearce. "Good."

West smiled. "I'd rather put a bullet in your brain."

Lexi was all for that. She'd hand him the ammunition and pass him more weapons.

Pearce let out a long exaggerated sigh and turned to her. "As I told you, he's not really human."

"I plan to cheer when he kills you," she said, and she would. She'd never been one to welcome violence. With Pearce, she prayed for it.

"I take it back. She might be the perfect woman for you." Pearce looked disgusted by the idea. "Too bad neither one of you will live long enough for us to know."

19

WITH EACH step West felt better, more like himself. The aches and pains combined until his body went numb. He ignored the throbbing in his shoulder and forced the haze from his brain. He silently bargained with his body for two solid hours of adrenaline-filled hate. That would fuel him to finish this assignment. He could collapse later.

Their footsteps fell uneven in thuds in the dirt. A series of lights attached to the walls and fed by thick wires lined their path as they walked through the maze of crates and past rooms filled with people working. The details flooded his brain. It seemed like they devised the dispersal method and were perfecting the toxin. That meant Alliance had time to end this, but not much.

The important thing: now he knew about the weapons. Leave it to Pearce to upchuck the details on some huge walk-through. The need to impress everyone with his brilliance had finally tripped him up. It was an amateur mistake. He'd bought into West being unable to move or process anything.

They made a final turn and stepped into a wider hall that dumped into a larger open one. This one held chairs and a table. Almost looked like a command center of sorts. But that's not what jumped out at West first.

"Raheel." West walked right up to the man. Seriously considered delivering a knockout blow, and would have if it didn't destroy the image he'd crafted of being near death. "What a surprise."

Lexi let go of West's arm and stepped in front of him. Put her body right between him and Raheel and verbally went after him. "You're in on this."

"Alexis. What are you doing here?" Raheel snapped out the words as other men walked around him on the way out of the chamber and into the hall.

Fury pounded off her as she balled her hands into fists. "Dying."

West reached over and took one of her clenched fists in his. He wanted to send her the silent message to calm down. Going after one of the men would bring all of them running.

Pearce joined them. "Is there a problem?"

Raheel held eye contact with Lexi for a few more seconds then turned to Pearce. "This is the man who attacked me."

West was sorry now he hadn't killed Raheel. Looking at Lexi's red cheeks and her scathing glare, he guessed she would have been in favor of that solution as well. She'd believed in Raheel. That sort of betrayal stayed with you.

"Then you'll be happy to know we plan to torture him some more before killing him," Pearce said as he circled the small group. He continued until he stood in front of the computers set up on the table by the far wall.

West couldn't see the screens but it looked as if Pearce was tracking something. West hoped Alliance had him twitchy and chasing his shadow. That would make it more likely for him to mess up again. Then he could pounce on Pearce. He saved his energy to do just that.

Raheel's gaze bounced back to Lexi. "And the woman?"

"Her, too." Pearce waved off the question. "Neither one of them is useful to us except as entertainment."

Lexi didn't show any outward reaction but West felt her shudder beside him. The woman amazed him. She'd seen a horror show and stayed on her feet. Letting her go was going to rip him apart, piece by piece, until there was nothing left but that killing machine everyone wanted him to be.

There was movement at the end of the hall. A man came into view. "Jake, show our guests in."

West drank in the details. This guy might be forty. Regular height, mousy brown hair. No distinct features. Dark pants and top, so no flashy clothes. He was the type who could blend in anywhere because nothing about him stuck out. Not handsome but not odd-looking, which would have drawn attention. Just your average accountant from Tulsa.

No introduction needed. "You're Benton."

West flipped through his mental Rolodex. What he called the "Asshole Contingent," a group of the world's most dangerous criminals. Nothing about this guy looked familiar. If he'd worked the system for years, he'd managed to weasel under rocks and pop up out of nowhere. Keep his identity hidden. Now, West added a face to the blank spot where only Benton's name used to be.

"That's not my real name, of course." Benton carried a metal case no more than six-by-nine inches but thicker than an average briefcase. He set it down on the table while it was still handcuffed to him.

Without question, he stored this new toxin in the briefcase. West made a mental note to cut the guy's wrist off and take the case.

"Who are you?" Lexi asked in a voice filled with confusion.

"A businessman." Benton rested his hands on top of the case. "Someone just trying to make a living."

"You're a piece of shit." West wanted to draw his attention. See what moves he'd make and how hard he was to shake.

The guy didn't disappoint. His gaze flicked to West. "You should learn when to be quiet."

An interesting response. His cool slipped when confronted. Not much, but enough to reveal that he was not trained. He didn't have the control needed to work in the field. That raised a whole new set of questions.

Benton lived on the fringes. In a cave here. In a compound in Morocco that West had helped reduce to a pile of rubble during the search for the guy. Benton had been named as the secret source behind international bombings and providing the weapons that tipped internal and border conflicts from one side to the other all over the world.

His fingerprints were on a list of terrorist activities, even though his actual prints weren't anywhere. He thrived on creating chaos and had the resources to bring that world's most dangerous people to the table to listen to his demands.

West watched him stand at the table now and couldn't figure out what it was about this man that made other men turn. Pearce had been at the top of his game and highly respected, yet he ended up serving Benton, a man who had come on the scene less than a decade ago without any fanfare and gone on to become an international enigma.

West had expected someone a little more impressive looking. This guy was . . . soft. Not fat, not thin. Nothing extraordinary.

Benton motioned for them to come forward. When West stayed put, Raheel pushed Lexi. As far as West was concerned, Raheel was inching closer and closer to a bullet. They'd taken his weapons but West watched every move and knew he could grab one. Then he'd light this motherfucker up.

"Jake showed you around. What do you think of the

place?" Benton held out an arm as if showing off a new mansion he'd purchased instead of a pile of rock carved into the side of a mountain that buzzed with the sound of voices and moving equipment.

"I liked your place in Morocco better." West smiled. "You know, the one I blew into a million pieces with some of your men inside. Shame you weren't there at the time."

Fury swept over Benton's features. "You shouldn't have reminded me. I loved that house."

Lexi beat him to a response. "Someone should blow you off the Earth."

Benton's smile faded. "That attitude is what started all of this." He nodded toward one of the open chairs. "Alexis, sit."

"If the army knows you're here, you're safe." She remained standing until Raheel pushed her into the chair. A move that earned him a killing glare before she turned back to Benton. "You can let us go."

"That's the problem." Benton tapped his fingers against the case. "I have purchased a few generals but it's hard to find loyal followers when you can't definitely state which side you'll sell the battle-ending weapon to. But that's my worry, not yours."

Benton shrugged as if to say "Oh well," and West had to beat back the urge to punch him. He acted as if dealing in death was no big deal. He might as well have been selling vacuums or time shares.

Raheel tugged on West's arm, then pointed to the chair. "Sit."

"Let Mr. Weston Brown stand." Benton eyed him, running his gaze over West as if assessing his opponent. "He strikes me as the type who would want to die on his feet, and tiring him out sounds like a smart idea."

"You've done enough." Lexi sat up straight with her hands on her lap. Every line of her body was stiff and tension seemed to edge her tone.

Benton leaned forward as if they were having a friendly chat rather than him justifying death and destruction. "I don't think you understand how much trouble West has caused me."

She made a face. "You sound like a child."

The expression on Benton's face went from pathologically friendly to fury. His features fell and the underlying anger punched through. "Do not talk to me about children."

Interesting. West stored that away for later. And there would be a later. He knew Lexi performed a mental countdown as she waited for whatever this guy had in store for them. Now that West had met him, he knew the chances of them surviving had increased. There was no way this unimpressive piece of garbage could outsmart Alliance. He might be ahead now because he'd had privacy on his side, but that was over.

Lexi continued to stare at Benton. "What is wrong with you?"

But he had to keep her alive long enough to get them out of there. He put a hand on her shoulder. "Lexi, stop."

"You should listen to him." Whatever bond Benton thought he'd make with her disappeared. He dismissed her the same way he seemed to dismiss everyone else. "I know our spy is injured but he's proven very resourceful. Tie them both up."

Raheel reached for Lexi, and West's hand shot out. He grabbed the other man's arm and squeezed, letting him know that even torture hadn't sapped his strength. "Do not touch her."

"This is no longer interesting to me. Tie them up." Benton looked from Raheel over to Pearce. "Well?"

The clicking of computer keys stopped as Pearce left the monitor to join them. He had a gun in his hand and aimed it at Lexi's head. "Is it time to start killing people?"

He sounded far too excited by the prospect. Whatever soul he'd once had was gone now. Traded for toxin and cash. But so long as the gun stayed on Lexi, West knew his moves remained limited.

"Torture the woman," Benton said.

Raheel's hands came down on her shoulders and she tried to squirm away from him. "No!"

"She means nothing to me." West forced his body to remain still as he delivered the information. Kept his voice and expression neutral. They only wanted her because of him. This was to punish him.

"Then you won't care what I do to her." Benton slid his case off the table.

"My men are on the ground." West knew the ploy

wouldn't work. This was all about keeping her as safe as possible while he stalled. His strength inched back and he silently worked on an exit strategy. He just needed time . . . and Raheel's gun.

"They won't find us." Benton's voice remained strong, but the fact that he kept talking meant something.

"I found you." West figured this guy had to fear something. West might even respect Benton if he were smart enough to connect the dots and realize he'd come up against the one intelligence group that would stop him.

Raheel bound his hands with a zip tie. The dumbass. West conducted drills seeing how fast he could shred one and get free.

Benton's gaze lingered for a few extra seconds before he turned to Pearce. "Take them away. We have work to do."

Raheel walked them back toward the cell. Lexi could almost hear West thinking. There was no way he was going to let them get trapped deep within the caves.

She'd watched him confront Benson and mentally write off Pearce. Injured or not, tortured or not, West was the man in control of that room back there. She just hoped his body could deliver after all it had been through. He should not be standing, let alone planning an attack of some sort.

And that was what he was doing. She could see the

wheels spin. She decided to help by taking her own shots at Raheel. "How can you do this?"

He waved her off. "Shut up."

West glanced over his shoulder at the armed man behind them. "Is your friend Javed in on this, too?"

"He told you to be quiet." Pearce turned to the left instead of the right.

Lexi didn't have to search her memory. This hallway led them straight back to the torture chamber. Her body reacted with a complete shutdown. Her muscles tightened and her mouth went dry. She tried to move her fingers but they'd gone numb.

"I have nothing left to lose," West said as they turned the corner.

"We'll see about that." Pearce gestured to Raheel, then to that horrid piece of fence. "Put her in the chains."

The words hit her like a shot to the chest. "West."

Raheel grabbed her from behind as Pearce kept the gun turned on West. "No smartass comment now?"

West stayed silent. Her insides whirled. She heard a screaming in her head and was surprised not to hear it echo through the caves.

"That's a shame." Pearce motioned for two guards in the hallway to come inside. "Tie him to the chair so he has a front row seat for this."

Raheel stepped forward with his hand still clamped over her wrist. "We should torture him, not her."

She hated that idea. Hated Raheel. Right now she agreed with West and hated this country.

"Watching this happen to her *will* torture him." Pearce grabbed the wire and handed it to the guard behind West. "See, West here has a savior complex. I'm sure there's some psychological reason behind it having to do with his fucked up childhood, but the point is that watching her bleed will be worse for him than ripping his own skin off, though that will happen eventually."

West stood there with his arms tied behind his back. "When did you get so fucking sick?"

Pearce just smiled. "I'm going to need a bigger knife for you." He headed for the door, but not before giving his guards new orders. "Shoot his other shoulder if you need to subdue him."

"Where are you going?" Raheel called after Pearce.

"I have something special in mind for West." Pearce stepped into the hall. "Get them ready."

Once he was gone, Lexi looked to West. He gave her a short nod and jerked his arms. The zip tie went flying. Then the room erupted in chaos. Something whizzed by her head. She didn't know what it was until one of the men behind West grabbed his neck and dropped to the floor. Her gaze flipped back to Raheel where he stood in a knife throwing with an empty hand where his blade should be.

In a blur of movement, West swung around and leveled the other guard with a punch to the head. The man stumbled back but stayed on his feet. The guard reached for his radio just as West nailed him in the chest with a kick. He made a half-choking, half-gagging sound as he hit the wall. West was on him a second later. Bent down only long enough to remove the knife from the other man's throat and plunge it into this one.

The flurry took only a few seconds but moved in slow motion in her head. She heard the grunts and saw the flashes of movement. When the world spun back to regular speed again, Raheel was beside her and West stood a few feet in front of her with fresh blood seeping from his wound and a knife in his hand.

West took a step forward, fury obvious in every line of his body. After a quick visual check of her and the cut of her binding, he aimed his homicidal glare at Raheel. "I should kill you."

"I saved her by throwing the knife." He visibly swallowed. "Saved both of you."

West nodded. "That is the only reason you're still breathing, but I can make that stop."

With their arms freed and men on the ground, the power balance had shifted. She saw one problem, despite the hammering of stress through her. "We're still stuck in here."

"I can get you out," Raheel said.

Before they could move, Lexi asked the one question that buzzed in her head, weighing down everything else. "Javed?"

"He was watching over the garage and saw you taken here. He found me and asked for help to get you out." Raheel's gaze flipped from Lexi to West. "That's why I'm here today."

"You seem pretty comfortable walking around," Lexi said. "No one is trying to kill you." And from what she could tell, the people manning this group liked to kill.

Raheel's attention never left West as he bent down and removed the weapons from the two dead men on the floor and pocketed them both. "The general I worked for brought me here."

That made sense in her head. She couldn't pin down the nationalities of the people here. She heard English and no accents, so maybe they were American. The few Pakistanis seemed, like Raheel, to have been re-cruited. This was not a homegrown operation. It didn't even feel like a terrorist cell. The Pakistani army would want this group out as much as she did.

Maybe this was nothing more than one man's insane crusade. She just knew from the look of the guards that they'd had military training and would not be easy to get around.

None of that absolved Raheel, and she reminded him of that. "You're in on this."

"I didn't know this was about chemical weapons." He shook his head. "I thought this was a secret army assignment."

No, he had wanted to believe that. She could see the truth in his eyes. He probably got extra money and looked the other way when confronted with the obvi-ous clues. "I don't buy it."

"Hey." West glanced out the doorway then back to Raheel. "Get us out of here and I won't kill you. That's the best deal I have for you right now."

"There are too many guards."

West aimed his gun at Raheel. "You have ten seconds."

20

WARD AND Josiah made their way toward the compound. They got beyond the fence without trouble and now had to get through a wall of men. They needed to get far enough so that when the diversion came they could capitalize on it and sneak into the caves.

For now, they hid between two trucks. The next stretch of this run would take them into the open. With his messed-up hand, Ward could shoot but not with anywhere near the accuracy Josiah could. That left one option for how to go forward.

Ward pulled out a second gun. He'd been practicing shooting with his left hand and now was the time to use his new skills. "I'll draw fire."

Josiah's concentration didn't break. He continued to scan the area. "No."

Running Delta, Josiah possessed a leadership mindset. He made decisions without hesitation. Ward appreciated that but he was in charge.

"That's the only choice. You get to the edge of that rock ledge." He didn't give Josiah a chance to argue. He took off. Slipped out just far enough for anyone watching to pick him out.

At first nothing happened, but Josiah didn't wait. Keeping low, he slid around the hood of the truck and darted out. Took off at a dead run.

He got ten feet out and the shooting started. Men fired from above.

Zigzagging, Josiah got to the next waiting place then turned and fired. He picked off the gunman at the end, then the one next to him as Ward ran across the open span. His sharpshooting skills hadn't lost their accuracy.

The sound of gunfire brought men running from every direction. An alarm sounded and bullets pinged around them. Trucks started and the open yard broke into chaos.

Josiah dropped down and pushed his back against the wall as he caught his breath. "I think we have their attention."

"Did you notice the men? Not Pakistani." Ward needed to get closer to take photos and check IDs. He had no problem killing them first.

The techs back at the Warehouse could run the facial recognition programs and lock down identities. Give them an idea where this stream of mercenaries originated from. There seemed to be an endless supply of guns for hire. They had no loyalty. They loved their paychecks and killing.

"Americans?" Josiah asked in his British accent.

"Some." Ward expected he'd know more once he got

closer and heard voices. Right now the yelling morphed together with the banging and shooting into a dull roar. "Time check?"

Josiah fired then looked at his watch. "We're on countdown."

Men moved in from two sides. They were pinned down by fire and needed the diversion. But with the communications blackout, they were stuck with the hard start time and had to survive until then.

"To your right." Josiah kept up a constant barrage of shots. He aimed and fired and men fell around them.

Ward glanced to the right and saw men pile into a truck. They signaled to each other and weapons were drawn. If the truck rammed the rocks, which is what he would do in their position, he and Josiah would be trapped. "We need to move."

"Nowhere to go."

Ward ducked and fired. One out of every three of his shots hit a target. Thank God Josiah's percentage was near perfect. But that wouldn't help if a truck ran him over. "This is about to get messy."

"We thrive on messy." A bullet ricocheted off the rocks and zipped across the side of Josiah's head. He grabbed his ear. "Shit."

"You hit?"

Josiah lowered his hand to a palm full of blood. "Just grazed."

Ward knew Josiah would play through it. But they had another problem. "I'm running out of ammo."

"Same."

Ward was about to call a second time check when the truck started rolling. Men hung out of the sides shooting. The rapid gunfire cut off all other sounds. Shots kicked up the dirt all around them and kept them hiding behind the rocks.

"Fuck me." Josiah reached for the weapon by his ankle.

"Time?"

Josiah shook his head without looking. "Not yet."

An engine rumbled and tires rolled. Ward knew the truck headed directly for them. The gunfire was meant to lock them in for when the hit came. Smart move. He was reluctantly impressed.

That didn't mean he'd give in. He lifted up, peeking around the rock. They had to jump out at the last minute and run. Then keep running.

Men closed in. A line of guards stood only twenty feet away, ready to pick him and Josiah off as soon as they moved. That cut off most of their options. He tried to work through a new one.

A huge boom cut off his thinking. One minute the truck headed straight for them. The next it flipped and burst into a ball of fire. Men on the ground dove out of the way. Bodies flew through the air and pieces of debris rained down.

"What the fuck?" Josiah pushed up beside Ward.

As they watched, men ran around on fire and the focus on the ground switched from attack to rescue.

Smoke billowed and flames crackled. The wind caught the fire and flames jumped from the vehicle to a tent.

Around the side of the chaos came a figure, running bent low and headed right for them. Josiah lifted his gun but Ward pushed the barrel back down.

"This one's with us." He would have recognized that cocky walk anywhere.

The fire roared, and the men were too busy screaming at each other as they tried to drag bodies away from the explosion. The fire dragged everyone's attention away from the caves, but they still had to find West and get out before the flames closed off access.

Mike slid in beside them in a cloud of dust. "How was that for a diversion?"

"Needs some work." Josiah took the extra ammo from Mike's outstretched hand. "You were early."

"You're welcome." Mike smiled as he glanced at Ward. "Nice shooting."

The men knew this was a sensitive subject. Ward appreciated the humor. "I hit stuff."

"Like Josiah?" Mike's question had Josiah reaching for his ear again.

Ward reloaded. "Thought about it."

"Thank Harlan for this light show. The guy is good with a stinger missile. Who knew?" Mike balanced on the balls of his feet. "He's ready for round two, so it's going to get fucking loud."

Josiah nodded. "Time to grab West."

"Let's go." Ward was already moving.

The three of them formed an inverted vee pattern as they jogged. Men poured out of the entrance to the caves. Josiah and Mike took them out one at a time. Something burned across Ward's forearm and Mike grunted at one point. But they kept moving.

"Where do we look?" Mike asked.

Josiah took out his knife. "Knowing West, he'll find us."

Ward hoped that was true.

The boom shook the ground. Raheel slammed into the cave wall. West put his arm around Lexi's head and tucked her against him. The pain in his shoulder pounded but he blocked it out, as he had been for hours.

The rocks muffled the sound but West recognized it. An explosion. Not just any explosion. One that sent people running. That could only mean one thing. Alliance had arrived.

Raheel steadied his body with a hand against the wall. "What is that?"

"The cavalry." The best group of operatives on the planet. The finest men West knew.

He should have guessed they'd blow Pakistan apart and risk an international incident and the higher-ups' wrath to bring him out. They wanted the intel and the information on the weapons. That was their job. But Ward made it clear that they would not leave bodies behind. Ever.

Raheel frowned. "What?"

"My team is here."

"Thank God." Lexi closed her eyes and whispered the comment against his chest.

Footsteps sounded behind them. West turned, ready to shoot, but Raheel grabbed his arm. He pulled them deeper into a side tunnel, tight against the wall in a claustrophobic space that should barely hold two of them, let alone an extra person and one at West's side. They squished in and waited.

A few seconds later a group of men rushed by. This time West picked up accents. Eastern Europeans. These were the nasty guns for hire. Looked like Benton had some interesting contacts.

As soon as the group passed, they stepped out of the small enclosure and Raheel started talking again. He kept his voice low but the urgency was unmistakable. "How do you know the explosion was for you?"

"No one knows how to make noise like the men of Alliance." And this was intentional. If Josiah wanted to go in quiet, he would have. They lit up the day for a reason. Possibly as a signal to let him know it was clear. West didn't care so long as they were going.

Ooh-rah.

Lexi pushed her hair back over her shoulder. "Let's hope they know who to shoot and who not to."

The sexy woman had a point. His team wouldn't shoot unarmed women for fun, but it was hard to tell the hostiles from the nonhostiles in this type of situation, with smoke billowing all around. With the men scurrying and the firepower in the building, not to mention the chemicals spread around, they had to exercise extra caution.

"New plan." He hated suggesting this but it was the right thing for her. It would keep her safe. He looked at Raheel. "You take Lexi and head out."

She pushed away from him. "You are coming with us."

Before his eyes she morphed into the strong, sure, confident woman he met that first night at the clinic and had run with since then. She wasn't taking any of his shit. He loved this side of her. All sides of her, really, but he didn't get her this far only to have her get clipped by a stray bullet.

"They will fire on me," Raheel said.

Now was not the time to discuss international politics and the Alliance understanding that a specific ethnic background didn't make you a bad guy. Hell, they'd been tracking Pearce, and he was an American asshole. Looked like Benton was, too. Being a bad guy knew no international bounds.

Besides, Raheel would have an advantage. He'd be holding one of the assets Alliance needed, and Josiah knew not to shoot. "They'll see Lexi and take her."

She waved a hand in front of West's face. "I'm right here."

He grabbed her hand and pressed it against his chest. "I need to stop Benton."

"You need help. You're injured and you said your men are right here. Let them handle this." She did not give an inch.

Not his style, but before he could come up with a response, a man popped out of the tunnel entrance in front of him and then quickly disappeared again.

This was not the place for a firefight, but they had no choice.

"Get back." He shoved Lexi against Raheel and both fell against the wall. West pressed back as tight as he could but he was an open target.

Three men came out shooting. Tom passed behind them and kept going, heading out into another tunnel that could go anywhere. West wanted to follow but focused on the targets he could see.

Gunfire rang back and forth. Something stung the skin on his upper arm, this time on the uninjured side. Just what he needed. He could shoot with either arm but needed at least one. Good thing it felt like it skimmed the fabric and little more.

They traded shots, Raheel and West taking turns firing and stepping back. The chaos and noise had Lexi wincing but she held out her hand in what West took to be a request for a weapon. He ignored that. But they couldn't keep this pace up. Eventually other men would come running and they could get trapped. West knew he had to move out, draw fire.

He looked at Raheel. "I'll swing around and shoot everyone. You cover me."

"Damn it, no." Lexi grabbed his arm.

The move put her in the firing line, and West lost it. "Get down."

As he moved in front of her, one of the hostiles fell forward. Wrong direction. The other two spun around, and the move gave West the perfect shot. He fired twice, one to the back of each head, and watched them crumple.

He heard shuffling then and prepared to unload again just as Javed stepped into view. He'd abandoned his uniform for street clothes. His pants and shirt were stained with blood and his eyes were wild, as if an adrenaline rush had him in its grip.

He motioned to them. "Come."

"You're here?" Lexi blinked but didn't move. She had a hand wrapped around West's arm, and her fingers tightened.

West was willing to give the guy the benefit of the doubt. He could always put a bullet in him later if this turned out to be a ruse. "Any more hostiles?"

"We'll have to shoot our way through."

That worked for him. "Done."

Javed turned and ran right into another man's chest. A familiar chest attached to a guy with a furious scowl.

West almost smiled.

Guns came up on both sides and the shouting started. Raheel looked ready to fire.

"Everyone stop." West pointed to Mike, Ward, and Josiah. "They belong with me. And, Mike, the guy you're trying to strangle is Javed."

"So?"

Ward stared at West. "You were a hard man to find."

"I thought we should leave you here." Mike didn't ease up on his grip on Javed. "And should I let this guy go?"

"Javed and Raheel are with us." Lexi straightened her shoulders and stepped up next to West. "They're Fearless Five."

She acted like they were at a fancy dinner instead of in a shithole in Pakistan. West had to touch her then. He put a hand against her lower back, ignoring the twinge in his shoulder when he moved it. The stares from his team members also blew by him. He'd worry about that later.

"Lexi, this is Ward, the boss, and Mike." He then pointed to Josiah. "You know this guy."

Mike pushed Javed to the side and looked at West. "You done being lazy and ready to get back to work?"

Lexi took another step. This one put her half in front of West. "He's been tortured and needs help."

"Do you?" Ward asked him.

Mike snorted. "That would be a first. Not the torture. You seem to get off on that."

West thought Lexi's wording—that he needed help—bordered on offensive, but the way she rose to his defense definitely did not suck. He put a hand on her shoulder and leaned down with his lips close to her ear. "He's kidding."

Mike's eyebrow rose. "Well now."

Josiah nodded. "Told you."

"This isn't an official Pakistani army operation." West decided talking quickly and ignoring the byplay was the right way to go. Plus, he needed the information out there. "Benton is here."

Ward frowned. "You've seen him?"

"Yeah." The other men nodded. They had the facts and would all know this was good news. They had a face now and could get to tracking. But Benton wasn't the only ass-wipe in town. "So is Pearce."

Ward waved that off. "Yeah, we let him out and sent him in your direction on purpose."

The strangled sound came first. Then Lexi brushed by West to stand right in front of Ward. "What is wrong with you?"

One of his eyebrows rose. "Excuse me?"

"West almost died."

"I'm fine." He understood the plan and admired Ward for taking the risk. And watching Ward handle Lexi when she was spitting mad was something to see.

West knew he should step in but he liked seeing her all fiery. He also knew since Ward lived with Tasha, he had plenty of experience with pissed off women who didn't back down. They were a special breed. West never thought he'd get lucky enough to spend time with one.

Then she turned on him. "You are not okay."

But there were limits to how much West could take in front of the other men. He had a reputation to uphold. "Enough."

"Interesting." Mike whistled and glanced over at Josiah. "You were right."

Josiah nodded. "Told you."

And that was likely the end of peace as West knew it. Once these guys got hold of something, they chewed it until they choked on it. He had never been in the hot seat but feared he'd take that role now.

Fine. He would not apologize for wanting her. That was something they could deal with back at the office. Right now they needed to find fresh air. "We need to move."

Ward held up his hand as he looked at his watch. "Wait for it."

"What?" Lexi asked.

The second explosion rattled the rock walls. Pebbles cascaded down and the ground shook as if an earthquake had hit. The team members stood there and rode it out. Raheel and Javed flattened themselves against the tumbling walls.

West had the best job. Holding Lexi, even as she squirmed to see what was happening.

He looked over her head at Ward. "Diversion?"

Ward smiled. "You impressed?"

"Pretty much."

21

THEY FANNED out in front of her as they led her through the cave tunnels. No one jumped out at them and the guns stayed silent.

Lexi went from trying to calm the fear bouncing around inside of her to battling back a false sense of being completely safe. Probably had something to do with the wall of hulking men surrounding her.

They were not out of trouble. Men and explosions and guns all wound around them, but as she held onto the back of West's shirt in a tight grip, she felt real hope for the first time in hours. The worries about West being electrified in front of her fell away. This group, the men and how they joked with each other through the stress, how lethal they all looked, had her mind turning from survival to something more. She wanted the men who hurt West to pay.

He called to her over his shoulder, "You okay back there?"

She wanted to hug him. Give him another kiss. Since Mike kept smiling at her, she refrained. She had a feeling he was waiting for a public display of affection so he could bug West about it.

She settled for leaning into him, almost touching her lips against his neck. "I'll breathe better back at the clinic."

For the briefest of seconds he rested his head against hers. "I'll be happy when you're on a plane to DC."

Not exactly a location that popped into her mind. "What's in DC?"

"It's where I live."

A new kind of hope bloomed inside her. Blame it on the adrenaline or the danger, she didn't care. Something was happening between them. What she felt for him was not gratitude for being alive. She wanted him. Wanted to get to know him and give them a chance. To do that, his comment would have to mean something.

"Do you two want to be alone?" Josiah asked as he and Mike shifted positions and Mike took point.

Accent or not, she was not in the mood. "Do you want me to kick you in the shins?"

Josiah shot Ward a quick look. "I like her."

Ward laughed. "You're not alone."

She decided that was a good sign and didn't push it. She also had to step back because she kept running up West's back and kicking the back of his boots with the front of hers.

They got to a fork and the first two men repeated the system they'd been using the whole way through this exit strategy. They checked first, and when they gave the all clear signal, they all turned the last corner. This time they broke into an open area just inside the tunnel maze. They'd made it the whole way from the back to the front of the cave without running into more gunfire.

When they moved into the fading sunshine, flames rose into the sky in front of them. She stared in awe at the destruction around her. It was as if a bomb had gone off. Overturned trucks and debris littered the area. There was a huge hole off to one side with scorched earth around it.

She saw bodies and a line of trucks driving away from the compound. "What happened?"

Mike gave her a quick smile. "That was us."

"We have men to catch." Ward looked at West. "We need to break apart, and you're the only one who's seen Benton."

"Raheel has too."

"Good." Ward grabbed Raheel by the shoulder. "You'll come with me and I'll take Mike."

West shook his head. "We need to get Lexi out of here."

Interesting how he could compartmentalize and forget all that happened to him. If he wasn't going to fill his team in on what happened, she would. "You still need a doctor."

"Aren't you a doctor?" Mike asked.

West cut him off. "Don't ask."

"There's no time for any of this." Ward glanced into

the distance. "We have to handle the remaining area and do it fast because the rest of Delta can only hold off the Pakistani army for so long."

Javed stepped forward. "What should I do?"

Seeing the exhaustion on her friend's face was a harsh reminder. She thought about all she'd been through over the last few hours, but it now looked like she'd be able to walk away. Javed and Raheel would be mired in this. There could be serious repercussions.

Ward continued to issue orders. "You need to figure out how to buy us time before more people come."

West shifted her behind him and stepped toward his boss. "Ward—"

"Sorry, man. She's still your asset." Ward blew out a long breath. "She's in this with us until we can get her out, and that's not now."

Asset? That was the one thing Lexi clued in on. "I have a name."

"We can spend more time chatting later." Ward clapped his hands. "Go."

West watched Ward and the others split off to the right. Then he took Josiah and Lexi and went left. Not that he could concentrate. Part of him needed Lexi out of the firing line. So many shots and none had hit her. That was pure luck. He didn't want to push it.

Not that he had a choice, but he could be clear on his expectations. "You don't move without me telling you it's okay, got it?"

Josiah shook his head as he stepped away and gave them a few feet of space. "You need to work on your romance."

As if he didn't know that. He hadn't even tried romance until her. "Shut the fuck up."

Josiah's head shot up again. "We ready?"

That depended on her answer. West looked at her. "Lexi?"

She shrugged. "I heard you."

"There." Josiah clapped. "Let's go."

They weren't even close to an agreement. "She's purposely not agreeing."

"Gee, I wonder why." Josiah turned around. "If I were Pearce, where would I hide?"

West wanted to stay on this topic. He thought about pushing the issue, but the determined look on Lexi's face told him she was not open to a reasonable discussion. "Wherever a weasel would go."

Josiah wiped a hand over his mouth. "Take a truck and—"

"He's in the caves." Lexi pointed at the opening to the tunnels.

They both looked at her. "What?"

"I saw Tom when West was shooting at those other men." She talked and her hands moved as she explained. "He slipped into a tunnel on the other side of where we are. We didn't pass by him again, so I'm thinking he stayed in there."

"I saw him, too." West searched his memory for

Tom's exact location the last time he saw him. "Pearce isn't moving without Tom, so I'd bet they're together."

Josiah frowned. "He had to get out."

"Why?" No, this strategy made perfect sense to West. When he got trapped here years ago, he had to find a place to hide. The army and search teams looked for people buried under the snow. He went from hiding place to hiding place and waited everyone out. "You hunker down and wait it out. Let us clear and then slip out before the army comes looking."

Josiah hummed. "Risky."

That didn't convince West. "Safer than dealing with us."

"I like your lack of ego," she said in a dry voice. "And I'm coming with you so don't even try to come up with some weird place to stash me."

Josiah smiled. "Time to rope-a-dope."

"What does that mean?" she asked.

They ran this drill all the time. West usually did it with Bravo, and he'd practiced with Delta before they got on the plane to come to Pakistan. But it all came down to the same point. "Josiah is going to try to get himself shot."

Lexi sighed. "I don't understand you guys at all."

"Not the first time we've heard that." West shifted again Lexi until she stood behind him. "You stay between us."

"You just do what you have to do and I'll be fine."

Josiah took over. "Here we go."

They stepped back inside. The whole thing struck West as nuts. It was like climbing out of hell then turning around and jumping back in. Of course, that described most of his time with Alliance. They were always walking in while others ran out.

After a few turns the caves all looked the same. West guessed Pearce was counting on that. Hoping they'd get lost while he snuck out. And he needed to go soon or risk getting trapped in there when the army arrived. That meant time and the advantage were on their side.

Lexi tugged on his belt. "Right."

The sensation had West's brain cells misfiring for a second. "What?"

She leaned in and whispered right against his ear, "It's the one on the right."

He thought so, too, even though nothing about the rock formation looked familiar. Every cave had the same things except for the few with the chemicals and rockets stored in them. West wanted to remove all of that but there was no way to do it. And finding his way back to the tunnel with those crates would involve a huge mental exercise.

He put her back against the wall and he and Josiah took positions on either side of the opening. He couldn't talk and risk being found out, so he lifted a finger to his lips and stared at her until she nodded.

Josiah signaled and held out three fingers to start the countdown. They went on one. Josiah slipped in low and moved fast. West followed, ready to fire. The area stretched before them. The space was long and thin. West couldn't see the endpoint at the dark end but he didn't want to stray too far from the opening and from Lexi.

Just as he thought about her, he turned around. Even though he told her to stay still, the silence bothered him. Something felt off. With a signal to Josiah, he headed back to her. He looked out into the hall and she was gone.

He snapped his fingers and Josiah turned around. He frowned in question. But whatever he saw had him hurrying back to West's side.

"She's gone." Fighting back the rage inside him, West managed to keep his voice calm and low.

"What the fuck?" Josiah mouthed the words more than said them.

They moved back into the hall. Nothing moved. No footsteps or talk. Anxiety ratcheted up inside West. He tried not to panic. Listened, hoping she would call out and give away where she went.

God, he wanted to believe she wandered off or was just standing somewhere nearby, but nothing about the woman he knew suggested that would happen. She was smart and understood the area and its dangers. Respected the people and did not take anything for granted.

He'd once thought her reckless, but he was dead wrong. She was pretty fucking brave, and all his. And he'd fight to hell and back to get her back.

Through a series of hand signals Josiah communicated the plan. They'd stick together and try to follow a trail. Problem was, there were footprints all over the tunnels. Marks in the dirt from the men rushing out after the explosion. Tracking one over the other would not be easy, but West had an advantage. Lexi was the only woman in here, to his knowledge. He looked for smaller prints.

It took a few minutes but he spotted the tracks. There would be a print then a slide mark. She'd been dragged backward. He let the rage over that simmer and build. When he found her, the person who had her would die.

They circled back toward the front of the cave. A few steps before the main room Pearce appeared in front of him.

"Looks like you lost your girlfriend," he said, nodding behind him. When he stepped aside, Tom stood there with an arm around Lexi's neck and a gun to her head. "We're taking her."

Panic flared in her eyes. West glanced at her, then away. He needed all of his control. "You aren't leaving here."

"The adrenaline has to be wearing off by now." Pearce made a face that on anyone else might be seen as sympathetic. On him it was just fucking creepy. "The pain. Damn, West. You have to be in serious pain. I turned up the electricity on those last two jolts."

Josiah shifted beside him. That was a signal because he knew not to move.

Pearce must have picked it up. "Nuh-uh. You come toward me and Tom drops her."

"She is not my concern." Josiah's aim moved from Tom to Pearce. "You are."

West tried not to show a reaction. Josiah was doing his job. And in terms of overall safety, Pearce should be their focus. But West's priorities had shifted. He wanted her. Cared about her. Would die for her.

Some of the amusement drained from Pearce's face. "You don't understand Benton's vision or how hard the Alliance will fuck you over when someone at the top—probably Tasha—decides it's time for you to go."

"Are you still spewing this garbage?" Josiah shook his head. "It's pathetic."

While they talked, West planned. He calculated the chances of getting to Lexi before a bullet slammed into her. Not great.

They were running out of time. If he knew that, Pearce knew it.

West knew he would only get one shot. It had to be executed perfectly. He'd take Pearce, and that meant he had to depend on Josiah to save Lexi. He hated that.

"Down!" The shout came from behind Tom and had him turning. Before West could get off a shot, he heard a bang and the compromised bodyguard dropped.

Javed now was with Lexi, who just stared down at the man at her feet. Knowing she was okay gave West the freedom to unleash. He had Pearce up against the rock wall with a gun aimed at the middle of his fore-head.

When he started to talk, West banged his head

against the wall. "I think I promised you a bullet in the brain."

"West." Pearce reached for West's extra weapon at his side but Josiah stepped in and grabbed it. Didn't say anything but kept watch while he held his own gun on Pearce.

The man was not getting out of this one alive.

"You cannot kill me." Pearce's voice bobbled. "I have valuable intel, and Tasha ordered Ward to keep me alive." When West didn't lower his gun, some of the confidence ran out of Pearce. He looked at Josiah. "Tell him."

"Right, I forgot." Josiah cleared his throat. "Tasha told Ward to bring you back in a box."

Not that he needed the green-light, but West was happy to get one. "There you go."

"You won't kill me in cold blood." Pearce shook his head. "That isn't you. It's not how Alliance works."

"Yeah, it is." West fired. Aimed and shot and didn't regret one second . . . until he looked into Lexi's eyes. They were wild and full of fear. He wanted to kick his own ass for killing in front of her. Again. "Lexi—"

She didn't even spare Pearce a glace. "He doesn't deserve a tattoo."

And just like that, West's world tilted right again. "No, he doesn't."

22

LEXI KNEW she should have been upset. Two more men dropped right in front of her. She'd become numb to all of the violence but refused to mourn the men who tortured West. She'd wanted to take a bat to those two.

Pearce deserved what he got. She knew the man for a day and despised him. She could not imagine the trail of destruction he'd left in his wake.

"Lexi?" Josiah stood in front of her. "We need to go."

She didn't realize she'd gotten lost in her thoughts until she felt the touch of his hand against her arm. She glanced down and watched West check Pearce's pockets and take a photo of him. She had no idea what the last part was for and she didn't care. She never wanted to think about Jake Pearce again.

"We can't leave yet." West stood up. "We need a sample of the weapon. The toxin."

Part of her knew he'd say something like that. He was here for a job, and somewhere along the line that got muddled. But she could barely stand on her feet.

She swayed back and forth. She had no idea, with the injuries and attacks, how he still moved.

Josiah looked from West to her. "I'll go."

"You haven't been in the caves." West rubbed his arm.

She didn't realize until she saw the rip in his shirt that he'd been shot again. "Are you bleeding?"

He turned his arm and looked at the area. "No."

Since she only saw a little blood and that had clotted, she decided to believe him. But that didn't solve the bigger problem. The one beating its way to them right now. She could help with that one. "I can get us there and back."

Stress pulled at the edges of West's mouth. "You are staying outside with Josiah. I'll run in and out."

There was no way he could run. Even if he could, he definitely shouldn't.

"No." Forget caring about him, which she did, too much, this was her talking as the medical professional who stitched him up several times.

"You don't get a say," he snapped back at her. "There could be more armed men in there."

He had about ten seconds to get rid of that attitude. "So, naturally, you should be the one who goes in and finds them. Heaven forbid someone else gets shot on this assignment."

Josiah laughed. "She has you there."

The clenched jaw suggested West was not impressed. "We need—"

"Outside." Josiah took a step toward the area and the entrance beyond. "We'll find Ward and figure this out."

"Seems reasonable." She didn't know if that was true or not. Didn't really care. The relief of having Josiah side with her was enough.

When West started to talk, Josiah piped up again. "And, for the record, I *am* in charge of you, so we're going."

Lexi loved the way Josiah handled West. "You I like."

Josiah shot her a smile. "I just like bossing him around."

"Who doesn't?"

West debated hunting down the toxin anyway. He didn't generally buck Alliance leadership. He listened and followed because the place was run by smart people with a serious purpose. This time he wanted to ignore that.

"West?"

He heard Josiah's voice. Thought about Lexi and the danger and capitulated. "I'm coming."

Josiah held up a hand. "Where's Javed?"

"He was . . ." Lexi looked around. "Where did he go?"

Josiah tightened the grip on his gun. "We sure he's on our side?"

West had asked that question over and over. He wanted to believe in Javed because he meant something to Lexi. And it didn't make sense that he'd step up so many times if he was really on Benton's payroll or someone else's. "He's helped us."

"Saved us." She looked from West to Josiah and back again. "Javed is a friend."

Josiah frowned. "Friend?"

She shot him a you-are-right-on-the-line glare. "I think you know what that word means."

West got to see her use that expression on someone else. He was happy not to be on the receiving end of that . . . this time. "Friends only."

There was a noise behind West, a shuffling and a thud. Both he and Josiah turned, ready to fire, pulling back at the sight of Javed with a bag in one hand and a satphone in the other.

He glanced up and came to a stop. Didn't say anything. Didn't go for his gun, which was the only reason West didn't put him down with a bullet to his brain.

But he did take aim. "This is interesting."

"This has been quite a day," Josiah said as he stepped up beside West. "Lucky for you, Javed, I'm in the mood to shoot one more time."

Lexi broke in between them and went toward Javed. She stopped before reaching him but her body swayed and her shoulders fell. Looking at the bag he held, she said, "What are you doing?"

Javed bit his lower lip as his gaze traveled around the area. "It's not what you think."

"I've defended you." Pain radiated from her body and her voice.

West wanted to hold her, take her out of there and away from the lying and death. If she could hold on for another hour he'd make it happen. He'd forget the idea of leaving her and find a hotel somewhere. Hot showers and a big bed. That was the fantasy scenario right now. A shower and her.

He gave Javed one second to come up with a story. "It looks like you're stealing weapons grade toxin."

The find didn't make sense. Nothing in Javed's record—and Josiah had checked it—pointed to this. The guy wasn't on anyone's radar and he'd been a career helicopter pilot, working his way up the chain to join the most prestigious squadron in charge of the highest places on Earth. To be one of the men who did what no one else could do.

Javed tightened and loosened his fist. Kept doing it. The silence ticked on and he didn't make a move.

"We can stand here all day," Josiah said.

Javed closed his eyes then opened them again. "It's my job."

It was the way he said it. Careful, with his accent fading. A new piece of crap was headed right for them. West could sense it coming. "You fly helicopters for the Pakistani army."

There was a buzzing sound and Javed looked at his watch. "We need to leave."

Looked like they were on a countdown for something. "Why?"

"Is the army coming?" Lexi asked.

"No."

West hit his endpoint. The cryptic bullshit pushed

him right past his tolerance level. "Talk or I shoot. Do not test me."

Javed tightened his grip on the bag. "CIA."

As soon as he said it the pieces made sense. Javed showed up at random times, which in hindsight might not have been so random. He knew how to get to the encampment. Shot the right people. Had an in and out of his base without question. Knew where to be and befriended Lexi. He could as easily be intelligence or Benton's sidekick as a guy lying to save his own ass.

West wanted to know now. "Explain."

"I'm Dr. Palmer's handler. He's my asset. Feeds me information."

Lexi's eyes widened. "What?"

West sympathized with her confusion but he couldn't stop to help her now. And he didn't accept Javed's half-assed answer. "The weapons?"

"I knew." West took a step forward and Javed started talking faster, this time directly to Lexi. "The go command is only there for when I'm not available. You couldn't know that, but if your dad had been there, he would have told me directly. I had it handled."

"You are begging to be shot," Josiah said.

"Okay, wait." Lexi talked slowly as the words stuttered out. "Someone needs to explain all of this to me."

Javed kept his gaze locked on West. "I have an assignment just like you do."

Speaking of that. "No one told us you were on the ground. You're saying we got sent out here, sat through briefings, all without being told about an asset in the field."

Josiah shook his head. "Not believable."

"Deep cover," Javed said. "Plus, until I checked in two days ago, I had never even heard of Alliance. Apparently, some of my bosses feel your group undermines the CIA mission."

"We're not CIA." Josiah said, clearly not believing this excuse.

The possibility of being kept in the dark and having the assignment thrown into danger due to intradepartmental wrangling pissed West off. That was part of the reason Alliance was born, to cut through the layers of crap to get to the intel. But that's not what got to him about the idea of Javed being CIA. "You didn't do anything to protect her."

Javed shook his head. "General Harif grew suspicious. Raheel warned me about his boss's concerns and I told him to move her out. The timing proved problematic. Harif went to the clinic and so did one of Benton's men."

"Problematic? That's the word you used?" Lexi got right in Javed's face. "Two men were killed in front of me. Anything could have happened if West hadn't shown up."

West knew it was so much worse than that. "And you had plenty of chances after that to fill us in."

"You were not read into the operation." Javed sure as hell sounded like CIA with that response.

"We should let her kill you right now," Josiah said.

"It is so tempting." She rubbed a hand over her face. "I don't get any of this."

West felt for her. In her world, undercover and special ops agents looked and acted like him. They killed people and walked into danger. She didn't know about the everyday people who passed information and picked drop sites. It was no surprise to him that the CIA would approach a U.S. doctor in Pakistan or put him in place, except for the part where that information should have been in the briefing.

Javed shifted the bag from one hand to the other. "Need to know."

West had lived most of his adult life in undercover operations and he still hated that catchphrase. "Don't give us that bullshit."

"Stop." Lexi faced West. The pleading look in her eyes tore at him.

"We'll go through all of this later. I promise." He knew he shouldn't. The information stayed confidential and protected and under wraps for a reason.

Javed stepped up until they stood in a small group. "Your men have the army on a chase but they'll get here eventually. Those explosions will tip off someone."

Josiah narrowed his eyes. "And?"

"We can't leave this stash of weapons here and unprotected." Javed lifted the bag. "They cannot fall into Pakistani hands."

"You're taking the weapons. This is all about the

CIA grabbing the weapons first." The way West saw it, this had CIA disaster written all over it. "And you've called in someone to take the rest of the facility out. You're grabbing the toxic material and leaving the other shit behind."

Pakistan didn't know about the dangerous materials on its soil. That meant no one could protect the people or prepare for the potential health fallout, not just the political one.

Josiah nodded. "You'll pick it clean then blow up the tunnels, leaving a mess behind."

West knew then Josiah was on the same wavelength. They both knew this could explode. Javed didn't seem to care, and for whatever reason, that made West believe his CIA tale even more.

Javed put the bag's strap over his shoulder and gestured toward the entrance. "We're leaving."

They got as far as the actual entrance to the cave. West could see light and sky. He could not let Javed go one more step. If he got out with that bag, CIA or not, Alliance would lose it, and that could not happen.

West stepped in front of him with a hand on his chest. "You're not going anywhere."

Benton spoke from behind them. "I agree."

23

LEXI SPUN around to face Benton. The man with one name. The same one who ordered that she be tortured. He stood there alone and all she wanted was for one of the men with her to pull out a gun and stop this nonsense. They could all do it, she didn't care so long as it ended.

"You're like a fucking cockroach." West slipped his hand around her elbow and slowly pulled her back to him.

She didn't fight it. She had no interest in being a hero or standing out front on her own. "He really is."

Josiah closed in ranks next to West and formed the other half of the shield in front of her. Normally she would have pushed her way through, not wanting to be left out or feel forgotten. Not this time.

Something about Benton scared the hell out of her. Pearce ran on greed. She hated him and didn't mourn his death. The world would run better without him. But she understood his motivation. Many people suffered from the need for more, but most didn't take it to the point of mass homicide, or at least she hoped that was true.

Benton was a different beast. He talked as if he believed he qualified as some sort of legitimate businessman trying to get by. Psychopath sounded closer.

Benton didn't spare her a glance. He kept his attention on Javed and the bag in his hand. "Give that to me."

"It's three against one, genius," West said.

"I am never alone." The second after he said it red dots appeared on West's and Josiah's chests.

Seeing those moving dots suggested to her that they were being targeted. Her stomach took off on another roller-coaster ride. Waves of nausea crashed over her as she tried to remember the last time she ate.

But she was the only one struggling with the newest threat. West and Josiah looked bored.

"What's in your case?" Javed asked.

Lexi hadn't noticed the box under Benton's arm. Or the thin chain leading to his wrist. It figured this guy would chain something to his body.

"Not your concern, but I can't let any trace of my chemicals get in the wrong hands." Benton looked around. "Understand?"

"Because then you can't sell your garbage for top dollar," Josiah said.

Benton put a hand against his chest. "I'm a businessman."

She guessed he actually believed the stuff he said.

Maybe somewhere along the line he started buying into the justifications he spewed. She didn't. "You're crazy."

He frowned at her. "Name-calling is not necessary."

Javed adjusted the bag on his shoulder. "We can all wait here."

"As to that . . ." Benton smiled as the red dot on West's chest moved to his forehead. "I am willing to offer an incentive to the speedy resolution of this."

Lexi nearly jumped out of her skin. It felt as if something was crawling inside her and trying to get out. "What are you doing?"

"You have one minute to hand over the bag or West gets a bullet. Then Josiah. Then the woman. I'll keep going until you are buried in bodies."

The words bounced around her head. The visual images so awful she could barely breathe.

"No one give it to him." West stood stock-still. Only his mouth moved. "The toxin stays with us."

"Then I will kill all of you and take the bag." Benton shook his head while he made a clicking sound with his tongue on the roof of his mouth. "Really, there is an easy way to do this."

"Either way we get shot," Josiah said.

"True, but maybe I'll spare her. Take her with me." Benton aimed all of his intensity at her. "Come here, my dear."

"Do not move, Lexi." West never looked at her but his fingers tightened on the gun.

He didn't have to look at her. She felt his will from

where she stood. The heat rolled off him and the anger vibrated in his voice.

One of Benton's eyebrows rose. "She comes to me or my men shoot you now."

"Fine." West lowered the barrel of the gun. "Do it. Come directly at me."

She almost jumped on top of him. "West?"

"You have a beef with me, with Alliance, take it out on us," he said to Benton, then dropped the gun the whole way to his side and stood there. "Only a weak man goes after women."

Benton laughed. "Are you trying to make me angry?"

"I'm letting you know how little you matter to me," West spit back.

"Lexi, now." Benton pointed to the ground. Ordered her around like she was a naughty puppy.

She shifted and West's hand came down across her body, holding her back. She thought about pivoting around him but Josiah stepped back, trapping her against West's side. There was nothing subtle about that.

"No, Ms. Palmer? That's a shame for your boyfriend." Benton let out a long dramatic exhale. "I had heard you were close."

He lifted his hands as if he were about to give a signal then stared at West with a dare in his eye.

"One more thing," Josiah said. "When your man shoots West, I'm going to shoot you."

"You think you have the angles all worked out, do you?" Benton asked. "I think not."

West's hand brushed against hers. At first she assumed he'd moved, but then she remembered his ability to hold still for hours on end. He could sit on stakeout and barely breathe.

When the brush came a second time, she knew it was a signal. But about what? Standing there with her heartbeat pounding in her ears and her stomach flipping inside out and hollow, she tried to concentrate on every word. Every sensation.

"Fuck this." West's gun came up and he got off a shot. "Down!"

The last thing she saw was Benton jumping to the side. Then her mind blanked as Josiah turned and tackled her. His weight barreled into her chest as his arms wrapped around her. The air shifted and her hair flew in front of her eyes. She went airborne and braced for the hard landing that never came. Her body bounced on top of his as he rolled, hitting the ground then tucking her under him.

Rounds of gunfire thudded over her, around her. The concussive bangs continued for what felt like hours. She struggled to lift up and check for West, but Josiah had her head tucked under his chin and his body flush against hers.

When the weight finally lifted and she opened her eyes, they'd rolled toward the opening of the caves. The walls provided protection. She stared at the evening sky as the clouds raced overhead. It took another second for her brain to catch up with the chaos. She sat up then. Javed sat crouched a few feet away and Josiah was already up and firing.

The shots seemed to come from every side of her except behind. She scanned the area but didn't see any sign of West. The rest of the Alliance team and Raheel were on the scene and battling with men hidden around the area whom she could not see.

The site looked abandoned. A burned-out truck and a huge crater in the ground. Bodies from one side to the other. She studied every still form, looking for that familiar gray shirt, but saw nothing.

Her vision blurred and the ache in her stomach built until she had to rock back and forth to ease the pain. "West?"

She didn't realize she'd said his name out loud until Josiah rushed back to her side. He wrapped an arm around her and leaned down. "Were you hit?"

"Where is he?"

Just as she got the words out a vision stepped into view. Through the smoke and the battle a man, tall and trim, someone she'd never seen before, came forward. He had something on his shoulder and it looked like it weighed his steps down.

She blinked a few times and saw the long barrel. But this wasn't a gun. She'd seen something like it in movies. A missile launcher or something like that. Something lethal.

Javed started yelling and waving his arms. "You can't. My people are coming."

"Lexi, move."

She recognized that voice and looked around for West. He was on the ground. Pinned down maybe. But he was alive.

The tug on her arm nearly ripped her shoulder out of the socket. One minute she sat near the entrance. The next she dove through the air with Josiah leading her. She thought she saw West again but through the banging and yelling and roar of the fire nothing made sense.

Josiah had her up on her feet. She had no idea how her legs moved or where they were going. She'd finally gotten her feet under her and steadied herself when she heard a strange whistle over her head. The sky lit up and then the crash knocked her down. Heat blanketed her and Josiah fell across her body, trapping her against the ground.

She might have blacked out for a second. She wasn't sure. When she focused again the fire burned out of control all around her.

Something heavy hit the back of her leg. Hard and rough. Then another. The sound of something rolling. She pressed up on her palms and struggled to shift around. She turned her head and glanced back at the entrance to the cave. All she saw was a wall of fire and piles of stones.

Her brain couldn't assess the picture in front of her. She figured she'd gotten turned around, the pile of rocks didn't look familiar.

She heard men's voices around her. Shoes pounded the ground as legs ran past. None of it made sense until she saw Ward drop to his knees, throwing rocks to the side with his bare hands. Digging.

He kept saying something and pulling on something. Something gray. She strained to hear, picked up the word "right" as she noticed the flash of gray under the bottom rocks.

West was buried alive.

He'd done some dumbass shit in his life but this was the worst. Just as he'd fired the gun and broke the chain holding the box to Benton's arm, he dove. His shoulder rammed into Benton's stomach and knocked him sideways as the box thudded in the dirt.

West had kicked it as he struggled to pull Benton's body over his. If someone was going to take a shot, then he would use this asshole as a shield. But the bullet never came. And Benton didn't fight like a man gone soft. He pummeled West's back with his fists and clamped a hand over his shoulder wound.

West yelled in fury as the adrenaline rush hit him. With one twist and a punishing grab, he body-slammed Benton into the dirt. The guy's head was knocked to the ground and his head lolled. Those eyes rolled back and West hoped they'd go closed forever.

He shifted and hit something. That damn box. He kicked it toward the cave's entrance and away from Benton's outstretched hand.

When he landed his first punch to Benton's chin it felt so fucking good he did it again. The blast hit on the third punch. West recognized the sound. A shoulder rocket launcher roared to life and fired like the sound of a plane passing right by his head. His attention shifted and Harlan stood there.

Without hesitation, Benton made his move. He scrambled to his knees and raced toward the box. West made it his mission to deny him whatever was in there. He jumped on Benton's back and flattened him into the dirt as the rocks tumbled. At first one or two, then it became a punishing rain. Flames kicked up and Benton screamed.

West could only see that box. He gathered it underneath him and put a hand over his head. His last thought was of Lexi and the flash of motion he'd seen after Josiah read the signals he'd made and dragged her to the ground before the explosion came.

At least she was safe. And he had the box.

Now he had to survive.

24

THE AREA had turned into a burial site.

Lexi dug at the rocks until her hands bled. She kneeled in the dirt between Josiah and Raheel and moved the pile from one place to another, throwing the smaller ones to the side. Ward and Mike worked from above to make sure no more rolled on top of West.

The cold air nipped at her skin and the protective vest shifted until it climbed up her throat and nearly choked her. She ignored it all. The flames and the grunts of the men around her. The paralyzing fear that she'd lost West, and the thick tension around her as his teammates worried for his life.

When her hand finally rested on West's back, fear and longing battled within her. She begged the universe to let him be alive as she slipped her hand down to his neck to feel for a pulse. Relief swamped her and her body fell forward when she felt a thump under her hand.

Josiah leaned in. "Lexi?"

She nodded, too lost in hope to speak.

They had to get him out. She didn't need to explain that.

His friends were already moving, clearing away as much of the rubble as possible. She yearned for the clinic and all the tools sitting in cabinets and on tables back there. If only they had the gurney to lift him to safety. Even the bag she carried before getting caught by Pearce had medical supplies in it. She had no idea where that was now.

Ignoring what she didn't have, she pointed at Josiah and Mike. "We need to lift him and you need to follow my instructions."

They didn't argue. As she shouted commands about his head and his back, they picked him up, with Ward rushing in to hold West's head and keep his neck steady.

As they turned him, a box tumbled out of his open hand. Javed leaned down to get it and Mike snatched it back. "No way. We can't even get confirmation of who you are."

In all the confusion and the craziness of the last hour, or however much time had passed, she'd lost sight of Javed and his role in all of this. The idea of him being CIA. Of her father passing information to the CIA or being paid by him or whatever Javed was insisting.

Her world went black at the thought. All those lies and all that subterfuge. She couldn't deal with any of it now and would have to wait to confront her father when they were both on safer ground. She planned to put that off for as long as possible while she worked through everything else.

But Javed. She'd never seen her friend in this state. He paced and mumbled under his breath. She took it for a few minutes, then that nerve behind her temples started to tick.

She turned on him. "Get ahold of yourself."

"Listen to the smart woman," Ward said as he peeled the shirt away from West's body.

With her outburst immediately forgotten, she dropped to her knees and took over. Ran her hands along his arms and legs to check for broken bones. She studied his stomach as she worried about internal bleeding. When she was satisfied that the worst of the blood covering him came from old wounds and not new ones, she bent over and put an ear to his chest. The steady breathing had her eyes closing in gratitude.

The mountain almost swallowed him once. Now he'd survived a second time.

She just needed him to wake up and talk to her.

"I need to leave." Javed walked over to Ward. "I can't break cover."

"You mean you have lies to protect." Raheel growled out the response from the other side of the cleared space. No one mentioned the CIA or undercover work to him, but Raheel clearly picked up on the clues.

Josiah stood up and brought Javed's bag with him. He held it out, balancing the strap on two fingers. "Not with this."

"Or the box," Ward said.

"You don't understand." Javed stared at Ward, then Josiah. Whatever he saw on their faces had him moving on to Harlan. "You know how this works."

Older and British, Harlan looked every inch the serious elder of the group. But he shook his head. "We all do."

"Let Raheel and me go."

Now Javed fought for Raheel. Guilt pinched Lexi as she thought about how she'd doubted him. He walked into the clinic to try to save her and she thought the worst. She'd have to apologize for that when the chaos subsided.

"I'm not sure your friend wants to spend time with you." Ward kept talking even as Javed started. "And even if he did, that's tough shit. You walked into the middle of my assignment."

Gone was Javed's easygoing charm. He stood firm as he aimed his anger at Ward. "I have been here, working this cover."

Ward held out his hands. "And you can stay here, but the bag and the box go with us."

"You already destroyed the cave and more than likely the crates in there." Javed's voice dropped to a harsh whisper. "Do you have any idea how much intel we just lost?"

The tone and the way he held his body. It all looked familiar to her now. The cockiness went with the job he did, and he had it.

"That was the point of the rocket launcher," Ward said. "No one gets the toxin."

She could go a lifetime without hearing that word. She went to work every day, slept in her bed, all while a deadly compound sat close by. Pearce had said something about perfecting it or trying to make it airborne.

She didn't remember the details but did remember the terrifying implications, and to see that Javed writing them off as no big deal made her wonder if she'd ever known him at all.

Javed eyed the bag. "That isn't your call," he told Ward.

"I made it my call." Ward didn't ruffle. He stood his ground and shot back an answer for every one of Javed's concerns.

Harlan stepped up. He'd been the one to launch the rocket, or whatever it was, and bring down the tunnel.

He climbed down off the rock pile to stand next to Ward. "And I backed him."

"You need—"

He didn't stop. Javed kept justifying. He started to sound like Pearce, and that made something in her head explode.

She held up a hand to ward off his ridiculous arguments and bat away the smoke from the nearby fire. "Shut up."

"Excuse me?"

"Don't give me that macho garbage. You are sitting here arguing about who gets credit, and West isn't opening his eyes." Her gaze shot back to the man at her feet. The one who'd come to mean so much in such a short time.

She didn't toss around the word love easily and it was far too soon, but she felt a tug that made her feel hot and comfortable at the same time, itchy and safe.

He touched off a flurry of emotions inside her, something that had never happened before, not like this, and she wanted a chance to investigate where it could go.

So Javed needed to shut up. "The only thing I care about is getting him out of here before whoever you work for arrives, or the army does."

Josiah stood next to her. "Me, too."

"How are you going to do that?" Javed threw his arms wide. "Look around you. There is nowhere to go and no way to get there."

Raheel picked that moment to pipe up. "Me."

"What?" Javed wore a frown.

She watched him now, wondering how she'd never seen it before. He turned the charm on and off. What had seemed so genuine before now struck her as a ruse. He'd told her this story about living his whole life in Pakistan and loving the land and the people. It was a passion they shared.

Now she'd bet he grew up in the U.S. or somewhere else. Every detail was in doubt.

"I'm a helicopter pilot," Raheel said. "I'll fly him out."

Javed's frown only grew. "Wait—"

Ward cut Javed off and talked directly to Raheel. "I go with West. Mike will double back with transport."

Now she wanted to put the brakes on. "I'm coming with you."

Ward shook his head. "You're not."

"I have medical training." That argument had to

work. West was breathing now but still unconscious. If something happened, she would know what to do.

Josiah threw her an apologetic smile. "We all do."

Of course they did. Why should that surprise her?

Ward nodded and the group started breaking apart, moving in different directions. "We're wasting time when we could be getting him help."

She kind of hated Ward for that. He picked the one argument sure to win her over, reluctant or not. And she knew he knew that.

She turned to the one person she thought might support her. "Josiah, I don't want to leave him."

"I promise I'll take you right to him once we get out of here." Josiah took her hand in his. "I am not lying, and I think you know that."

She glanced at Ward, thinking that if this deal fell apart it would be at his end and from above. "You should know I will shoot him if he doesn't."

He smiled. "Got it."

The next fifteen minutes passed as slow torture. They strapped West in and jogged with the gurney to the helicopter. She wanted to stay strong and act cool. But when she leaned down to kiss West on the cheek, a tear fell. She didn't burst into tears but knew she probably would the minute she had two seconds alone.

The past few days and hours ran together. She'd been through so much and all of it at this man's side. Letting him go now broke her. Something inside cracked and crumbled.

She held his hand until Josiah appeared beside her and helped her let go. "He's going to be okay."

The men loaded in and the chopper blade began to turn. The engine roared to life with deafening precision. She put an arm over her head as her hair flew in a hundred different directions.

All the emotion and frustration backed up on her, but she waited until the helicopter lifted and the men dispersed before she turned on Josiah. Harlan stood there, too, but she didn't care. She needed to make this point. "He thinks he's a machine."

Josiah's expression turned serious. "What?"

"He's convinced he shut down his humanity. I look at him and see this brave, strong, decent man. He doesn't see any of it."

Josiah shook his head. "How do you see him?"

"As all man." She remembered the first time she saw him. "I picked him. I stood in that clinic and demanded he be my bodyguard."

Harlan glanced over at Josiah. "Really?"

He nodded. "She did."

She had no idea why that was some big surprise. West was big and hot and had this presence that made an impact. She'd pick him over most—make that all—other men. "He shouldn't kill on demand." When Harlan and Josiah glanced at each other, Lexi's confidence faltered. "What?"

"We all do." Harlan hesitated before finishing, "It's part of the training."

They were missing the point. "But he goes in first. He told me everyone has a set of skills. I guess that's his."

Josiah took a step back as he shook his head. Debris crunched under his feet. "That's not true."

"He can shoot and get information out of people better than anyone I know," Harlan said.

West was so much more than that to her. He had the tattoos and awful reminders. He'd now lived through a new set of injuries and torture. All of those focused on things that had happened to him. They had so little to do with who he was inside, the man she knew, who kissed her and protected her.

But she had to wonder, if they all had the same skills and went through the training, why West took on the danger that made him the target. She needed to understand. "Why him?"

Josiah shrugged. "Because he's good at it."

These men shrugged all the time. It was their go-to expression whenever she asked a question that was even a tiny bit hard. But the words registered. West had a home with Alliance. From his messed-up childhood he'd learned skills that made him not just effective but essential to the team. They had been to her.

Maybe he saw his role as that of emotionless shooter. She knew better. From the looks on his friends' faces, so did they.

Harlan cleared his throat. "Not to get technical here, but we need to tread carefully. I'm not sure internal team information is your business."

She probably would have accepted that excuse when they first met. Not now. "West is my business."

"Does he know that?" Josiah asked with a smile.

She thought about all the things they'd said to each other and the information they'd shared. Some facts sat out there, but she did hold back. That's what you did when the attraction spiked but enough time hadn't passed. But that was a temporary state.

"He will."

Josiah's smile grew wider. "You plan on fighting for him, then?"

This wasn't the time or the place. She should have the conversation with West and not his friends. But hiding her feelings . . . not happening. Not after seeing him buried in a pile of rocks. Not after almost losing him.

Not after she just started to love him. "Yes."

Harlan made a strangled sound. "You didn't pick an easy guy."

That was the story of her life. Never easy. "I don't do easy."

"Then you need to know one thing, Lexi," Josiah said.

She was almost afraid to ask. "What?"

He winked at her. "He really is going to be okay."

25

WEST LAY in the hospital room in Islamabad and counted the ceiling tiles. He'd been transported to a top secret location and would be flown out of the region, probably to Germany, as soon as he stabilized. The move needed to be timed to happen as soon as possible, for his protection and that of the entire Alliance team.

But now he measured tiles. Across and down then multiply them together . . . then start all over again. Each tile block had tiny holes in it. Soon he'd be counting those.

The door was pushed open with a *wift* sound. He held his breath, waiting for the face to appear. When Mike and Josiah stepped inside, West tried not to look disappointed. He'd adopted the same expression several times today. A member of the team would walk in and he'd hope, but no.

All of Bravo called and told him to get his ass home. He missed those guys. No question he admired Josiah and the way he ran his team, but West's heart was back in DC with Bravo.

His friends stepped up to the bed, one on either side. Mike scanned the equipment, taking in the flashing lights. Josiah shifted his weight around, something he never did, and generally looked uncomfortable.

West found Josiah's fear of hospitals vastly entertaining. The guy had sniper skills, negotiating skills, and the kind of in-the-moment smarts you wanted in a leader. Yet the sight of cotton balls made him dizzy.

"You okay?" Josiah asked.

"I'm ready to go home." He was ready to never check in. When he woke up on that helicopter he'd done two things—threw up and asked for Lexi. They were unrelated things but at least one stemmed from his head injury.

"You're staying at least two nights." Josiah shot him a look that said, *I dare you to disagree,* so West didn't.

"About Lexi . . ." Mike put a thigh on the edge of the bed but jumped up again when something beeped.

Josiah rolled his eyes. "Ah, you Americans. So subtle."

"She tried to give Josiah a lesson in about who you really are." Mike skimmed his fingers over the tubes running from the machine next to West's bed and leading nowhere since he refused the pain medicine. Not his style.

But that didn't explain the comment. "What are you talking about?"

Josiah jumped back in. "She told me you're not a machine, which I knew. I think she meant to remind you, not me."

"She doesn't get what we do," West said. Even though he hadn't noticed her weeping for any of the attackers he'd taken down. She ran and fought beside him. Impressed the hell out of him.

"I thought maybe you asked her to send us a message." Mike followed one tube to the end and held it up. Then he started folding it in half. "You retiring and forgot to tell us?"

Even though he wasn't using the equipment now, he might be in the future, and having Mike's hands all over it seemed like a bad idea. West knocked the tube out of his hands. "Of course not."

"She thinks you see yourself as nothing more than a killer."

This was not a conversation West wanted or needed to have. He'd blocked so much after the avalanche. Seeing so much death and being unable to stop it messed with his head. He'd stepped back and focused on the shooting. Honed his skills.

Then she walked into his life. Sassy and tough, ready to take him on and not afraid to fight back. She had him spinning and reassessing and wanting her until his need for her pushed out everything.

He didn't understand why she blindsided him or where the resurgence of emotions came from, but he did understand his role on the team. He went in first and never questioned it. He wouldn't have it any other way. "It's my job," he said to Mike.

"Being a killing machine?" Mike made a face. "Not really."

But it was. "You know what I mean."

They all had strengths, and that was his. A pretty simple skill that served him well and made him invaluable to Alliance. He could kill and push away any conflict in his head.

Josiah stared at the clock next to the dark television. "She's right, you know. You are not just a guy who can shoot. None of us see you that way, and if you do, you should let Lexi convince you otherwise."

No, he couldn't afford to have them questioning each other. He had no intention of leaving Alliance. "I'm happy with my job as it is."

"Listen to him, dumbass." Mike shook his head. "Whatever you think is wrong with you? It isn't. Got it?"

West wasn't sure how to take that but he knew the reassurance, coming from Mike, meant something. The guy didn't throw around compliments or hand out hope. "Thanks. I think."

"What about your personal life?" Mike pushed buttons and spun the machine around.

He slid that in there. Subtle and quiet. He put Lexi on the table as a conversation topic.

West tried to pretend he didn't hear. "What?"

Josiah shot him a don't-be-stupid look. "She cares about you."

"She lives in Pakistan." Damn, West hated that. If she were in the states, he could swing through. In a country he planned to visit, he could make arrangements or they could meet.

But he was done with Pakistan. Nothing against the

people, but he'd been buried alive there twice, and testing it by going back again seemed to be asking for it.

"We all know that's about to end. The military and police are going to rip Skardu apart." Josiah ticked off the harsh realities. "Her father's role as an informant is over, and since Ward finally reached the guy at Everest base camp, I can report the good doctor is pissed. And Javed could be in danger."

Mike nodded. "Bottom line, there's no way she can go back there and be safe."

"I wonder if I get to decide that or not." Lexi spoke from the doorway. She didn't come in or scold. The smile on her face suggested she enjoyed catching the men talking.

Mike gave her a little wave. "Hello."

"We'll step out." Josiah reached across the bed, grabbed onto Mike's sleeve and pulled him to the end of the mattress. "Leave you guys alone."

"I'm not kicking you out." She watched as they passed by her.

"I think you have the balls to do it," Mike said.

Josiah stopped for a second on the way out. "I kept my promise."

Her smile grew even wider. "You get to live."

The door shut and he was alone with her in the small private room. Outside, bells dinged and the intercom went off every few seconds. Nurses raced from here to there, and the smell of antiseptic could knock you out. But in this room there was only him and her.

When she didn't move in any closer, he decided to push it. He crooked a finger at her. "Come here."

She continued to stand there rubbing her hands together. "You need rest and—"

"Lexi, now."

A bit too much, he knew, but watching her touched off something inside of him. Since the first time he met her, that smile and face reeled him in. Now she hovered in front of him with shiny clean hair and slim jeans. Her coat ended at the top of her pants and showed off her slim waist.

Dirty, clean, he did not care. He loved the rough side of her that could take an emotional hit and get right back up. He also liked the sexier side that knew how to pick out a pair of jeans.

He wanted to crawl all over her. Take those clothes off and get to the impressive bare skin beneath.

"I'm not really a fan of the bossiness," she said as she stepped up to the side of his bed.

He took her hand. Rubbed each finger before kissing the back. "I'm injured."

'You're playing the victim card?" But she didn't sound too surprised or upset by that.

He'd never tried it before and was a bit disappointed in the results. "Whatever it will take to get to kiss you."

She smiled. "That's easy."

With one hand braced on the mattress by his pillow, she bent down. Her hair fell in a wave over her shoulder and teased his cheek. By the time her mouth covered his, his breathing had ticked up. His fingers tangled in her hair as her lips crossed over his.

She pressed and conquered, then her mouth slipped open. It was an invitation he couldn't resist. He licked inside her mouth as the kiss seared through him. When she lifted her head he followed and kissed her again. One last time.

He fell back into the pillows. "I heard you talked with Josiah."

"That's between him and me."

"It was about me." When she shrugged at that, he tried again. "I love my job."

"I know that."

But it scared her, and he got that. She was human. The work he did straddled the line and a lot of people would say he went too far. He'd tried to hide those aspects of work from her and failed. "It's dangerous and keeps me on the road."

Her head snapped back. "Are you giving me the *speech*?"

He didn't know what it meant but it pretty much made him sound like a dick. He circled around and tried again. "I'm trying to explain that the man in front of you can kill a man without guilt."

"Your tattoo says otherwise."

He was half sorry she saw that thing. All sorry he answered any questions about it. Thing was, she nailed the answer and his mind-set in getting it. It did function as a form of penance. He tried not to add to the marks, and having those deaths on his conscience did drive him. He never took a life with glee.

Even with Pearce, a man who needed to die, West didn't celebrate. He did what he needed and moved on. Though that one had a touch of revenge linked to it.

Since he didn't want her worrying and certainly didn't need her to analyze his job and decide he came up short, he tried to explain. "Every member of the team has a specialty. Mine happens to be that I don't flinch."

"I'm not sure what that means, but okay."

"You do know." She did. She'd seen it, and the truth was, she was lucky to be alive because of it. They both were.

Her head tilted to the side. "Is this the part where you tell me to go find a nice doctor or graduate student?"

The words shuddered to a halt in his brain. Even if he should send her away and hurting her was the way to get it done, he couldn't. Some lines did not need to be crossed. "The idea of you with another man makes me want to hit someone with a bat."

Her eyes widened. "That's pretty intense."

"So are my feelings for you." He clamped down to keep from saying anything else. That was already too much. She did not live here and deserved a life. He couldn't give that to her, and that meant letting go.

"But?" she asked.

"What you see is what you get. Injured, near death."

Even though he felt better, the last few days had taken a toll. He could run then slide to his knees. That didn't mean he should or that his eighty-year-old future self would appreciate it. "I'm the guy who would bring danger to your doorstep."

"Technically, I brought the danger to you this time."

She'd made a call. The rest unfurled in a way no one could have predicted. "Lexi, you know what I mean."

She ran a hand over his leg and stopped at his knee. "I can handle it."

The gentle touch burned him through the thin hospital blanket. "I can't handle the idea of anything happening to you."

"If the goal is to get me to leave—"

It would be best. Smart and focused. But his mind went into a spin at the thought. "I'm trying to be honest."

She snorted. "No, you're not."

That pissed him off—the comment and the sound. "I know what I feel."

She picked up his hand and pressed it against her chest. "Do you want to know what I feel?"

She tempted him in ways he'd never experienced. With her, he thought about having a house and a dog. He'd bent all his rules when dealing with an asset. Hell, it made him sick to even think of her in those detached terms. "Lexi."

"This is the start of something incredible." She rubbed her thumb over his leg. "I am falling, and falling hard."

The honest words filled him with a blinding sense

of rightness. The panic shot right behind that. "God, don't."

Her hand dropped to her side. "So, you're saying I'm falling by myself."

"I didn't—" His blood pressure machine beeped. The cuff checked it automatically, and West hated that. "I'm trying to be realistic."

"You're being safe. You're cutting yourself off from emotion."

"Is that so wrong?" Some people craved normal and safe. She was using the words as a weapon.

"I am not going to be buried under an avalanche. I'm hoping I won't be in a position to be shot in the head again either." She leaned down a bit. "I know you clamped down on feelings years ago, but I want you to let me in."

"You want in my head and it's a mess in there." He tried to make a joke but it fell flat.

She snorted. "At least you admit there's something in there."

"Meaning?"

"You are not a machine. You are a man. All man." She put a hand over his chest. "Flesh and blood, heart and soul, Hot and so sexy. And if you give me a chance, I'll convince you."

"It's not that simple." But, damn, she made it sound easy. As if he could just walk away from the horrors that came before and walk into the light with her.

Sadness filled her eyes. "Love doesn't come with a safety switch. It's messy and scary."

A pretty sentiment but in practice a disaster because his version of messy included bodies and blood. Even now he nursed everything from a head wound, to a gunshot wound, to injured ribs, to all sorts of aches and pains and sprains.

Unless she planned to travel with him and be his personal physician, it amounted to a shitty life for the person not doing the shooting. "My life isn't normal."

"Mine hasn't been either."

He knew she had things to work out with her dad and carried guilt about her mom. He didn't want to downplay that, but problems as a teenager didn't compare to the real-life adult work of figuring out how to move forward. She had moved on and he couldn't. "We are talking about two different things."

"No, we're talking in circles." She put her hand in her pocket and pulled out a small card. "Here."

He turned it over in his hand. "What's this?"

"The key to my room."

He almost dropped it on the blanket. He knew he should say something but the words jammed inside him and he couldn't come up with anything.

"I won't bother with giving you the address because, apparently, I'm in some sort of safe house with the rest of the team, but you probably knew that."

He did. He worked up to asking about her and refused to undergo any tests or say anything until he got the reassurance about her being safe. She had a room between Josiah and Mike, two guys who would battle to the death for her, in a rooming house that provided cover.

West had been debriefed about what happened and briefed on all he missed. He knew about the sleeping arrangements. He knew she'd contacted her dad. He knew Alliance had maintained control of all of the toxin and the CIA was pissed. He knew Pakistan didn't like the explosions and cried about sovereignty through back channels.

And he knew no one could find Benton's body or any sign or his trail. That part killed West.

Seeing her, thinking about her, was the one bright spot in a pretty shitty couple of days. "How long are you staying in Islamabad?"

Intellectually, he knew she should go now. But he rarely just thought with his head when he saw her. Now, his heart got tangled up in this. He didn't even know he still had one of those until she walked into his life.

She sighed at him in a way that now felt familiar. "I'm tempted to answer that by asking how long it's going to take you to come around and use that key."

"Lexi—"

"Right, well, when you get out, when you feel brave. Come to me." She stuffed her hand back in her jacket pocket. "But hurry because I am ready to reboot my life, and you need to decide if you want to be in it."

And then she was gone.

26

LEXI LEFT her room for twenty minutes. The safe house had a shared kitchen, and she'd heard rumors about coffee being in there. The plan was to pop downstairs and come back up. Popping proved tough when she ran into Ward and he filled her in about Raheel and Javed. Both were fine but Javed would more than likely be pulled, which was an intelligence blow.

Hearing about how much still remained unsettled frustrated her. Only seemed right, since she'd spent a frustrating two days alone in Islamabad. Not that she had anywhere to go. After the explosions there'd been a security crackdown in Skardu. The clinic was a crime scene, and people still looked for her, which explained why she had to limit her movements to the safe house and the hospital.

With Josiah's help she finally reached her dad. He'd gotten to base camp when she delivered the news, or as much as Josiah said she could on an unsecured line. He'd been furious about the risks she'd taken. He yelled about the clinic and how he'd have to start over. He talked about how she never should have taken the risk and made the report.

Mostly, he blustered, but underneath that she picked up the concern. He wanted her out of Skardu and Pakistan and somewhere safe. For him, their relationship traveled the same path. He would figure out when he saw her that it had changed. The years of feeling inadequate were behind her. No weak person could survive the week she had.

The only positive part of her life lay in a hospital bed a few miles away. She'd left West's room after issuing a challenge. He didn't respond then, nor had he since. Oh, he texted to check on her. Notes filled with mundane chatter and little else. He never used that key she gave him, and that chipped away at her until she wanted to crawl back into bed and hide.

She put her key in the lock now and closed her eyes. What she'd see on the other side could hold the answer to everything. She did what she did every time she entered: hoped he was standing there.

After the beep the lock clicked. She pushed the door open and walked in. No broad-shouldered man waiting for her. No sign that he'd been there or that he cared.

Man, he was stubborn.

She dropped the coffee cup on the edge of the chest of drawers and went to the window. The temptation to stay there and wait him out pulled at her, but she'd be safer to move on. Waiting around for something that might never come would eat away at her self-esteem until she had none. She didn't want to go back to that place.

Good thing the bed called. Yeah, it was the middle of the afternoon and she should be working or planning or setting a new course for her life. She preferred the idea of sleeping. She'd had so little lately. That soothing cleanse of rest.

The doctor who checked her out, at West's insistence, explained about delayed symptoms and possible depression. He'd read off a list of symptoms and offered medication. Most of all he recommended rest and gave her a pamphlet on ways to clear her head.

Lexi dropped down on the edge of the bed. Falling into that big stack of pillows sounded so good. Who needed wine and chocolate? She had cool sheets and a dark room.

She kicked her shoes off and curled her legs to the side. She was reaching up to grab those pillows and pile them around her when she saw it. A note on white paper with black writing.

Her heart jumped and the excitement built. Maybe West had stopped by, and with her stupid luck she'd been listening to Josiah instead of here waiting.

Lexi flipped the envelope over and pulled out a page. The block lettering was so perfect that it could have been done by a machine. But it wasn't. This message was too personal and too clear.

I will see you again soon—Benton

A half hour later West stormed in. He knocked once then used the key. That was probably good since she was in no condition to get out of the chair by the window. She'd been sitting in it with her feet curled under her since she'd made the call.

West stopped right in front of her, close enough so she had to lean back to look up at his face. He put his hands on his hips. "You called Josiah."

It had been a work thing, and keeping that separate from West struck her as the right thing to do. "There was a note—"

"And you didn't call me." He crouched down and balanced on the balls of his feet. Winced as he did it. The position put him slightly lower than her, but his tone didn't leave any room to wonder who he thought was in charge.

"You didn't seem interested." It was an unfair shot but she wasn't feeling all that charming right now.

His jaw made a cracking sound. "Don't do that. You know it's not true."

"You have a problem with sending mixed signals." One minute he wanted to be the one she called. The next he wanted her on a plane and headed away from him. She couldn't keep up. The emotional running around in circles made her dizzy.

He had his hands clasped together and his knuckles were tight enough for her knuckles to turn white. "If you need something, you come to me."

The answer to that one was too obvious. "I gave you a key."

"I'm trying to be smart."

"Really? Because you seem like an idiot right now. I don't get your choices at all." She had to stand up then. She needed to pace. Maybe she needed some air.

It was unfair, really. He walked in and her exhausted body switched on. He talked, lectured, or ordered, and she wanted to punch something.

He stood up next to her with his palm up. "Let me see it."

A note dropped in her locked room by a stranger suggested she should not screw around waiting. She didn't see a reason to anyway. She wasn't looking for games or attention. She wanted West, and that was different from whatever sickness was behind the letter and the subtle threat inside.

Turning, she reached over and plucked it off the nightstand. "Here."

West read it then flipped the card over then seemed to read it again. It was no more than a line. It didn't take long to absorb, so she wasn't clear what had him so enthralled.

He dropped it back on the nightstand. "We can't find him," he said. "Ward is pretty sure he got injured in the fire. The only good news is he didn't get away with any toxin."

As little as she wanted to hear about Benton, she did have one question. "What was in the box?"

"A rough formula for the basic chemical compound, and samples. Between that and the containers Javed took, we can see he was still in the testing stage." West exhaled. "Pearce's talk about them being ready to start bombing appears to have been overblown."

"How is Javed . . . or should I say who is he?"

"CIA." West made a face. "About your dad—"

"I can't talk about that yet. Josiah wouldn't let me ask questions on the satphone, and I need to hear the rest straight from my dad." She really didn't need to. When she took a breath and sat down, put the pieces together in her head, it all made sense. The travel, the houseguests, the decisions he'd made over the years. He did some sort of covert work, and she didn't really want to know what.

"So, how did Benton or someone working for Benton get into my room?" Because that was the burning question that would keep her up all night.

"He seems to have contacts everywhere. We weren't followed and it wasn't luck." West sat down on the edge of her bed. Rubbed his palms up and down his thighs. "You're safe now."

"Lucky me."

If he picked up on the sarcasm, he hid it well. "There are guards everywhere inside and people watching from the outside."

He assigned others. Not him. He stayed away as if she'd scared him. Maybe she had.

The thought made her stomach roll. "People I know?"

"Pretty much all of Delta is here and watching."

Her real concern was about the name not on protection detail. "You didn't volunteer."

"Being near you, I lose my concentration. That's not a great characteristic in a bodyguard."

At least he didn't lie or come up with some excuse like a new assignment. She'd half expected to hear he ran out of the country and was hiding out on a new job somewhere without a phone or any communication. "You hide your feelings well."

He shook his head. "What do you want from me?" He sounded defeated and confused.

But the answer was so simple. "Everything. I at least want you to try."

"You know—"

"Maybe I want you to want it." She didn't want to hear whatever he had to say to that. No more excuses or pretty words. "Are you attracted to me?"

"Oh, come on."

That was fair. He'd never pretended the attraction didn't bounce back and forth between them. He just had an astounding ability to ignore it.

She was determined to hit it head on. "Do you want me?"

"More than I want air." He shot the answer right back to her.

The quick response gave her hope.

He rubbed a hand through his hair. "I'm trying to be—"

"Smart, yeah I know." There was another word she could add to her Most Hated list.

Words weren't working anyway. She started unbuttoning her blue long-sleeve shirt.

His eyes narrowed but something else happened in there. The heat he kept banked flared to life. "What are you doing?"

"Getting a little stupid." If this was all she would ever get, then she'd enjoy it. Sex promoted intimacy and added to the experience of falling in love. But mostly it felt really good. She needed to feel something— anything—right now.

When she reached the last button, she pushed the shirt off her shoulders, letting it tumble to the floor. Next she reached for the button at the top of her jeans.

He stood up and covered her hands with his. "Lexi . . ."

She slipped her fingers out from under his. They slid under the hem of his sweater. The V-neck was snug but not too tight. Her hands roamed across his chest, and this time he didn't try to slow her down. But he didn't take part either.

Her palm slid over his nipple. "Say no and I'll stop."

He didn't say anything for a few seconds. She used the time to learn every inch. They'd made love in Pakistan but that was on the run and with the tick of danger around them. The moment likely added to the intimacy. This time she wanted him, just him. No distractions or fear of being caught. They could do what they wanted, and that freedom both enticed her and frightened her.

Her mouth went to his neck. She slid her tongue around the bottom of his chin and held his body tight against hers.

She could feel his excitement. His erection pressed against her and his breathing grew shallow. The quick gasps of breath and the way he cradled her body between his thighs. She was not alone here. So long as he could admit it.

"I brought two condoms."

Relief ran through every cell. "I like a man who's prepared."

"Do you like one that's naked?"

This was the West she missed. She understood that his job stayed with him and he couldn't joke all the time. But he hid his charm. Buried it down deep. She loved these peeks, the moments when the guard came down and he made her smile.

She pushed the sweater up and over his head. The tee came next. Then she had miles of broad chest to caress. The battlefield of scars had intrigued her before. She'd touched them and asked about a few. Others she recognized for what they were. A stab or a gunshot.

Having seen him in action and as the person he dragged out of danger, she viewed them differently now. They were about bravery and honor. He stepped up and walked in. More than once she'd seen him volunteer to take on the violence so someone else didn't have to.

It was a spectacular skill, and so hot. It was hard not to love a man who would literally die for you. She knew because she'd tried. The last thing she wanted to do was fall for a guy who spent his life on the road, away from her.

His arms went around her and his mouth touched hers. A quick kiss at first, then it deepened. His mouth slanted and devoured. There was nothing neutral about it. He dove in and dragged her with him.

Sensations whipped around her. She grabbed his shoulders and tried to hold on. Even as she worried this meant nothing but the slap of bodies to him, it meant everything to her. She craved the closeness and his touch. And when he kissed her, she melted. Actually turned into a pile of goo.

Something tugged behind her, then the bra was gone. His palms slid up to cup her. One thumb rubbed across a nipple. Then the other. He broke off the kiss to stare down at her as he pressed her breasts together and flicked his tongue over both nipples.

As he kept going, one to the other, she sucked in air but could barely breathe. He switched to long licking strokes and her head fell back. Tonight might kill her. That was her last thought before her back hit the bed. He pushed her deep into the pillows and climbed up her body, making each step on his hands and knees count, with his mouth wandering as he went.

Without any signal from her brain, her legs fell open. Her skin felt tight. She wanted them out of their clothes. She let him know by brushing her hand over the zipper of his jeans. A bulge rose behind her hand and she rubbed and squeezed to bring it to life. Through it all she kept touching, letting his jeans provide the friction.

He gasped and looked down at her hand. "Damn, Lexi."

Her mouth over his ear. She nibbled and licked until she couldn't stand the bits of clothes that still separated them. "Take them off."

He nearly ripped the fabric. He shoved the jeans over his hips and stripped them to his ankles. One yank and they went flying over the side of the bed.

She wanted to help but that reaction set her off. The fact that he wanted her so badly to wait fed her ego. Made her care about him even more, and that was saying something since she couldn't get enough of him already.

Then his mouth started its tour. He kissed a path over her stomach as one hand cupped her breasts. He caressed and massaged. The gentle touches mesmerized her. She almost didn't hear him lower her zipper. It clicked with each tick. And that hot mouth continued to follow those hands.

When he got to her hips, he touched her underwear. Slipped two fingers inside to rub her. Back and forth then in circles, anything to get her wet.

She lifted her hips and he pulled her pants down, inch by delicious inch. The rough fabric rubbed against her bare thighs. She thought it might be the most sensual touch ever until he licked up the middle of her bikini underwear. A groan escaped her and her head fell to the side.

She was so close. So primed for him. Ready to feel him inside her without footsteps echoing in the yard. And it needed to be now.

Her legs fell open as far as they could. Her hands slipped into his hair. One of his fingers slipped the elastic band to the side as he continued to kiss her. Each time he pressed a finger inside her, her hips rose off the bed.

Lost in a haze, she gave herself over to the sensations. Forgot about everything but the feel of his hands and the lick of his tongue.

As her bones turned to jelly, he tugged her panties down. The crotch was wet and her body was ready. "Find the condom."

He slipped it out of his back pocket and held it in his teeth while he adjusted what little clothing he still had on. Then he was back. Rolling it on and pressing against her. He didn't enter her. God, if he was looking for permission, he had it. To highlight that, she squeezed her legs tighter around him.

The move had his head shooting up to stare at her. "Damn."

He lifted his body off her for a second. She heard the jingle of a belt and then skin touched skin.

"Now, West." Another second and she might explode. Her body had pulled tight and her inner muscles cried out for release. His finger felt good. She knew from experience she could feel better.

Their breathing bounced off the walls and something pulsed in the air. She needed the sensation of him entering her. The tightness as he squeezed in.

Then he was. He pressed her thighs apart and lifted her legs at an angle. By the time he slid inside, her body rode a fine edge. And when he pressed into her again, deep and slow, her eyes closed.

A slow thrust. Then another before the speed picked up. He was wild now. His body moved over her, in her. She pressed her hands against his hips and drew him in deeper.

Her body clenched and the spiraling inside her sped up. When he reached down and touched her at the same time he pressed deep inside her, she came. Her back rose off the bed and her breath stuttered. All the tension inside her waded into a ball, then burst.

She came as she screamed. The joint feeling of him inside her as he kissed her had her body bucking. She rode it out as he held her. And when she squeezed her thighs and those tiny inner muscles together, it was his turn.

He plunged and retreated. In and out, caressing her everywhere. When he collapsed on top of her, she wrapped her arms around his waist. Tiny pulses moved through her and the world felt as if it tilted right again.

This was hot, sweaty sex, just as she liked it. His mouth and hands. And with it over, she could barely hold up her head. He'd exhausted her. Drained the energy right out of her.

And she loved it. She also loved the feel of his skin. As she held him, her fingertips brushed over his skin, learning and touching his back and arms.

She'd started to doze off when she felt him move. The mattress shifted as he sat up on the far edge of the bed and put his legs over the side.

She could pretend to be asleep or face it. She went back and forth, trying to hold onto the warm satisfaction of what had just happened but considering the cold reality of him sneaking away.

"What are you doing?" She asked because she wasn't doing anything wrong and refused to feel like she was.

He glanced over his shoulder at her. His gaze traveled down her legs and back up again. "I need to leave."

Her heart collapsed but she would not show it. "Okay."

"It's about work." He stood up and his pants came up with him.

Sure it was. "Your job is important. Go."

He scooped his sweater off the floor and wrestled his way into it, stopping before lifting it over his head. "You know you matter more to me than anyone, right?"

Those words meant almost nothing if he followed them by walking out the door. But she had no way to make him understand that. And she didn't want to. He had to figure this out, to want it for himself. "But not enough."

"What?"

She waved his question off. "Nothing."

He stared at her, hesitating. "Good night."

She waited until the door closed behind him. "Goodbye."

27

WEST SAT at the Alliance conference room table four weeks later. Most of the injuries had switched from unrelenting pain to dull aches to memories. He hadn't experienced any permanent damage, but the shoulder injury came close. A few more inches and he'd be retired and unable to shoot.

The most vivid reminder of his failure on that mission sat in front of him. He flipped open the briefing file about Benton. They had a sketch now of his face and a few leads. The guard who helped him escape on this side was talking but didn't know much. West guessed that's how Benton's empire worked. That he followed the drug dealers' game and only let a limited number of people know anything.

The important thing was they got the toxin samples. They took Pearce out, discovered a bit about his business, and took the toxin he was so desperate to use on innocent people.

They'd also raised the wrath of the CIA, which did not take kindly to having their agent embarrassed. Javed's cover held, so far. Dr. Palmer was not as lucky and he was annoyed about being cut off. The only thing saving them from hearing his full wrath was that he really was on Everest with an expedition and everyone decided he was safest there, so no one rushed to bring him back.

West didn't give a shit about lost jobs and who got credit for things. If people wanted praise they could go into another business. Covert work was, by definition, not the place to be.

Tasha stood across from him with her palms balanced on the back of a chair. She faced him and shot him a disapproving glare every now and then. He didn't ask questions because it was clear she was gearing up with a few of her own. He wasn't sure how he got to be so lucky to be chosen out of all the Alliance members for this meeting.

She finally talked. "I'm wondering how much longer we need to deal with you being miserable and generally looking like a kicked dog."

He blinked a few times as the words sunk in. "Excuse me?"

"You've been downright depressed lately."

Never in his life. Sure, he dragged his sorry ass out of bed every morning and spent half the night rolling around thinking about Lexi, but that would pass. God, it had to pass or he'd be in a hospital. "I've been recuperating."

"Oh, please. I've been in the field. I know you." Tasha snorted. "Hell, I was you."

This was the weirdest debrief he'd ever experienced.
"I don't understand what's happening here."

"I'm disappointed in you."

He had fought and kicked and lived through rounds
of torture and lost his woman. What the hell else did
Tasha expect from him? "What are you talking about?"

Tasha had a file in her hands and trapped against
her chest as she crossed her arms. "I've talked with the
guys, especially Josiah and Mike, and I don't get it."

He didn't usually work with Delta but he couldn't
believe they'd whine to the boss behind his back. And
about what? "What are you saying, exactly?"

"You let someone like Lexi go?" Tasha frowned at
him. "Really?"

Not her business, but Tasha had struck a direct hit.
Zoomed in on the biggest regret of his life. He'd actually walked out after sex. He really was a dick sometimes. Didn't mean to be but his feelings for her grew
and swelled until he didn't know what to do with them.
With him came danger and uncertainty, and she deserved better.

He typically dated women who were interested in
some fun for a few weeks. He didn't go for the home
and hearth type, or even the baby type. With Lexi, he
threw that all out the window. Broke every personal
rule.

He hadn't been kidding when he told her he didn't
sleep around for fun on a job. He worked and studied
briefings. He'd come up with contingencies and meet

with the team. Make sure his body and mind were in the best possible shape.

He didn't rescue a woman and then think about nothing but how she would taste. But that's exactly what happened with Lexi.

She was the one person who didn't make him feel like a machine.

"You know her?" He couldn't imagine where Tasha, a former MI6, and Lexi, would cross paths, but the idea of them being friends wouldn't exactly stun him. They both blew through life the same way. They didn't take any male nonsense. For some reason he loved that.

"Ward told me she's pretty and nice and can stand up to you. Josiah thinks you're a fool to walk away from her. Hell, even Mike likes her, and he doesn't like many people." Tasha pulled out a chair and sat down. "Frankly, with those recommendations she sounds like a keeper."

West knew he had to buckle in. This wasn't a drive-by chat. No, Tasha wanted some time with him. Not something that was generally a good thing. She might be living with Ward but she was the boss, and West didn't mess with that. She had his respect. Right now he just wished he didn't have her attention.

Ward stepped up to the table with Josiah. They didn't turn around and leave again.

West was starting to hate this day. "Why are we talking about my personal life?"

Tasha smiled up at him. "I'm impressed you admit you have one."

"About her." Josiah hit West on the good shoulder. "Go get her back or we're sending you in for a psych exam."

West thought about crawling under the table but was pretty sure they'd notice. "This is why I'm here?"

Tasha tapped the top of her file. "About Lexi."

"No thanks."

When West stood up, Tasha pointed at the chair again. "Sit."

"My relationship with Lexi is personal." How he felt about her had nothing to do with a case. Sure, they met during one, but he saw her as a woman and not a file number. He didn't have a bias problem. He had a wish-she-were-here issue.

"Personal?" Josiah scoffed. "Uh, no."

"She was an asset," Ward added.

West really wanted to kick them both out of this talk. "Can we not use that word to refer to her?"

"Fine." Tasha tapped her hand against the file in front of her. "What should I call her?"

That one seemed kind of obvious. "Lexi."

Tasha did not break eye contact even for a second. "Aren't you clever?"

West battled with the urge to stand up again. "We both know me being with her would be stupid."

"Well, one of us thinks so," Josiah said. "I saw her when she realized you were under that pile of rocks. Seems pretty serious to me."

West hated talking about her. He couldn't stop thinking about her, and his home had turned into a battlefield. He crawled into his bed and wanted her there. Thought she'd be interesting to talk with across the table. Now Tasha was dragging the woman into work, which meant he would never get a second of peace.

"Why do you all care about this?" He was referring to his love life but figured they were smart enough to pick that up.

"She's way out of your league but likes you." Ward shrugged. "Or did."

"What kind of answer is that?' West honestly didn't know. It didn't make sense to him.

"She's hot." Josiah held up a hand when West's expression turned homicidal. "Don't scowl at me. She is."

Despite it being a Saturday, the office buzzed with activity. They had a constant stream of assignments. One team or the other was always on call and about to be dispatched. The tech crew was in the room searching for Benton clues, which was why West showed up today, not for an informal game of twenty questions.

"Apparently you ticked her off." Tasha opened the file and scanned whatever notes she wrote inside.

None of that made any sense. West just stared at his boss. "What?"

"She's left messages," Tasha explained. "Left them at places you don't work, like the CIA, which ticked an alarm with our techs."

"I don't get it." It was that simple. He had no clue.

Ward paged through the plastic sleeves. "You left her and she was looking for you."

"Was. I doubt she is now." Josiah looked up at the ceiling as if he were struggling to remember something big. "How long has it been?"

West could take the countdown to hours. "I'm still lost."

"I know you're a loner," Ward said, "and believe you should have to go through life alone, or at least unattached." He shook his head. "But take it from me, that's not true."

The amusement left Josiah's face. "We've all seen death and lived through some really awful shit, but you get to have a life."

The room flipped on West. He was ready for one topic, but they kept jumping around. "Is my job in trouble?"

"No, dumbass."

"Ward." Tasha glared at him before turning back to West. "The exact opposite."

"Okay." West picked that answer because he wasn't sure what else to say.

"Lexi thinks you believe you're nothing more than a trained killer for us. I think she used the word machine." Ward looked like he was searching for the right word to say. "If we gave you that impression we messed up and will fix it."

The conversation had West squirming. He'd never complain because that wasn't who he was. But the truth was, every now and then he'd sit down and assess. He'd become the kill leader. Not really a title he ever wanted.

But he loved his job. It was letting himself feel again that scared the shit out of him. "Look—"

Tasha jumped right in. "I'm going to shortcut this because Lexi is on a flight tonight to Ecuador."

That news hit like a kick to the nuts. "She's what?"

Tasha glanced in the file again. "It looks like she's headed back to work. You might want to give her a reason to find a job here."

Josiah gave West another shoulder slap. "Step up."

West looked from one person to the next. He respected everyone at the table but they were confusing the hell out of him right now. "Huh?"

"This woman is beautiful, smart, and talented," Ward said. "Your life didn't scare her and she never left your side." He leaned forward in his seat with his elbows resting on the table. "You don't let that kind of woman go."

West had run through a similar list last night. All the great things about her. It convinced him that walking away from the hotel room had been the right thing to do. "We only knew each other a few days."

Ward frowned. "So?"

The argument there made sense. West knew that Tasha and Ward had only known each other for a few days on an assignment before moving in together. But West would never compare himself to Ward. "She can—"

Tasha lifted a finger and pointed at him. "If you say

Lexi can do better than you I am going to beat the shit out of you."

That went too far, even for her. "Excuse me?"

"I know you had a shitty upbringing," Ward said, "but wake up, West. You are a good man. Loyal and strong. You protect and rescue. You always put the group's needs ahead of your own."

West had never heard his boss, or anyone, say anything like that about him before.

"In other words," Tasha said, "Lexi would be getting a good catch with you."

Josiah hit his hand against the table. "So, go stop her from leaving."

They all made it sound so easy to ignore the danger and the other load of crap that came with this job.

"Unless you really don't care." Ward kept talking. "Then let her get on the plane and find a nice Peace Corps volunteer, fall in love, move to Kansas. Leave her alone."

He'd hit on the one argument that made West's brain boil. He knew walking away meant she would find someone else. He always got to that point in the logic and then fumbled.

"Ecuador." His new least favorite country.

"Here's where she is right now." Tasha slid a file across the table.

West opened it and paged through. Saw the flight confirmation and an address. There were more pages of documents as well. "How do you know all this?"

Ward shook his head. "It's almost sad that you asked that."

"Let me put it this way." Josiah started yelling. "Go get your woman."

By the time he finished, most of the Warehouse floor was staring. Not West's favorite thing, but he hated the idea of Lexi leaving, and possibly deciding not to come back sucked even more.

She'd once said something about falling hard. Now he knew what she meant.

He stood up and swiped the envelope of intel off the table.

Tasha smiled "You're going?"

He wasn't sure what he was going to do or say but he knew one thing for sure. "I have to talk with her."

"Do yourself a favor and do more than talk," Josiah said.

One thought ran through West's mind: that's why Josiah is the leader.

28

Lexi ignored the knock on the door. No one knew her in Baltimore. She'd never met any neighbors at the executive apartments. Most of them were businessmen on short-term assignments. She was there because the place came furnished. With everything she owned trapped back in Pakistan, her choices were limited, and the one choice she did want to make couldn't happen because he didn't want to take a chance on them.

For weeks after West walked away she blamed herself. Fell back on old patterns and stayed mostly to herself. Her shaky relationship with her dad didn't help. But the truth about West soon hit her. She was great for him. They could be great together. His fears, not hers, held them back.

The knock came again, this time more insistent.

She dumped her plane tickets on the bed and stepped around the luggage she'd packed for the trip. Her hand hit the door handle as it turned. She jumped back and the door opened.

West stood there, all fire and fury.

"You unlocked my door." She couldn't figure out whether to be appalled or chalk it up to one of West's eccentricities. The fact that he could open locks was just one more skill to add to his many others.

"You didn't answer." He slipped his hands into his back jeans pockets. He may have even rocked back on his heels.

She was too stunned to say or do anything. After a few beats of silence she finally got something out, though in her head it barely made sense. "I'm leaving soon for about six months."

He stepped inside and shut the door behind him. "No."

His response confused her even more. "What?"

"You can't go to Ecuador." He nodded after he said it, as if he'd been practicing.

"How do you . . ." She inhaled, trying to separate the things worth getting ticked off about from the things that didn't matter. "Okay, that's annoying."

He didn't pretend not to get it. "My office looked it up."

In West's world that answer probably made sense. "Do you think that makes it better?"

"You could go and decide to stay and not come back."

Maybe she should have been happy with the comment but it ticked her off. "And you were so concerned about not seeing me, as evidenced by the fact you haven't tried to for an entire month."

"I fucked up." That time he did rock. It was subtle but it happened.

She had to focus on the mundane because if she looked at the big picture—what she felt for him and how little regard he had for that—she would lose it. She'd tried to reach him, which proved impossible. There wasn't exactly a listing for Alliance in the phone book.

That led to unraveling. She'd spent so many hours wondering what could have been and trying to figure out how she fell so fast. He was just a man, but when she thought about him she ached with the need to see him. His face popped into her mind and she wanted to grab on, to talk with him. She missed their banter and the kisses. Hell, she even missed the fighting.

Thinking about those days now brought that familiar pain back. The soreness in her chest and trouble breathing. Okay, yeah, she was going to need to sit down for this. She cleared a space on the bed and dropped down.

"Well?" he asked.

She wasn't sure of the question but apparently it was her turn to speak. He really was not good at the communicating thing. "No kidding you screwed up."

"I didn't think you'd agree that fast." After some quick rearranging of duffel bags he plopped down on the bed next to her.

The wall she'd been erecting against him wasn't holding. This close, she could smell him. Unlike in Pakistan, he smelled good. Fresh and crisp. He'd washed his hair and his clothes were clean. No blood anywhere. She'd been sucked in by the scarier version.

She feared what would happen to her control after a few minutes with this version.

It helped to remember how he'd acted at the end. She'd been so sure he was dead, and blinded with relief when he wasn't. But he'd pushed her away. Used the lame I'm-not-good-enough excuse. "You were a pretty big jerk."

He stared at his hands. 'Yes."

Then there was the rest. She started to say what she needed to but the words choked up on her. She got them on second try. "Leaving my room right after we—"

"Yes."

She had no idea what kind of game he was playing. He didn't offer excuses or come up with justifications. He sounded as sad and desperate as she felt when she offered to volunteer at a clinic in Ecuador. Anything to get away from West.

"Why do you keep agreeing with me?" she asked.

"Because you're not wrong."

This made no sense. He'd gone without a word for a month. Didn't try to reach out, and now he was sorry. No thank you.

She got off the bed and went back to the door, mostly because she needed to move. "You can go now."

"I don't want to leave."

The simple words spun up inside her. What *he* wanted. Forget what *she* needed.

All that frustration and pain came bubbling up to the surface. She tried to bite it back but the look on his

face had her changing her mind. He just . . . sat there.
Nothing showed in his expression except for the lines
around his mouth. She didn't remember them but they
must have been there before.

"I gave you everything," she said. "I offered a relationship." The words tumbled out of her now with a
load of fresh pain behind them. "I knew about your job
and accepted it. I understood you and didn't want to
change you."

He stood up and reached out to her. "Lexi, listen—"

She shifted away from him. "Look, I know my feelings on this are too intense. We didn't have a relationship or anything—"

"That's not true"

"—but you refused to even try. I stood there and admitted that I was falling for you and you ignored it."
The humiliation rolled over her again. She wasn't the
type to spill her guts. She didn't fall for a guy after
a few days. The whole thing was new and scary and
weird, and he made it all worse with his reaction.

He touched her. Fingers wrapped around her arms,
gentle and reassuring. He started to bring her closer to
his body then stopped. "I panicked."

"What?"

"Yeah, me. The guy who can jump out of a plane and
rappel down a mountain." He exhaled and their bodies
moved in closer. "You saw so much killing. Watched
me be the guy I am at work instead of the kind of guy
who takes you to dinner."

"I watched you protect, and I never saw you rejoice over death."

"The machine thing."

"I was right. You have emotions and feelings and keep them bottled up because it's easier." The whole amateur psychologist move wasn't her finest hour, but she was right. All of that mattered to him and it impacted how he viewed his contribution. If she had any money she'd bet it on that.

"I did do that. It was self-protection." He shook his head as he spoke. "But I don't want to hide from you."

Her indignation dwindled. It was tough to be angry and guarded when he stayed off the offensive. "Are you just agreeing with everything I say so I sleep with you again?'

"I don't want you to get on that plane."

She would have given anything to hear those words even a week ago. "You haven't even tried to see me in weeks."

"Lexi." His hand went to her waist and the other tucked her hair back behind her ear. "I have no idea if I can be a boyfriend or whatever you want to call me. All I know is that being with you is the only time my life has made sense. Without you has been miserable."

The words flooded through her. She wanted to push them away and pretend they didn't matter, but they did. They changed everything. "Really?"

"I won't point out that you're smiling."

She tried to swallow it. "Then I won't point out how much the last few weeks sucked."

"For both of us." He leaned forward and pressed a kiss against her hair. "God, I missed you."

"Why didn't you come to me? You obviously knew where I was or easily could have figured it out."

"I hate the idea of you in danger." He closed his eyes, and when he opened them again the pain was mirrored there. "It rips me up."

"Do you like the idea of me dating someone else? Because that will happen at some point." She couldn't imagine it, but she wanted a life. She could only wait around for him for so long.

"I'd probably try to use the full power of the Alliance on any date of yours." His fingers tightened on her waist. "That includes the rocket launchers."

"I can't wait around and I won't be the girl you see now and then."

"I get that."

She inhaled nice and deep and went for it. He stood there saying the right things. If he was going to bolt it would be now. "When it comes to you my resistance is low . . ." She stumbled over the words. "I fell for you fast and hard and stupid. Without any sense of self-protection."

She almost wanted to close one eye and wait. This would be a bombshell for any guy, but for someone like West with his limited friends and painful upbringing, it would all be too much.

He smiled at her. "I'm in."

Everything inside her stopped. She struggled not to slip out of his hands and onto the floor. "What?"

"I wake up thinking about you. I miss you all day and then think I can smell your hair at night." He kissed her forehead, then her cheek. "If that's not falling for someone, I don't know what is."

"West." She cupped his cheeks in her hands and kissed him. Not a peck. This one lasted. Lingered a little while it burned. When she lifted her head again her breath came out in short pants.

"Does this mean you'll stay?"

She was a tagalong, not a permanent worker. She needed a way to fill in the time as she got ready to go back to medical school. That gave her leeway, and for him, she would take it. "Yes."

He wrapped her up tighter and her feet left the ground. She didn't get sucked under yet. There was still so much to work out.

"But you should know that will mean I'm unemployed."

He made a face that made it clear this was not an issue for him. "No problem."

"I don't have a place to live." Which freaked her out. She'd lived a nomadic existence for part of her life and accepted it, but she was ready for roots. Craved them.

His smile could light a small city. "You do. With me."

"I've thought about medical school and why I dropped out." She waited for him to jump in. When he didn't, she inhaled and kept going. "It's important to me that I finish. On my terms, not my dad's. For me. I'm actually looking into returning and doing the applications and tests and all of that."

He winked at her. "I like the idea of dating a doctor."

"You're ready to accept that I'll be in your life and bossy and—"

He held up a hand. "Bossy? Wait a second."

"It's not too late for me to kick you."

"Yes it is." He kissed her chin. "But I was kidding."

Her arms went to his neck and her mouth brushed against his. "You understand that I probably love you."

The reality is, she knew she did. At first the feeling was new and uncertain, but once he'd walked away the feelings hit her with full force. She did love him. She was stupid with it. It explained all the danger she accepted and made sense in terms of how much she wanted him and what she was willing to do to satisfy that need.

Sex in the middle of a battle zone? Looking back, that blanket might not have been a good idea. She didn't regret it, but she did have to watch because when it came to him her boundaries stretched.

He pulled her in tighter and gave her a real kiss. Forget the brushing. This one exploded through her. "And I probably love you back."

If it was possible for words to turn on a switch. For light to flood and everything to feel brighter and sweeter. It had just happened. "I have to make a billion calls about my change of plans."

"Later." His mouth went to her neck. He nibbled and kissed.

"I don't . . . oh." That was the spot. "This works, too."

"You know, there is a big bed right there." He cleared his throat. "It would be wrong to waste it."

"Let's see if we can upset the neighbors with all the noise."

He laughed then. "I like your style, Alexis Palmer."

"And I like you." She did. Liked so much about him, even the annoying stuff.

His mood sobered as his fingers grazed her lips. "Just kept falling."

"Done."

Three days later West sat at the conference stable in the Warehouse with Lexi by his side. He thought they'd been called in about protocol or a late debrief about Pakistan. He'd hoped there was news about Benton and his new venture that would keep them chasing him.

But no. The visit was part personal and part business. The offer blindsided him, but the more he thought about it, it made sense. Except for the danger. He couldn't tolerate it.

Tasha set the white envelope down in front of Lexi. It had her name on it but no other sign of its contents. And she wouldn't be able to leave the building with it. The letter would stay here as she considered the terms.

Welcome to covert ops.

"All of the details are in here." Tasha tapped the edge of it.

West waited for Lexi to say something. Instead, she stared at the envelope then at Tasha again. To say she looked shell-shocked was an understatement. It was as if she'd run into a wall and rattled something important. The fact that she was blinking more than usual probably made him think about it.

After a few seconds of silence that seemed to stretch into minutes, Lexi picked up the envelope. "You're offering me a job?"

"You have medical skills. That's invaluable." Tasha pointed at him. "All of Delta agrees you were amazing in the field."

He had to ask again because this question mattered the most to him. Danger was a bright line for him. "Would she be—?"

"She'll be back with the techs. It's very safe." Tasha waited until Lexi looked down at the envelope again and then winked.

"Josiah told me you all have medical training," Lexi said.

"Not at your level."

Tasha started to say something then stopped. She waved off whatever the other thing happened to be. "Look, I know this is a couples' decision, and you do both have to agree. If the answer is no, that's fine."

West thought about giving a knee-jerk reaction. Push her back into medical school. Classrooms seemed safe to him and danger lurked everywhere else.

He knew he was overprotective and that experiences shaped how he viewed this issue. He'd already promised Lexi he'd work on it. In return, she promised that she'd continue to ignore anything that sounded like she needed to obey.

When no one talked, Tasha jumped back in. That's what she did. Filled the dead space. "We look for people who will fit in and who have skills. You are one of those people."

Lexi glanced over at him then back to Tasha. "I appreciate it. I really do."

"But?" Tasha asked.

Lexi put her hand over the paperwork. "I need to finish medical school. Prove I can. It's unfinished business and I'm not doing that kind of thing anymore."

West had to fight the urge to reach over and kiss her. He also saw the wheels spinning in Tasha's head. "I like that even better."

He was almost afraid to ask. "What?"

Tasha stayed focused on Lexi. "You can do some contract work for us while you go to school. After graduation or whenever, if you want to work here on some level, great."

Lexi turned to him and smiled. "We'd work together."

That didn't bother him. They actually had a pretty good set of role models for that particular problem. "Ward and Tasha make it work."

"For the record." Tasha held up hand. "I am very tolerant."

"No comment." Yeah, West thought of about fifty ways he could get in trouble right now. Ward had stories and West had heard some of them. He suspected he wouldn't love all of them being told.

"Take a few weeks and think about it," Tasha said.

Lexi slid her fingers through his under the table and squeezed. "I have to figure out what my schedule will be, but I'm definitely free now. We just need to figure out if this is a problem for our relationship, since that comes first."

God, he loved when she said stuff like that.

Tasha nodded. "As it should be."

"But, thank you." Lexi's voice was filled with gratitude.

"West happens to be one of my favorites." Tasha leaned in. "Don't tell the others."

"I am?" That was news to him. He'd always gotten the impression she tolerated him and little more. Not that she was rude. Just determined and focused.

Tasha's attention stayed solely on Lexi now. "And I'm happy he found you. He needed a strong woman."

Lexi smiled. "I agree."

"So do I," he said, and he meant it.

"You guys are going to be fine, job or no." Tasha looked across the office and frowned.

West followed her gaze and spied what looked like a football game being played inside by Bravo. Yeah, she was not going to like that happening near the multi-million-dollar computers.

"How can you tell?" Lexi asked.

For a second Tasha looked confused but then her expression cleared. "Easy, I knew West before you and after you. He'd be an idiot to let you go."

Lexi laughed. "I like that."

"And that is why she's in charge," West said.

"A woman in charge at work and one in charge at home." Lexi whistled. "I like it."

So did West. "Just as it should be."

ACKNOWLEDGMENTS

I've never been to Pakistan or tried to climb K2 (or anything higher than a ladder, for that matter). With this general lack of knowledge, I normally would not have taken on this setting, except that I saw a reference in *Buried in the Sky: The Extraordinary Story of the Sherpa Climbers on K2's Deadliest Day* by Peter Zuckerman to Fearless Five, the helicopter crew that helps to rescue stranded climbers off some of the highest peaks in the world. Intrigued and in awe, I started spinning a tale . . . and much research later the backstory for *Falling Hard* was born. My book is totally fiction and not about Pakistan at all. Zuckerman's book is nonfiction, and you should all read it.

My heartfelt thank you to my fabulous editor, May Chen, for not saying "Do you know anything about Pakistan?" when I told her where this one was set and for suffering through computer issues with me as we tried to get this manuscript back and forth to each other. You are terrific and I'm lucky to have you and everyone at Team Avon.

Thank you to my hardworking agent, Laura Bradford, and my fantastic readers, who make it possible for me to do what I love for a living. I am truly grateful.

As always, thank you to my husband, James. You're more amazing than any fictional hero I can create.

*G*ive in to your Impulses!

**These unforgettable stories only take a second
to buy and give you hours of reading pleasure!**

Go to *www.AvonImpulse.com* and see what we
have to offer.

Available wherever e-books are sold.

AVONIMPULSE